ENDLESS HOOD LOVE

SHANICE B.

Cole Hart
SIGNATURE NOVELS

Endless Hood Love

Published in the United States of America.

Published by Cole Hart Signature, LLC.

Mailing List

To stay up to date on new releases, plus get information on contests, sneak peeks, and more,

Go To The Website Below...

WWW.COLEHARTSIGNATURE.COM

YANNI

Word on the street was that my nigga Quantavious was cheating on me. Personally, I didn't give a fuck. I have never been the type to believe anything that came out of a jealous bitch's mouth. The main ones who were spreading rumors were the main hating ass hoes who would sell their soul just to get a taste of Quan's dick. If I didn't see my nigga cheating with my own two eyes, then I wasn't going to accuse him of shit. Quantavious and I had been together for three years, and I wasn't about to walk away from him just because of some funky ass rumors.

Every bitch in Warner Robins wanted Quan. He was fine as hell, and the nigga was laced with money out the ass. Rarely do you ever catch a nigga who was sexy and had so much swag to damn match. Quan was about 6'2 and dark chocolate in complexion. He was a dread head who rocked a silver chrome grill in his mouth and flexed around town in his custom-made 2018 Black Dodge Challenger. He had never held down a nine to five job. He always told me that he wasn't about to slave for no white man. He started hustling on the block at an early age. Once he saw how much money he was making selling dope, he never looked back. He has always been about his paper, and when he met me, it only intensified. I wanted him to have it all and pushed him to new heights, I motivated his ass every chance I got. Failure was never an option in our relationship.

I knew in my heart that there was no other bitch on this planet that could replace me. I was sexy as hell and could have any nigga that I wanted. I was milk chocolate in complexion, I was around 5'3 in height, and I was thicker than a snicker. I had pretty brown eyes with soft kissable lips. I kept my hair done and never wore cheap weave. I was a classy bitch and I had shown Quan my loyalty. All these other hoes just wanted a free ride. They wanted to sit on their ass and let a nigga take care of them, whether they knew it or not, it was the year 2019 no nigga was about to take care of no bitch. If she was smart, she better grind with her nigga so they could both win.

Even though my nigga was a hustler, I worked as a CNA at The Lodge which was a nursing home. I had been working there for almost two years and wasn't about to give up my job no time soon. Even though Quan didn't want me to work, I always told him that I was going to keep a job. I wasn't dumb. I wasn't about to depend on him because what would happen to me if we ever broke up? Where would that leave me? Yeah, not working was not an option for me.

I pulled my 2017 Candy Apple Red Ford Focus into Taco Bell parking lot and cut the engine. I finger combed my Brazilian weave as I waited for my lil' cousin to clock out. Shontaea and I were first cousins, but we acted more like sisters. Neither one of us had a good childhood, but we made the best of it. We both grew up in the projects and lived down the street from one another. Growing up in the hood wasn't for the weak minded. Most of the people who lived on the same block with us ended up being sprung out on dope.

Shontaea and I always stayed away from that shit, even though both of our mamas were addicted to the coco.

My mama got hooked when my daddy ended up dying of a brain tumor. I was only ten when my father passed away. My mama couldn't cope without him. He was the provider of the family so once he was gone my mama stopped giving a fuck. We lost everything and ended up moving to the projects when I was eleven.

I was only twelve when my mama got her first hit from Taea's mama, Tanya. My aunt Tanya had always been an addict, she just couldn't stay away from the dope, no matter how hard she claimed she tried. For the longest, I hated my auntie for getting my mama hooked on drugs, but as I got older, I finally found it in my heart to try to forgive her.

Taea and I practically raised ourselves because our mamas damn sure didn't do it. Was I bitter about the shit? Hell yeah, I was. I wanted my mama to get herself clean, but to this day, she stayed getting high. It was just something that I had to accept. I couldn't keep dwelling on the past. It was time that I lived my own life and make sure that I didn't follow in the same footsteps as she did.

Reminiscing about my childhood always put me in a foul mood, so I was grateful when I spotted Taea walking towards the car. She hopped in, and I started the engine.

"Hey boo, how was your day"? I asked my cousin as she clicked her seat belt in.

"I swear I almost just lost my damn job."

"What the fuck happened?" I asked her as I pulled out of Taco Bell and merged onto Russell Parkway.

"This bitch believes she runs some shit, I swear, since this hoe done got promoted, she thinks it's okay for her to talk to me any kind of way."

"Who the fuck you talking about?" I asked her.

I stayed ready to pull up on bitches. I didn't play when it

came to Taea. In this world, she was all I had, and I wasn't about to let nan bitch get wrong with her or disrespect her on any level.

"This fat bitch named Mookie. She was just wiping piss off the bathroom floor last week, but just got promoted to shift leader. Now she thinks she can talk to me any kind of way. The bitch has lost her damn mind, I cursed her fat ass out and smacked her ass one good time."

"Bitch let me turn this damn car around so we can go get this bitch straight. She must don't know she fucked with the wrong one today. All you gotta do is say the word, and I will whip this bitch back to Taco Bell."

"Nah, I'm good boo, I handled her fat ass. The bitch was two seconds away from getting pushed through the fucking Taco Bell window if she would have kept popping off at the mouth," Taea replied loudly.

I couldn't help but laugh at her ass, she was reckless with her mouth and had a badass temper. It didn't take much to set her ass off. Even though Taea was thin and didn't have much weight on her, she was strong as hell. Taea always stayed having to beat a bitch ass. I guess because Taea was skinny they thought they could bully her, but Taea wasn't allowing any of that. Taea was slim, about 5'2 and was a yellow bone. She had naturally long shoulder length hair and didn't have to wear weave. She was naturally beautiful, and I believe that was what most bitches hated about her. Nothing was fake about my cousin she was the realest you could have ever known.

"Taea, you need to tell me how all this shit popped off. I want details," I told her as I weaved in and out of traffic.

"Omg, you so fucking messy, but I'm ready to tell it all," Taea laughed.

"You know I get off at five all this damn week, well I was about to damn clock out when her fat ass walks up on me and tells me that she wants me to get off at eleven tonight, I looked at the bitch like she had bumped her head. I've been at Taco Bell since eleven this morning, a bitch is tired and ready to go home. The general manager wrote the schedule out with me getting off at five this week. Mookie wanted to throw her weight around, talking about she was going to write me up if I left. She started talking shit, I did my best to stay calm until the hoe told me that she was going to fire me if I left. Bitch, I lost it and went on attack mode. I smacked the shit out her ass. I slapped that hoe so hard she fell to the damn floor."

"Taea, you slapped the bitch?"

"Hell yeah, I slapped the taste out her mouth, and I don't regret the shit, the hoe was asking for it."

"Taea, you already know that bitch going to go and try to get you fired."

"I know she is, but look though, I'm not the only one who don't like her ass. Nobody on my shift likes her dumb ass, so it's basically her word against all four of us who were working. Taco Bell love talking about they have cameras, but them bitches don't even fucking work.

"How in the hell do you know if they work or not?"

Taea laughed.

"After I smacked her ass, I went back in the back to see if I could erase the whole incident but turns out the bitches wasn't even on. If she goes flapping her mouth, ain't nobody gonna snitch on my ass, and the cameras don't work for them to go back and see shit, case closed."

I swear I couldn't help but laugh, my lil cousin honestly didn't give a fuck, she was willing to catch a fucking charge if it meant she was earning her respect. Taea and I both were willing to beat the breaks off a bitch if she ever disrespected one of us. I don't know what other bitches do to get their respect, but I was willing to die for mine.

"Enough about my fucked-up ass day, how was your day Yanni?" Taea asked as she pulled her shoulder length hair into a messy bun.

"My day was good, I worked my ass off, but it was worth it. It's just so fucked up how some people can stick their loved ones in a nursing home and never come visit them. I have this one patient named Mrs. Lottie Mae, she been there since I first started working there. Every fucking day, she sits in the entertainment room and just stares out the window.

"Ugh, girl that shit is depressing as fuck, I don't see how you work there. I honestly can't do the shit; I can't stand the smell of old folks."

I chuckled.

"It's not for everybody. I love my job, but it can be draining at times. It's just my heart breaks for her every day. The fact that she hasn't had one visit since I been there is what hurts the most. One day last week, I walked over to her and asked if she wanted to go play bingo with some of the others. She politely looked at me and told me no, she said that she was waiting by the window because her daughter told her that she was going to come to see her."

Tae shook her head.

"Did her daughter ever come?" Taea asked as she flipped through her phone.

"Hell nall. Her daughter was the one who signed her into the nursing home when I first started working there, she told Mrs. Lottie Mae that she was going to come back and visit."

"Let me guess the hoe never showed back up."

"Nope, never seen the skinny hoe again."

"Damn, well let's not judge her daughter, maybe Mrs. Lottie Mae wasn't shit when she was younger, so as soon as she got sick, her daughter stuck her in there. I mean I'm not going to fucking lie to you cuz, as soon as Tanya ass gets to the point where she can't do for herself, I'm signing her ass right on up," Taea admitted.

I understood why Taea felt like her mama didn't deserve any mercy. Tanya had destroyed our whole damn family, but even though my mama had taken me through hell and back, I honestly didn't believe I could just throw her away in a nursing home to die alone.

"Oh, shit, you got that look in your eyes," Taea muttered.

"What you talking about?" I asked her.

"I know you, Yanni, when I told you I was going to sign Tanya ass up in the nursing home when she got down in her health, you didn't say shit about what you would do when Lisa got old.

"I mean, I know Lisa has taken me through hell and back, but I don't think I can get rid of her and not see her at all.

"Taea," scuffed.

"You better than me, Tanya practically dead to me."

I didn't comment, because Taea had every right to be angry with her mama, but that didn't make it right. Trying to change Taea's mind wasn't going to happen, so it wasn't any point in me speaking on it, I changed the subject instead.

"You coming to my crib?" I asked Taea as I merged into the left lane.

"Nah, I'm going to have to catch up with you later. I want to shower and just rest up for tonight."

"What you got going on tonight?"

"The plan is to stay home with Jontavian and chill."

"And you got to rest up for that shit?"

"Bitch, hush. We going to catch up on a few movies that we wanted to see on Netflix, I can't be going to sleep on the one night that he decides that he ain't going to be out trapping."

Jontavian and Quantavious were homeboyz and had known each other since they were teenagers. When Quan got in the game, Jon followed along with him. When Taea first met Jontavian, she didn't give him any play, but it didn't take long for Taea to start fucking around with Jon on the regular. Next thing you know they were in a committed relationship and all in love and shit.

I pulled up at Taea's crib that she shared with Jon ten minutes later. Taea hopped out the car and was just about to slam the door when I stopped her.

"You working tomorrow?" I asked her quizzically.

"Unfortunately, I am," Taea replied.

"Do you want me to pick you up or are you going to drive yourself?"

Taea glanced over at her 2018 Toyota Camry that Jon had gotten her for their third anniversary and then looked back at me. I may try to drive the bitch, but if I change my mind, I will text you to let you know if you need to pick me up.

"Okay cool."

I waited until Taea had made it into her crib safely before I pulled off. I shook my head as I thought about Taea and her fear of driving. I'm not going to lie, Taea couldn't drive worth shit. Jon had brought her about three cars already with the Toyota Camry being the third one. So far Taea hasn't fucked it up because she been too scared to drive the bitch. Either she was running into someone, or someone was hitting her ass when it came to the previous cars.

After pulling out of Taea's driveway, I immediately headed home. Twenty minutes later, I pulled up next to Quan's Black Challenger. I was shocked to even see him home so early. Normally he didn't get in the house until late. I didn't bother by getting out the car, instead, I cut my car off and took a deep breath so I could relax and unwind.

As I sat there in silence, I began to thank the man upstairs for looking out for me. I had made a huge come up in my life. Here I was at the age of twenty-three and was living in my own four-bedroom home with three bathrooms. I never thought that my life was going to turn out like this. Growing up in the projects with the gangbangers and dope fiends, I lost all hope for my future. But when Quan came into my life, everything began to change for the better. My relationship with him seemed like a fairy tale, I felt like another Cinderella, even though I knew that was far from the truth.

I honestly loved him with all my heart because he loved me when I couldn't even love myself. When I first met him, I was twenty years old with no direction. I didn't know what I wanted to do in life, I had no motivation to go to a four-year college and wasn't interested in going to a technical college either. Even though I was smart as hell in school, I didn't feel the need to do anything with it. Instead of going off to a high price college like most of my classmates, I started slangin' dope on the corner so I could get the things that I needed for myself since I couldn't ask my mama for any of it.

I did this for about a year before my mama fucked around and snorted up over half of my dope that I was supposed to sell, while I was out shopping with Taea.

I was pissed when I found out what she had done. I knew I was fucked, and I was going to be punished for fucking up the dope man's profit. When my supplier Tito called a meeting about two blocks from my house, I already knew I was about to get beat the fuck down. Tito didn't give a fuck about me being a bitch, he always told me if I want to hustle like a nigga then he was going to treat me like he did the niggas who were in his crew.

When he called my ass out and started asking me where the rest of the money was for his dope, I immediately began to panic. Once he realized that I didn't have it Tito nutted up on my ass. Just when I thought I was going to get the beating of my life, Tito put his fist down when someone demanded him to stop. Tito was a big dark ass nigga, if he would have punched me, I would have never come back from that lick.

The fact that Tito and Quan were cousins was the only thing that saved my life that day. When Quan realized how I lived and how I was hustling to make ends meet, he quickly took it upon himself to step in and take over things. I went from stressing and crying and wondering how I was going to survive to living comfortably. He quickly swooped in, snatched me up, and made me his.

He always made sure I had enough money in my pockets to pay the bills in the house and to get anything that my heart desired. As we started to get serious, he eventually dropped a stack off for my education so I could take CNA classes and get my license. This nigga showed me love from the very beginning, even when he didn't have to, that alone was why I was so in love with him. I never knew real love until Quan came into my life. Just the thought of him always seemed to put a smile on my face.

I was just about to take my ass in the house when the front door opened, and I spotted Quan coming out. I squinted my eyes when I noticed he wasn't alone. My heart felt like it had fallen right out my chest as I watched him interact with some bitch.

Warner Robins was a small ass town. If you were doing some fuck shit, eventually the shit was going to get out.

I have never hung with KeKe, and we weren't cool because she was messy and was on that hoe shit. She lived in some low-income apartments on the Eastside and was known as the Eastside Thot. Everyone had run up in that and to know Quan had this nasty hoe up in my house was what really had my soul burning, and it wasn't in a good way either.

Honestly, I didn't understand what any of these niggas saw in the bitch, she wasn't cute in the face, the bitch just had a lot of ass. She was one of them light skinned ass hoes who thought she was automatically fine because of her skin tone. She was medium in height, with a bunch of tattoos on her arms, chest, legs, and neck. She had some weave in her head that stopped at her ass, and was wearing a pair of black booty shorts, with a grey tank top, that left nothing to the imagination.

It was something about how they were looking at one another that bothered me. Quan was so busy with his conversation with this hoe that he didn't even know I was parked right outside. I hopped out my car and walked over to them and instantly noticed the shocked expression on Quan's face.

"Hey, baby, what you doing home so early?"

I looked at him, and then I stared at the nasty bitch who was standing beside him.

"I'm not home early. Matter fact, I'm home late due to the fact I had to pick Taea up from work. Now what I want to know is what this musky ass bitch doing up in my crib?" I asked him as I pointed at KeKe.

"Baby, will you calm all that shit down, she just came over here to pick something up," Quan defended himself.

"Who the fuck is you calling a musky bitch?" KeKe asked.

"Bitch, ain't nobody talking to your ugly ass, get the fuck off my damn property," I spat at her.

If KeKe was smart, the bitch would have taken her happy ass on somewhere, but nall she wanted to pop off at the damn mouth.

"See bitch, that's why I don't like your ass, you think you so fucking much, bitch you wouldn't have shit if you weren't with Quan. He should have left your raggedy ass on the Northside in the projects with your crack head mama. Bitch you ain't shit, and once he leaves your ass, you ain't going to have shit either!" KeKe yelled.

I swear the bitch had gone too fucking far. I didn't even think twice about knocking that bitch slam out. One blow and that hoe were on the floor. I didn't hesitate to go to work on her ass. Quan tried to get me off of her, but I wasn't having that shit, I hit his ass right in the nose and continued to slam that bitch head into the ground. I kicked and stomped her a good number of times before Quan snatched my ass off her.

A few of our neighbors had come outside just to be nosy and see what was going on. Once KeKe got herself together and stood up I tried to attack her dumb ass again, but Quan held me firmly in his arms.

KeKe looked from me to Quan before she spit some blood onto the ground.

"You may have won the fight bitch, but that nigga who holding you is everybody's nigga. You a dumb ass bitch, if you for a second think this nigga has been loyal or faithful to you."

"KeKe get the fuck out of here!" Quan yelled at her.

"Nigga, I ain't going no fucking where this bitch thinks her shit don't stink. She thinks just because she got a little job wiping piss and shit off them old folks that she better than somebody. Let me tell your ass something, you ain't his only bitch and never will be. Matter fact, I just fucked that nigga in your house. Go smell that nice ass leather couch hoe, I bet you smell nothing but my sweet pussy juice on that bitch."

I tried to push Quan away from me, but he wasn't having that shit. He held me firmly, and he better be glad because I was ready to beat the brakes off that hoe.

"KeKe, get the fuck out of here before I blast your fucking ass. You don't have shit else to do but start some shit, ain't nobody fucked your ass! I don't want your ass, what the fuck I look like cheating on my bitch with the East Side Thot?

Now get the fuck off my property before I pistol whip your ass."

KeKe didn't say shit else, instead, she turned around and started walking to her car that was parked on the other side of the road.

Just when she was about to open her car door, she turned around for a brief moment and stared at me.

"I'm not the only bitch he fucking, he got others, you got a whole line of hoes you going to be fighting!" KeKe shouted at me before hopping in her beat-up Honda Accord and pulling off.

When Quan finally let me go, I wasted no time slapping the dog shit out of his ass.

"What the fuck was that hoe doing in my fucking house? Tell me the fucking truth. Nigga don't damn lie to me; did you fuck her?"

"What the fuck kind of question is that? I wouldn't dare put my dick in that bitch, that hoe lying. Who are you going to believe her or me?"

I looked around and noticed a crowd had gathered outside. I was beyond irritated because I hated for people to be in my business.

"All ya'll can take ya'll nosy asses back in the fucking house, it ain't shit to see here!" I yelled out to the neighbors.

I pushed past Quan and headed into the house. I slammed the door once he got himself inside and I wasted no time cursing his ass out.

"Nigga don't stand here and try to lie your way out of this shit. Admit, you told that hoe to come over here so you could fuck her because there is no other way, she would have any reason to bring her ugly ass over here. You know I don't like people at my house and never have you brought anyone over here."

"Look, baby, my stomach was fucked up today. I been

shitting all day. I ain't moved my car at all today because I was scared that I was going to have to shit while I was out and about. The bitch hit me up talking about she was on my side of town, and she wanted to buy some pills. Shid, I ain't about to turn down no fucking money, so I told her to pull up, and I was going to serve her. I lost track of time bae, I was trying to hurry up and get the bitch out of the crib before you pulled up."

I already knew that nigga was lying, but my heart wasn't ready to accept the truth just yet even though common sense had already kicked in. Normally I would ignore all the bullshit when it came down to a bitch talking about, they had fucked my nigga because I felt like the hoes were lying, but this time was different, something just wasn't right, and I was ready to get down to the bottom of it. I was tired of being in the dark, I was ready to see shit for what it was.

"Okay, you say you ain't fuck her then prove it to me. Pull your shorts down. Let me see your dick."

Quan stared at me like I was crazy.

"Baby, what's that gonna solve."

"Do what the fuck I asked you to damn do. You say you ain't fuck the hoe so you won't have a problem pulling down your shorts and letting me look at your dick."

Baby, I swear to you that I ain't touched that girl, I wouldn't never hurt you in that way. I'm not about to pull down my pants for you either, you just need to trust me.

"You must think I'm some stupid bitch, nigga either you pull them down or I will do it for your ass."

He took a few steps back from me and in my heart, I knew he was lying, but I still wanted the proof.

"Do it or I swear you will never have to worry about me ever again.," I spat at him.

When his shorts and boxers were down to his ankles, I walked over to him and got down on my knees.

I guess this nigga thought I was about to suck his dick because his manhood instantly started getting on hard.

"Pipe all that shit down, I'm not about to give you no fucking mouth service until I know the truth. I grabbed his dick with my hand and smelt it just to see if it smelled like he had been fucking.

The first whiff I took I smelt nothing but pussy. I stood up and pushed that nigga away from me.

"Baby, let me explain."

"It ain't shit that you can tell me to make this shit right! I've been loyal to your ass since day one and this the shit you do. All these hoes around this bitch who've been beefing with me and spreading all these rumors about you and turns out none of these hoes are lying. You really been out here fucking these hoes?"

Quan just stood there and stared at me.

I mean the nigga couldn't say shit, it wasn't anything that he could do or say to me to make any of this go away.

"Do me a favor, get the fuck out of my face before I hurt your ass. How I feel right about now, I swear I don't mind catching a life sentence."

Quan pulled his shorts back up and didn't waste any time grabbing his keys and dipping out.

He knew me all too well, talking to me when I was this upset wasn't going to lead to anything but one of us being six feet deep. I was the nicest person that anyone could meet, but once you crossed me, my beast mode was activated, and I didn't give a fuck who I hurt. After the door slammed behind him, and once I heard his car crank up, only then did I break down and cry.

QUAN

I was a boss ass nigga, but I also was loyal. Most niggas didn't know what loyalty was, but that was something that I grew up having. I was loyal to the streets, and I was loyal to the niggas I used to hustle with on the block, but never have I ever been loyal to my bitch. I know the shit is fucked up, but it was hard to stay faithful when I had so many bitches wanting to fuck me. Don't get me wrong, I was crazy about Yanni and would murk a nigga if they ever tried to fuck her, but I still did me, and she ain't know shit about it until KeKe opened her big ass mouth.

"Fuck," I muttered to myself as I slid into my Dodge Challenger and pulled into traffic.

Hoes came with the territory of being a dope boy and having money. I can pull any bitch that I wanted, but Yanni was the only one I wanted to be my main. The rest of the hoes that I fucked around with was just something to do. Yanni and I had been rocking together for a good minute, I was never going to leave her for anyone because I knew she was one of a kind. It was no replacing my shorty. I had fucked up bad, I was sloppy as hell to let KeKe loud mouth ass come over to my crib knowing that my shorty lived with me.

I never brought anyone to my private spot, normally I would get a hotel room and smash hoes there, or I would go over to their crib and drop some dick off in them, but today it was poor judgment on my part. I told KeKe to pull up, we got high, and I lost track of time. The little bitch gave me some fire ass head which only led to me bending her over my couch and fucking her raw.

Damn, I had taken that shit too far. I never fucked a bitch raw, but today had been different. I wasn't thinking clearly, and now I had to suffer the consequences. There wasn't a lie in the world that I could tell to make shit right with Yanni. She was super pissed at me, and she had every right to be. Niggas were gonna do some hoe shit at times, but most do hide the shit to make sure their bitch don't find out. I had fucked up, yeah, I knew that much. I just hoped Yanni didn't stay mad at me for too long. There was no point in me trying to talk to her at the moment, she was pissed, the best thing for me to do was let her cool off.

Fifteen minutes later, I pulled up at the Hampton Inn and booked me a room. Going back home tonight wasn't an option. I hopped out my whip, and all eyes were on me. It was crowded as hell and bitches were standing outside smoking and drinking. I nodded my head at a few and headed inside to pay for a room at least for that night.

"Good Evening, how may I help you?" the desk clerk asked me as she stared me down.

I knew by the way she was checking me out that she wanted to fuck with me. The bitch was standing behind the counter smiling hard as hell as she bit down on her bottom lip. She was chocolate in complexion, with big full lips, her teeth were pretty and straight, and her eyes were a soft brown. I already knew her hair didn't stop down her back, but at least her weave wasn't nappy as hell. I swear that shit wasn't attractive to have a bitch smiling in your face with a nappy head.

"Do ya'll have any rooms available?" I asked her politely as I ignored her flirtatious glares.

I didn't want to stare at her for too long because I didn't want her to think I wanted her. She was cute in the face, but her body was made up wrong. One then I didn't like was a skinny ass bitch. I wanted my hoes to have some weight on them. This bitch was skinny as fuck, she was that white girl skinny which was a turn off to me. Even though she was checking me out, I was ready to shut her down if she thought she was about to pull me, it wasn't going to happen.

Plus, I was already in the dog house, fucking around with another bitch in my city was only going to make shit worse. All I wanted to do was get a damn room so I could lay low for the night until my boo cooled down. Once Yanni calmed her ass down, hopefully, we were able to talk, and I would be able to sweet talk her ass into forgiving me.

"I do have one available room. It's a King-sized bed that's for smokers."

"Perfect," I told her as I pulled out my black card.

"How much?"

"Ummm, seventy dollars for one night."

I swiped my card and waited for her to hand me my key.

When she handed me the key, she had the nerve to brush her hand across mine. I wanted to laugh, but I refrained. Instead, I snatched my key card from her and walked off. Just before I walked out the door, I turned back to her and told her some real shit.

"You cute and all baby girl, but you don't want these problems."

The flirtatious smile that she had earlier dropped from her face immediately as I headed out the door.

I slid back into my car and was just about to pull off when I got an alert on my phone that I had a text message. My heart began to pound heavily because I thought that it was Yanni messaging me, but anger filled my body once I saw that it was KeKe. I read the message almost three times before I cursed that bitch all the way out.

KeKe: Nigga how you gonna not defend me? I only told your bitch the fucking truth. She needs to know the damn truth. You a hood nigga, you everybody's nigga, it's time she knows the shit. You the one who told me to come through, we fucked so what? I can't help she came home and saw me.

Me: Fucking with you was a fucking mistake bitch. You were supposed to have kept your mouth closed, but since you wanted to be messy then I'ma have to cut your ass all the way off. Maybe she wouldn't have tapped that ass if you would have left when she told you to. Do me a favor, stay away from me, lose this damn number.

I was just about to block that hoe number until she sent me another message with a bunch of laughing faces along with a message talking about, she was gonna tell her brother what happened. I told her ass to tell her pussy ass brother what she wanted because I didn't give a fuck. He wasn't going to do shit about it. I never laid a hand on the bitch; her mouth got her that ass whooping that Yanni served her ass.

I guess KeKe thought telling her brother was going to put fear in my heart, but it didn't. I wasn't scared of no damn nigga. I ran the Northside of Warner Robins. I sold the best dope and pills that money could buy. Her brother Ken was a dope boy on the North side who couldn't pull in the type of money I was making. He was a knock-off version of myself. He was about six feet in height, with a slim frame. He was light skinned and had that type of vibe that he was a pretty boy but wanted to be hood.

He never liked my ass because I had the connect that he

wanted. He was a regular ass dope boy still slangin dope on the corner. He was trying to make a come up, but after all these years he still wasn't hitting on shit.

Ken and I both grew up on the North side and never got along. We went to the same school but didn't run with the same crowd. He was always a pussy ass nigga even in high school. Yeah, he sold dope back in the day, but he wasn't about that life. I can remember when the police locked his scary ass up for selling dope in school. We all know how cops can be, they be wanting to know who all helping you sell the dope and who supplied it to you.

Anyway, word on the street was that when they locked his ass up and he started singing like the little bitch that he was. He snitched on all his homies, and all of them did a little time in the juvenile detention center. We all were in the 11th grade at the time when this shit went down.

When his homies got out, they stopped fucking with his lame ass and started running with my crew and me. So basically, the beef with me was he was still pissed that I took his little squad. But ain't no real nigga going to want to follow a pussy ass nigga who a snitch.

Me and his homies who came to my team dropped out before we even got the chance to go to the 12th grade. We were making so much money that everyone agreed to just say fuck school. Fast forward ten years later, I'm twenty-seven years old with a strong crew that consisted of four loyal niggas.

I was doing well for myself, but still had a bunch of niggas hating on my ass. I kept to myself, didn't fuck with anyone who wasn't from my squad and made sure to stay away from anyone that fucked with Ken. Messing around with Ken's sister was the biggest mistake that I made, but I didn't have to worry about no heat coming from him because he was a pussy ass nigga. He wasn't going to step to me about his sister. I didn't do shit to her ass. She did that shit to herself by running her mouth and trying to check my bitch. From now on, I needed to stop fucking around with these bum ass bitches who didn't have shit to lose.

From what I had last heard, KeKe didn't have a nigga. I understood I mean what nigga you know going to wife up a thot. I guess some niggas would because they were dumb as hell, but no real nigga going to want to wife that bitch. She got her money by fucking around with these ballers around Warner Robins and Macon, she stayed fucking somebody's nigga because she couldn't pull her own due to the fact her pussy had way too many miles on it.

After blocking the bitch, I hit my homeboy Jon up just to see if he could come through later tonight and chill with my ass. I mean, I had gotten myself kicked out my own crib and needed someone that I could talk to. Jon's phone ranged a few times before he picked up.

"What up nigga? I heard you in the dog house," Jon said into the phone.

"Damn, Yanni already hit Taea up and told her everything?"

"Hell yeah, nigga. Yanni super pissed she talking about leaving your ass for real."

I rubbed my face with my hand and groaned into the phone.

"Shit, man I fucked up bad."

"Yeah, I know your ass did. What in the hell were you thinking when you told that loud mouth ass girl to come to your fucking crib?"

"Man, I wasn't thinking at all bruh, I was on some bull-shit, I got to get my baby back man."

"Forget that shit nigga, let her ass cool down because she ain't with the talking shit right about now. Taea on the phone with her now, she still trying to calm shorty down. Where your ass at anyway?"

"I'm out riding, I was trying to see if you wanted to get up later."

"Nah, I can't get out tonight, I made plans to stay my light skinned ass home so me and bae can have some alone time. She has been bitching about how I ain't been spending time with her lately. She says I been in the streets way too much, with the shit you just pulled, she up here side eyeing my ass thinking I'm out here fucking other bitches. Nigga, I don't need that type of heat. They both know we like brothers, shid, by you doing shit like you did, Taea probably thinking I'm doing the same. You done brought heat to my door with this shit."

"Nigga, don't even start that shit, you always been faithful to Taea crazy ass."

"Hell yeah, nigga, I know I got a good thing, I'm not about to fuck that shit up to smash no hoe. My bae crazy, she will kill that bitch and kill my ass too."

I chuckled into the phone.

"Bruh, you can cheat and smash other hoes, you just got to know how to do it."

"Nah, I'm good on all that shit. Bae got good pussy, I ain't trying to cuff no other bitches."

"Respect," I told him.

"Look, I know you going through a lot and need someone to talk to, but let me give Taea some time, and I'm going to try to get up with you later on tonight. Where are you going to be at?" Jon asked.

"I just paid for a room for the night at the Hampton Inn."

"Cool, how many nights you paid for?"

"Only one."

"Well bruh, you might want to pay for a whole week cause shorty just that pissed."

"Fuck all that shit, I'm not about to stay away from her ass for no damn week. I ain't never stayed away from her, not even for two days."

"Shid, well, it can always be a first time for everything."

"Bruh, Yanni and I always getting into it and fussing, all I have to do is go in another bedroom and close the fucking door. I lock the door if I have to when the fussing gets too rough. I don't want to hurt shorty, but at the same time, I don't like leaving her alone for too long. You know I got a lot of enemies out here in these streets."

"I understand all that Quan, but nigga this ain't your normal argument, she found out you been cheating on her ass with all these raggedy ass hoes. She super pissed about that shit, like I said, just give her a little time, and you need to get your shit together in the process. You don't want to lose the one who's down for you because you want to fuck other bitches."

I ignored everything Jon told me and told him to hit me up when he was ready to pull up at the Hampton Inn.

I threw the phone on the passenger seat and headed towards KFC. I understood everything that Jon was saying, but I wasn't yet ready to really take all that shit in. I knew what I had to do, I had to stop fucking other bitches and be a faithful ass nigga. This shit wasn't easy, especially when you have never been faithful to no bitch. The shit was going to be hard, and it wasn't something that I could do overnight.

I pulled up at KFC and cut my engine. I normally would go through the drive-thru, but after a few times of them getting my order wrong, I decided to take my ass inside just to make sure they fixed my food right. I stepped into KFC and headed over to the counter and waited for someone to take my order

"Welcome to KFC. How may I help you?"

I stared at the bitch a few times because she looked familiar.

"Quan is that you?" the bitch asked me quizzically.

I knew that the little bitch looked familiar, but I couldn't remember her name for shit. Damn, I needed to stop smoking so much weed, I thought to myself.

"You may not remember me, but my name Aisha, we took a few classes in the eleventh grade."

I thought back for a little bit, and it all came together. Aisha was a fine little chick that I had a major crush on in high school. We took history together, and I always tried to sit beside her and work with her on all the class projects we had to do. I never told her how I felt back then because I knew a bitch was the last thing I needed to be dealing with. The only thing I was focused on was making my money, bitches could wait. The fact I came from a rough household was partly why I had a fuck all bitches and get money attitude.

Just imagine you growing up and your pops raising you because your mama out hoeing in the streets the entire time. My pops were one of them bitter ass niggas who didn't give a shit about me because my mama was a little thot. I mean damn, I understood my pops loved my mama, but I felt like the nigga loved her ass more than his own child. I was the only child, which was a blessing if you ask me.

I didn't have the best childhood, but it could have been better if I had responsible parents. My mama didn't work, she was the type of bitch that felt she was too good to work and spent her time hoeing around while pops worked. I believe that was what made my pops bitter about their situation. She didn't seem to be interested in anything and only cared about herself and what made her feel good. and didn't have money of her own, but she would gladly spend his and complain that he wasn't making enough. My pops were a mechanic. He was just an ordinary nigga who fixed people cars in the hood, so money was tight when I was growing up.

If I didn't hustle and grind, I didn't get the shit that I needed. So that's how I got in the drug business. I was only seventeen when my big cousin Tito took me under his wing, and I never looked back since. When my pops found out he didn't even lecture me or act like he cared, the only thing he said was I hope you save enough money so you can get the fuck out of my house.

A year later my pops ended up being killed at a gas station. He was hit by a stray bullet which punctured his heart, he died instantly. The shit was sad, but it was life. To this day, my mama was still doing her own thing. Yeah, my mama was hurt when pops died the way he did, but not once did I see her shed a single tear, she held all that shit inside.

After dropping out of high school, I ended up going out on my own and getting my own place. There was no way I wanted to stay with my mama. She had way too many niggas she was fucking around with, and I was a little hot nigga back in them days. I didn't want to end up popping a nigga for being on some fuck shit or thinking they were going to come in and try to run some shit.

My pops wasn't even in the ground good before I moved out my mom's crib. The relationship wasn't the best back then, but now that I was older, I didn't give a fuck about any of that shit. I hate in my heart for my mama. I made sure to look out for her whenever she needed something, I had forgiven her because having all that hate in my heart wasn't going to get me anywhere. Even though all had been forgiven, I never forgot what either one of my parents took me through when I was growing up.

Aisha continued to stare me down and finally began to blush when I told her that I remembered her.

She bit down on her bottom lip, and I got lost in her pretty hazel eyes.

Aisha was a redbone, with hazel green eyes, with pretty pink lips, and had her haircut similar to Halle Berry.

"I ain't seen your ass in ten years," Aisha added.

"Yeah, I know it's been a minute," I told her.

Aisha nodded.

"Are you still living here?" I asked her curiously.

"I just moved back here, I left after graduation and went off to Georgia State University. I went for business. I found a good job and was doing good for myself until mama got diagnosed with cancer about two years ago. I decided to move back home to be closer to her."

I eyed her up.

"What you doing working at KFC shorty?" I asked curiously.

I wasn't trying to be rude, but I was trying to make sense of the shit. You went to school for business but you up here working at KFC as a team member, the shit wasn't adding up to me. My mama always told me when I was growing up, if I wanted to know something then I better ask.

She didn't seem like she took offense to my question because she did answer it.

"Well, I have to pay my bills, and I'm not making as much here as I did in Atlanta. I'm working two jobs. During the day I work at the Air Force Base in the office, and at night I work here," she muttered.

"Damn, you grinding. You were like that in high school, that was what I liked about you back in school."

Aisha seemed shocked.

"You liked me back then? I had no idea you ain't act like you did."

"Shid, I was crazy about you back then. I just was more

focused on getting my money than trying to get a relationship."

"Right that's understandable, well what would you like to eat today?"

I smiled.

"Um, give me one of them five-dollar fill-ups. The two-piece I told her."

She rung my order up, and after paying her, she gave me a shy smile before telling me she was glad to see me.

I looked around and noticed that she had a long line and I wasn't about to keep the line held up trying to shoot my shot.

I boldly asked her for her number and saved it into my phone.

"What time you getting off tonight?" I asked her.

"Around ten," she replied.

"Okay cool, maybe we can meet up when you get off."

"Sure, I would love that," Aisha replied

I stepped aside to wait for my order as she busied herself ringing up the rest of the people that were standing behind me.

After grabbing my food, I headed out the door and hopped back into my car.

I turned my speakers up as I blasted *Plies' Drip 4 sale*. I nodded my head to the music as I pulled out of KFC. As I came to the red light with my Challenger banging, an old white couple had their windows down. They both looked at me and shook their heads. I couldn't help but laugh inside. These white folks didn't know shit about this type of music. I bet they were just cursing my ass out for banging so loud. My speakers weren't no joke, them bitches were so loud you could hear my music before you even saw my whip.

I pulled up at Hampton Inn about fifteen minutes later and headed in my room with my food. I checked the time and noticed it was already close to nine p.m. I hurried to eat because I wanted to head down the road to find me a something to wear since I didn't bring any of my things with me. When Yanni told me to get the fuck out, the last thing that I was thinking about was the clothes that I was going to wear.

After smashing my chicken, I grabbed my keys and headed back out. I went down the road to the nearest store which was Walmart and found a parking spot. I hated coming to Walmart on Watson Blvd because the bitch was always crowded and it was always hard to find a damn parking spot. After over ten minutes of roaming the parking lot, I finally found somewhere to damn park.

I hopped out my car and headed inside towards the men section. I didn't care how much money I had; I wasn't the type of nigga who felt I was better than anyone. Some niggas when they got their money right, they felt they were too good to shop at Walmart. Not I; I didn't give a fuck. Yeah, I wore all the latest gear as far as the clothes and shoes, but a nigga also had a little Walmart shit in my closet as well.

I grabbed a shopping cart that I had found and went to work on finding me a few clothes to wear until I was able to go back home to get some of my things. I found me about five shorts and a few shirts as well. I grabbed me a pack of black socks as well as a pack of boxers. After getting everything I needed out of the clothes department, I made sure to get me some Listerine to wash my mouth with, a toothbrush, and also some soap. I headed to the self-check-out line because I didn't have all day to be waiting around for someone to check me out. Walmart had all these cash registers and had only about four registers opened. The shit was ridiculous. I wasn't the type of nigga to have a lot of patience, so I always went to the self-checkout no matter where I shopped at. If they had it, I was going to use that bitch.

After paying for my items, I headed back to my car and started putting the items that I had just brought in the backseat. I was just about to get inside the car when I spotted a vehicle backing out. It was an old black man who was getting way too close to my car. I didn't waste any time blowing my horn to get his attention.

He was driving one of them old town cars and was wearing some big ass glasses because his ass probably couldn't see. He looked like he was about in his seventies, but I didn't know for sure. His ass looked way too fucking old to be driving by himself that was all I knew.

I swear these old folks caused a lot of accidents because they ass wasn't paying attention or they had cataracts in their eyes and shit. I didn't have time to be riding around here with a damn dent in my shit because somebody's granddaddy done ran into me from the back. When the old man heard me blow at him, he threw up his hand to let me know he saw my car and drove off.

I shook my head and slid into the driver's seat. I swear these folks in Warner Robins couldn't drive worth shit. All these nice ass cars these people rode up here, and all of them mostly had dents from them hitting someone or them being hit for pulling out in front of cars and shit.

All these hoes and niggas were rocking dents in their brand-new cars, and I was sitting here rocking a clean ass whip with no dents and no scratches anywhere.

I pulled out of Walmart parking lot and headed back to the hotel for the last time that night. I wasn't planning on getting my ass out anymore that night. When I stepped back into my hotel, I threw my bags on my king's sized bed and was just about to take me a shower when my phone alerted me, I had a text message. Yet again, my heart pounded because I figured it had to be Yanni, but it wasn't. Instead, it was a message from Aisha letting me know she couldn't wait to see me. She told me that she was getting off in another hour and that she was going to shower and change before she came over. I told her that was fine and I made sure to give her the name of my hotel that I was staying at and also my room number.

I threw my phone on the bed and headed towards the bathroom so I could take me a shower. Even though I had fucked KeKe earlier and had caught a nut, I was still down to nut again, but that was only if Aisha was down to break a nigga off some of that coochie.

The fact that I always wanted to fuck her was what really had my dick bouncing and ready to catch another nut. I undressed and stepped in the shower so I could take care of my hygiene before she pulled up.

After cleaning myself, I stepped out the shower, brushed my teeth, and pulled my long dreads into a rubber band. I grabbed a pair of my boxers, slid them on with a pair of my grey basketball shorts, and made sure to put a pair of black socks as well. I tore the tag off my plain black t-shirt and pulled it over my head. After I was done getting dressed, I made sure to put on a little cologne before I grabbed my phone to see where Aisha was at.

I already knew what I was doing was wrong, but I wanted to smash one last bitch before I begged Yanni back. I had always wanted to fuck Aisha, and I was finally about to get the chance to do it. I wasn't about to turn down the opportunity to blow her back out. From how she was looking at a nigga at KFC I knew Aisha wanted the dick.

Yanni and what we had going on was going to have to wait, because I knew deep down inside Yanni wasn't going to really leave me. Yeah, she was super pissed, but something in my heart let me knew that once she calmed down, she was going to want to talk things out. No way my baby was going to throw away nearly three years just because I fucked someone else and she found out about it.

Yeah, I fucked up this one time, but I was willing to do whatever to get her back with me.

An hour later I heard a knock at the door.

I hurried to open the door and stepped aside to let Aisha inside. My dick instantly grew hard when I noticed what she had on. She was wearing a pair of baby blue booty shorts a white tank top which showed off her titties and erect nipples. I could tell by how her booty shorts was fitting that she wasn't wearing any panties either. Damn, Aisha wasn't playing with my ass, she already knew what was about to go down, and she was down with it apparently. I loved bitches like her. My dick was throbbing and aching for a release, and it all came from just looking at her. I ain't even had the chance to feel her up yet.

When the door closed behind me, I took a seat in a chair as I watched Aisha start removing her clothes. No words were spoken between us, our bodies were doing all the talking at that moment. I licked my lips as she stood in front of me butt naked. Her body was perfect, and I took in every curve that appeared on her thick frame.

She walked over to me, and I sat back in the chair as she began to slow dance on me. Her pussy scent filled my nose as she lifted her left foot on top of the armrest of the chair and started popping her pussy into my face. I smacked her ass a few times as she continued to tease me. A nigga was ready to fuck, fuck all that playing shit. I stood up out of the chair I was sitting in, grabbed her, and pulled her down to her knees, as I pulled down my boxers and shorts. I stroked my dick a few times just before she slapped my hand away and slid my manhood into her mouth.

I groaned as her mouth wrapped around the head of my dick.

"Fuck," I muttered to myself as I rubbed my hands through her low-cut hair.

She sucked and slurped on my stick like she was sucking a lollipop. I felt no teeth, I felt nothing but her hot mouth devouring my dick. When she started deep throating my sausage, I swear she had my toes curling up. I gripped her lil' short ass hair and yanked on it, that bitch mouth was the truth.

I slid my thick pole in and out of her hot mouth as she played in her pussy. When she started licking and sucking my balls, I knew she was going to be a beast in bed because her head was about to kill my ass. It was like she was trying to take my fucking soul if I allowed her to. I pulled her away from me because there was no way I wanted to catch my nut this fast, especially not from just head. I wanted to sample the pussy too, I wanted to be able to always remember this shit because after tonight I doubt, I ever see shorty again.

We were going in two separate ways in life, I was tied down to someone already, and I wasn't about to leave Yanni for no one. I loved her way too hard, but I was infatuated over Aisha. I always wanted her, and I was finally about to stamp that pussy, so she could always remember me, no matter who she fucked with after tonight, they were never going to be me. She was always going to think about me; whether she wanted to or not.

After pulling my dick out of Aisha's sweet mouth, I pushed her ass down on the bed and sucked on each of her erect nipples as she moaned out my name. When I was done with her nipples, I lightly sucked on her neck, as I slid a finger into her honey pot. Her moans intensified as she begged for me to fuck her.

I pulled away from her rather briefly with a smirk on my face. I slid her legs apart and dipped my tongue deep into her love tunnel.

"Fuccccckkkk," Aisha moaned as I applied pressure on her clit.

I slid a finger deep into her love tunnel as I continued to lick on her clit.

I didn't stop until she started creaming. I licked and sucked her filling from between her legs before I distanced myself from her. I grabbed my wallet out of my nightstand and pulled out a condom. I rolled it over my enlarged dick as I stared down at Aisha.

"Shit, your pussy so sweet," I told her as I tapped my dick on her pussy about three times.

"Thanks," Aisha choked out as she waited on me to slide into her.

As soon as I slid inside her love nest, I already knew that her pussy wasn't going to be trash. Her coochie was good, juicy, and tight. She fitted my dick like a glove. I started out giving her some deep, slow strokes just so she could get used to the thickness of my dick. I was a good nine inches and was thick with it as well. I could tear a bitch down if I wanted to, but Aisha wasn't some little thot off the street, she was more than that, I was going to fuck her respectfully.

"You like that baby?" I asked as she started crying out my name.

I grunted as she wrapped her legs around my waist and started throwing her pussy at me. When she started doing that shit, I knew it was time for me to step my game up. She didn't want me to slowly stroke her, she wasn't that type of bitch, she wanted to fuck fuck, and I was down to do just that. All that slow fucking got boring after a while. I always was down to tear a pussy up.

I looked deep into her hazel eyes as I began to wear her pussy out.

She was screaming out my name and busting cream all over my pole.

Never have I ever smashed a bitch who could nut back to back like she was doing. I slid out of her a few moments later because if I would have kept on hitting her with her legs wrapped around my waist, I was going to end up busting. I wasn't ready to nut just yet. I wanted to enjoy myself tonight. I have never been a selfish nigga in bed. I always made sure to please anyone who I broke off this dick to.

I flipped Aisha over on her stomach as she placed her face in the pillow.

"Ass up," I instructed her.

Her arch was just right, and I could see cream oozing out her coochie.

"Baby girl, your pussy so fucking good," I told her just as I slid into her from the back.

Her whimpers filled the room as I dicked her down

"Fuck me, Quan," Aisha cried out as I continued to pound her.

I slid my dick out her coochie a few seconds later and flipped her around to face me. I stuck my tongue down her throat as I caressed her body.

I took her place on the bed and told her to get on top of me so I could see if she could ride some dick. Aisha didn't waste any time getting into position. Instead of her riding me facing forward, she flipped herself around and was getting ready to ride me cowgirl style.

I placed a hand on her hips as she slowly slid down on my monster dick. I laid there in utter disbelief as she started twerking on my manhood. I couldn't help but grab her juicy ass and play with it as she started to slowly grind on me. I nearly lost my mind when she started bouncing on my dick and yelling out my name.

If this bitch would have had a wig on her head, I swear I would have snatched that bitch clean off. That was just how good this girl was fucking me. When she started nutting on my dick, she started slowing down for only a brief moment. I was near cumming, I was ready to bust even though I didn't want to. But what brought that nut up out me, was when this little bitch fucked around and did a split on my dick. I nearly passed the fuck out right then and there. The nut that I was holding back shot out of me. I held her ass down just so she wouldn't move as I filled her pussy with my cum.

When we were done, she hopped from off me and headed into the bathroom. I watched her as she wet her a rag so she could clean herself off. I stayed there not able to move because that bitch had fucked my soul from out my body. I mean I just couldn't believe that someone could have good head and have even better pussy.

That bitch pussy was the fucking devil. I needed to stay away from her ass. Even though I had said I was only going to fuck her one time, I was beginning to wonder if that shit was even possible, her pussy was so good. I was putting Aisha in the same category as Yanni because both of them had some good pussy. I always was in search of different pussy, but I wasn't expecting this shit.

So much was running through my mind that I didn't even hear Aisha come back into the room until she wiped the extra nut from off my dick. She grabbed my boxers and basketball shorts and handed them to me. I was so weak I could barely stand up to put my clothes on.

I watched Aisha as she began to put back on her clothes when she was fully dressed, she walked over to me and placed a kiss on my cheeks

"I'm so glad that we found one another," she told me sweetly.

"Shid, I'm glad we did too. You got my number still? I ask her curiously?"

"Of course, I do. I wasn't planning on deleting it," she replied.

"I'm not going to lie to you, but I got a girl. We on bad terms right about now, but things going to iron out in a few days. I just wanted to fuck on you to see what you were working with, but I'm not trying to get hooked."

Just when I thought Aisha was going to pop off at the mouth about me not telling her I already had someone before we fucked, she did the total opposite, Aisha laughed instead.

"Okay cool, I already knew you probably had a bitch some damn where. Ain't no nigga with as much money as your single," she told me honestly.

"Yeah, you right on that," I replied.

"Well, since we being honest with one another, then I guess you should know that I got someone too."

I'm not going to lie, I felt like I had been slapped because I wasn't expecting her to say some shit like that. I guess I thought in my mind she was going to be single because her pussy wasn't worn out like most females who did a lot of fucking.

"Don't give me that look, when you came in KFC, you ain't ask me if I had a man or any of that shit."

"Right, I didn't think to ask at the time," I told her truthfully.

"Who's the nigga you fucking around with, he someone from here?" I asked her curiously.

I mean I didn't want to pry into her personal life, but I wanted to know who she was dealing with.

"You don't know him; he came with me from Atlanta to help me take care of my mama."

For the first time, I looked down at her hand, and that's when I noticed a silver ring on her left finger.

I had been so busy checking her fine ass out that I didn't even think to check her finger to see if she was married.

"You married to the nigga?"

"Nah, we engaged though. We going to get married next month," she told me as she grabbed her purse off my bed.

She was just about to head to the door when I stopped her.

"Do the nigga make you happy? Are you sure marriage is what you want to do?"

I could tell how she was looking and her body language that I was only a quick nut for her. Nothing more was going to come out of any of this, and I was cool with that. I had someone, and she had someone whom she loved and wanted to spend the rest of her life with.

"Look I'm going, to be honest with you, I love my man to the moon and back, I ain't never cheated on him until today, do I feel guilty hell yeah, but I ain't going to tell him shit. What he doesn't know won't hurt him, but what we just did can't happen again."

I smirked at her as I pulled her close to me.

"Shid, I understand," I told her before placing a kiss on her pretty lips.

As she walked out the door, I stood there to make sure she got in her car safely. After she had pulled off, I closed the door behind her and took a seat on the end of the bed.

I wanted to love Yanni and give her everything she needed, and I was willing to do just that. Fucking around with Aisha was just something to do, she loved her nigga that she was with and I loved my bitch. She had shit to lose, so I knew what we did was never going to get out to anyone. She wasn't about to risk her relationship for no one, she made that shit clear when she told me that us fucking couldn't happen again. A nigga couldn't get mad because I had someone anyway. At the end of the day, Yanni was the one I wanted to spend the rest of my life with.

I never understood why it was so hard being with one bitch, but from this day forward I wasn't going to be breaking off any more bitches. It was now the time to be the man that Yanni wanted me to be.

KEKE

I couldn't believe that Quan had let Yanni whoop my ass without defending me. Rather he knew it or not, he had just signed his death certificate. He had fucked with the wrong bitch. Apparently, he was used to fucking around with these clown ass hoes, but I wasn't one of them. I wasted no time pulling up at my brother's crib so I could tell him what had just gone down. I pulled up in my brother driveway but noticed that his car wasn't there. Instead of getting out and using my key, I decided to wait in the car for a little while longer.

Even though my brother had given me a key and told me I could come over anytime I wanted but I rarely ever used it. Today was just one of them days, that I felt I didn't want to barge in his house. Sitting outside and trying to clear my mind seemed like the best option for me today.

I pulled out my cell and shot Ken a text too let him know that I was at his house and needed to talk to him about something important.

The fact that Ken already had beef with Quan and didn't like him was something that I was going to use to my advantage. I was always told growing up that a lie goes farther than the truth, today I was going to test that theory.

I might was a thot in a lot of niggas eyes but I deserved respect. I wasn't about to let no one disrespect me. Yanni may have beat my ass, but the bitch wasn't going to be prepared for what I had coming towards her ass. I had a plan and I was ready to execute the bitch. Even though I always had a thing for Quan, I was ready to put all those lustful feelings away. I had a point to prove and I was ready to prove that I wasn't just come easy ass thot that he could disrespect.

I groaned in pain as I touched the lump that was beginning to form on my forehead. My lips was busted and my face were in pain. I sat in the car for a few more moments before my brother finally pulled up. Coming to the Westside and talking to my brother was the best way to get the plain set into motion. One thing I do know, was that Ken didn't play about me. He would do anything for me, I was his baby sister and he had practically raised me himself. We grew up in a household with no one but ourselves to depend on. Our parents were dope heads who didn't give a fuck about either one of us. The only thing they did was give us a place to rest our heads. We grew up on the Northside in the projects in a roach infested two-bedroom apartment. I hated my life growing up, but in the end, it showed me how to hustle and be able to take care of myself.

I grew up fast and used my looks to get what I wanted from men. I considered myself sexy and very alluring. I could easily attract any man just by my appearance. I was high yellow in complexion, medium in height, with wide hips a big ass, full juicy lips, and pretty white teeth. While my brother Ken sold dope to put food on the table, I came up with my own hustle to make cash. I was only a teenage when I first started sucking dick in the hood, most of them were dope boys. I went from sucking dick to busting it wide open for any nigga who had enough money to afford me; that's how I got the name of the Eastside Thot because almost every nigga on the Eastside had sampled my pussy. I didn't give a fuck what anyone said about me. As long as my bills was paid that all I cared about. The only people who had something smart to say was the hating ass hoes who was pissed that their niggas as fucking with me. I was the thot could fuck their nigga and send him back to them sexually satisfied. They should have been thinking me for helping them with the shit they felt they didn't want to do, but no all they wanted to do was hate on me. Even though I had fucked a lot of niggas Quan was someone I never got a chance to fuck with until today. I knew him because of the beef that my brother had with him, but I also brought my drugs from him when my bother didn't have what I wanted.

My brother was in the dark about a lot if shit that I did and I wanted it to stay that way. Buying weed from Quan was one of the first things on my list that I never wanted my brother to find out about.

Today was a normal day for me. I woke up with the urge to get high, but I wanted pills instead of weed. I was going to get some pills from my brother but he was out of pocket so I hit up Quan. I understood my brother hated Quan but Quan had some quality product. Honestly, I didn't give a fuck on who I brought my product from as long as I got that high that was all I was looking for.

Right now, Quan was the only nigga that I had been with that I regretted fucking. Going over to his crib had been a mistake. I knew Quan had a reputation for being a nigga who was always dropping dick off to bitches and I wanted to sample from for myself. He fucked me good that's for sure, but the dick didn't have me where I was going to let him treat me like some scum on the bottom of his shoe.

The tapping on my car window was what pulled me out

of my daydream and brought me back to Earth. He was dressed in a pair of black cargo shorts, a white and grey shirt that said Atlanta on it with a black Atlanta snap back hat. Everyone in Warner Robins, knew that Ken was my big brother because we looked so much alike. We both were high yellow in complexion, with soft brown eyes, and full lips. He was about six feet and kept his hair cut low with the sides faded.

I stepped out the car with tears fall down my face.

"What the fuck happened to your damn face?" Ken asked angrily.

I licked my lips and sniffed before I was able to respond.

"That's why I'm here. Quan did this to me."

"What the fuck? Oh hell nall, this nigga about to fucking die. What the hell you doing around that fuck nigga anyway?" Ken asked furiously.

There was no way in hell I was going to tell him what had really gone down, instead I lied to him.

"I ran into him coming out of Buffalo Wild Wings. He was trying to holler at me, but I turned his ass down. I'm not about to fuck no nigga who got beef with my brother. I guess Quan got pissed, you already know this nigga thinks he is God's gift to women, so I assumed he couldn't take no for an answer. He started calling me names which pissed me off. I smacked his ass and that's when he jumped on me in the parking lot. No one came to my rescue; Quan got this whole town scared as fuck."

I saw nothing but rage in Ken's eyes. I knew I was wrong for fucking Quan and lying to my brother but it had been done. It would have never come to this if Quan wouldn't have done what he done. Tears fell down my cheeks as I played my role. I already knew Ken was going to take care or Quan which only left Yanni.

I didn't want Yanni to die because her suffering was so

much satisfying. She thought she was so much, but I was curious to know how long she was going last once Quan was gone. I wasn't about to fight the bitch again, but she fucked up when she put her hands on me. If she didn't know she was soon going to find out that I fight dirty.

"Don't cry sis, I'm going to handle his pussy ass. I already don't like his ass, but for him to put his hands on you, means war."

KEN

Seeing that my baby sister KeKe beat up and bruised really had me heated. I wanted nothing more than to hope in my box Chevy and pull up on Quan. I already didn't like his ass and this gave me every reason to dead him. My sister was all I had and I was going to do whatever to protect her. All I cared about was making money and taking care or KeKe because no nigga in Warner robins was going to look out for my sister. All these niggas wanted to do was fuck n her and give her a little money to pay her bills but they wasn't' trying to wife her. I hated that she was thotting around but KeKe was grown and that was what she wanted to do for money while I chose to slang dope on the corner. We both had our hustle, I just hated hers.

What I couldn't stand about Quan's arrogant ass was that he thought I was some pussy ass nigga who wouldn't do shit. I had the reputation of being just a knock off version of a hood dope boy. Niggas thought I was a pretty boy and wasn't about that life, but that was where they had me fucked up at. Just because I was a light skinned nigga bitches fell for me hard. I was slim, tall, with pretty brown eyes that bitches grew weak for. Just because I was considered to be good looking didn't mean I went around fucking all these hoes in the War-Town. I only had one bitch I was pressed for and that was Carissa. She was a fine ass Mexican bitch that I had been rucking around with for a hot minute. I thought she was going to be the one I could settle down with, but she fucked that shit up when she left me to fuck around with Quan right hand nigga Jon. That shit tore me up inside. I tried to reason with her but she wasn't hearing that shit. When she told me she wasn't in love with me anymore, I knew then that I had lost her to Jon.

Jon had more money and could give her more and at the end of the day that was what she wanted. I was angry and upset because Quan and Jon had taken everything from me. Selling dope was all I had been doing since high school and Quan had taken over the War-Town with his product. I thought moving to the Westside would put me on top and put more money in my pockets but I had been wrong. I didn't have the same connect as Quan and my product wasn't as good as his. A few of the dope heads who brought from me always complained that my shit wasn't strong enough for them. Trying to find a good connect was touch business, but I had never been the type of nigga to give up. I knew eventually my time to shine as going to come once Quan fell. I wanted him dead along with his partner for stealing my bitch away from me. once they were dead, War-Town would be mine. The dope heads wouldn't have a choice but to buy from me. I wasn't a dumb ass nigga, I knew murking Quan would start a war, I had to play this shit just right. When he had involved my sister, the nigga was as dead. I didn't need no crew to back me up. All I needed was myself and my bitch Carissa to set some shit up. The fact that Carissa was in love with Jon was going to be the only issue. Right now, it was going to be hard for her to turn her back on Jon, but I was going to do everything in my power to make the shit happen. If my knowledge served me correctly Jon was still with his bitch Taea, I highly doubted Carissa meant anything to him, she was just some new pussy he was fucking for the time being, if I waited long enough I'm sure he was soon going to break her heart and she was going to be eager to help my ass with taking him down.

Once Quan and his right-hand Jon was out of the picture, I knew I was going to make money and make Carissa fall back in love with me.

I wiped the tears from my baby sister eyes and told her to follow me in the house. She took a seat at the kitchen table and continued to weep. I had to think rationally I didn't have time to make mistakes. If I played this shit right, I would end up the richest nigga in the War-Town, but one wrong move would only lead me and the people I cared about dead.

I walked over to the fridge and pulled out two beers. I one mine and passed the second one to KeKe and took a seat at the kitchen table along with her. I pulled a small baggy of weed from a glass bowl that I kept on top of my kitchen table and took my time to roll us both a blunt. A few moments later, I passed KeKe her blunt and lit it for her and told her to calm down. I lit my blunt next and took a few puffs before sitting it in the ashtray that was sitting beside the weed bowl.

"Quan is going to pay for this shit. He and Jon have got to go and I have the perfect plan to make this shit happen."

KeKe wiped her eyes and gave me her full attention. She hit her blunt none more time before giving me an evil smile.

"What's the plan bro?"

CHAPTER 5

TAEA

Even though I had a fucked-up ass childhood, I was determined to not let that shit define who I was today. Growing up on the Northside in the projects not knowing who my father was, was hard for me. When you add a dope fiend as your mama, it made it unbearable. The only thing that got me through any of this was my cousin Yanni. She was there with me every step of the way to make sure that I stayed sane. I contemplated just ending it all and killing myself back when I was in high school, the pressure had gotten just that hot. My mama was hitting the dope so bad that I would never be able to reach her ever again.

The mama who gave birth to me and showed me love was no more. She was someone I barely even knew. Tanya hasn't always been a dope head though. At one point in time, she was a great mama, and she was someone I wanted to one day be like when I grew up.

Before she got hooked to the white powder, my mama was working at Northside high school as a librarian. She was taking care of me and giving me all the motherly love that I needed to be successful out of life. Even though she wasn't making a shit load of money, she always made sure that I was straight. I didn't have to want for anything, name brand shoes, I had that shit. My hair stayed combed, and I was rocking some fresh as clothes to match. My life was perfect at least I felt like it was. We lived in a two bedroom home just down the road from the projects. But just because our house was in the hood didn't mean shit, my mama made sure that I didn't mingle with any of the kids that weren't getting what they needed at home. She always stressed to me that she didn't want their bad habits rubbing off on me. I was only nine years old and knew right from wrong. I knew not to do what the other nine and ten-year-olds were doing. Some were smoking dope, selling it at elementary school during recess, and most was having sex. The girls were busting it wide open, and the boys would talk about how they were getting their dicks sucked on the playground that was behind our house.

Everything changed for me once my mama ended up fucking around with a nigga who lived a block from our house. He was a hood nigga and had a lot of money. She fell in love hard. I still can remember when she first introduced me to him. I didn't like him from the jump, it was something about him that didn't sit right in my nine-year-old head, but I couldn't point out exactly what it was.

His name was Big Joe, he was a big ass nigga, caramel in complexion, rocked the gold chains, and the juiced-up Box Chevy with the chrome rims to match. He wore a box cut and had a shit load of tattoos all down his arms and a few in his face. Honestly, the nigga was ugly as fuck, that could have been some reason why I ain't like him.

Even back then I had a mouth on me. I was never the type of kid to sugarcoat shit, I was far from fake. I was the realest kid that you could have known. Just for having that personality trait alone was why a lot of kids stayed far away from me. I didn't have friends. I spoke, but I kept it moving. I wasn't trying to get myself hung up on the lifestyle that they were headed in. We were all young kids at one point; some of them didn't stand a chance of doing better with their lives.

When my mama sat me down and told me how much she loved this ugly ass nigga, I stared at her like she was crazy. I mean I wanted to ask her so badly, what she saw in him, but instead, I just kept my opinion to myself. My mama knew from jump that I didn't care for Big Joe, but she didn't give a fuck, it was all about her and what she wanted. At the time she wanted him, and it was fuck what I felt or thought.

You're a child and you going to stay in a child's place, was what my mama used to scream at me when I tried to speak my mind.

When my mama found out I didn't care for the nigga, she started acting cold towards me, she started treating me like I was some ugly ass kid on the streets instead of her nine-year-old daughter.

I'm not going to lie, I was hurt because I always thought a mama was supposed to choose her daughter over a nigga, but my mama was opposite of that. She wanted to be happy and didn't care if I was happy about any of her decisions.

I guess after the failed attempt of finding my pops, she was ready to move on with her life. I didn't blame her, I always wanted my mama to be happy, but not with no drug dealer though, my mama had too much going for herself to stoop to that level, but I guess the nice cars and the cash and the jewelry was what tempted her to settle for Big Joe in the first place.

It wasn't even six months into their relationship before my mama started snorting the white shit that he brought over to our house.

I can remember the very first time that my mama took her first hit. I had just gotten out of school and was coming through the door as Big Joe was stepping out from the kitchen with one of our silver dish trays with a few white lines that had been perfectly sectioned off. I threw my book bag on the couch and cut on the TV like I normally did when I got home.

My mama and Big Joe spoke to me and asked me how my day was as I flipped the channels to some cartoon that I was eager to watch. They made small talk with me until they noticed I wasn't responding back to them. They finally started to whisper to one another which I found to be interesting because I was a nosy ass little kid. I knew when adults got to whispering, they were talking shit a child wasn't supposed to listen to. They were so deep into their conversation that they didn't even notice when I cut the TV down. I grew still as I listened to him persuade my mama to snort a line of the white stuff, he had just lined up for them both.

I turned around when I heard her sniffing, and I knew then that my whole life was going to be changed forever.

Even though I was young as hell, I knew what drugs were and knew the effect that it could cost you if you couldn't handle it. One hit and my mama were a full-blown addict. It kilt me to my soul to know that she had gotten herself addicted to her nigga's supply. It started out two lines a day, and she eventually started to increase as she began becoming accustomed to it. Big Joe kept my mama high any chance he got, which was what made me hate him even more than I already did.

By the next following year, my mama had lost her job due to failing a drug test and not coming to work like she should. After losing her job, everything went downhill after that. Big Joe moved us to his crib because we lost our place and things went from bad to shit in a matter of a few weeks. All they did was get high all day and fuss and fight about petty shit. I hated being home, but I had nowhere else to go. Eventually,

Big Joe started beating on my mama which really sent me into a deep depression. I begged her to leave. Instead, she looked me dead in the eye and told me she couldn't, she loved him way too much to go.

I can remember the look she gave me and my heart still hurt to this day because her soul was already gone. She was in love with a dope boy who didn't mean her any good, and she was hooked on the worst drug, cocaine.

Yanni was all I had back then, she was the only one I could go to for help, her life at home wasn't the best either because not long after Tanya got on drugs, she got Lisa on drugs right along with her. So, both of our mamas and Big Joe was getting high together. Just when I thought things couldn't get worse, it did.

The day Big Joe died of an overdose; my mama changed. She was empty inside, her companion the man whom she loved probably more than me was finally gone and she didn't know what to do to cope. I would have thought that after learning of his overdose she was going to stop using but no this wasn't the case, this only made her only pick up on her drug use even more. We ended up moving to the projects and Yanni's mama Lisa followed suit right behind us.

To this day my mama was still getting high, and I was just waiting around for a phone call to tell me she had OD'd. I didn't wish any harm to my mama, but that didn't mean it wasn't going to happen soon. She wasn't taking care of herself, and she wasn't even trying to do better. It was like she had given up on life after Big Joe died. What I needed wasn't important to her, I had to make it the best way I knew how because she sure wasn't trying to get me where I needed to go in life.

Yanni found her hustle selling dope, and I found mine by stealing whatever I needed. If I needed clothes, shoes, and even maxi pads I would steal all that shit. My mama never questioned how I got my shit because she was too busy focused on how she was going to get the money to get her a hit.

But everything changed for me when Jontavian walked into my life I met him at the mall when I was only eighteen. I was in the middle of stealing some clothes out of Rainbow when he walked up on me. When our eyes connected, I found myself speechless. Jontavian was fine as hell and I wanted him from the moment we first met at the mall. He was about 6'1 in height, he was slim, had a low cut, and had sexy full lips with pretty white teeth. He resembled the basketball player Stephen Curry.

I felt as if I was in a trance, but I quickly snapped myself back into reality and gave him the cold shoulder. I didn't know shit about this nigga, so I politely told his ass to get up out my face. Instead of leaving me alone like I asked him to do, he told me to get anything I wanted out of the mall, and he was willing to buy it for me.

I laughed in his face because I thought he was playing, but after a while, it finally clicked that he wasn't. I grabbed everything I wanted and as he promised he paid for it. I had never seen him before, so I figured he was a nigga that was passing through and that was it. I could tell by how he was dressed that he was a young dope boy. I wasn't looking for a nigga to turn me out like my mama had fucked around and got. I wanted more out of life than that.

After he had brought everything that I wanted, he pulled me aside and told me that I was too beautiful to be out here stealing and shit, he encouraged me to get a job and do shit the right way. I found it funny that a dope boy could tell me to get a job when he was illegally selling dope to people and killing them in the process, but I didn't question him. Instead, I did exactly what he told me to do.

He walked away from me that day, and I thought that I

would never see him again, but that was far from the truth. Two weeks later, I was over my cousin Yanni's house with her new boo Quantavious. I had no clue that Quan had called one of his partners over to hang with us that night until I heard a knock on Yanni's door.

When that nigga stepped through the door, I nearly passed out. I wasn't expecting to see him again and there he stood right before my eyes.

Yanni tried to introduce us to one another, but we both told her that we didn't have to be introduced, we already had met each other just two weeks before. That night things changed for me.

Fast forwards three years later, and at the age of twenty-one I was living the life that I had always dreamed about. I was working at taco bell while he hustled all day long. We were living on the Northside not far from my cousin Yanni and her bae Quan. We had just gotten us a three-bedroom two-bathroom house with a garage. A bitch was too happy with the life I was living because I had come from the bottom, but Jon upgraded my ass and put me to the top.

No one was considered to be perfect, but Jon was perfect for me. He made me happy and would give me the world if I asked for it.

Even though I didn't agree with the lifestyle he chose far as making money, I was down for that nigga to the very end. Most dope boys were out smashing hoes and catching STD's, my boo wasn't on that crazy shit, yeah, he had bitches throwing themselves at him every chance they got, because he was light skinned and resembled Stephen Curry, my nigga was sexy as hell, but he already knew what would happen if he gave my dick away. I was a crazy little bitch and didn't mind catching a charge for fucking his ass up. I would happily go to jail and do my time and get my ass out and start me a new life.

He knew not to fuck with me, and he respected me. That was all I ever asked of him to do, respect me and love me and all would be fine in our relationship. But Yanni wasn't so lucky. Quan wasn't anything but a hoe and even though Jon tried to play it off like Quan was this faithful ass nigga I had read enough text messages and had overheard plenty of phone conversations to know Quan wasn't shit.

On a few occasions I had hit Yanni up to let her know what was up, but she basically told me that she and Quan were good and she didn't suspect that he was doing anything.

I knew right off to leave the shit alone, Yanni was in denial about what Quan was capable of doing. So instead of pressing the issue and always trying to tell her what I had heard or seen far as text messages between her man and mine, I left all of it alone. Eventually, I knew Yanni was going to wake up and see the shit that Quan was spitting to her was nothing but sweet lies, now she was beginning to see shit for what they really were.

A knock came at the door. I already knew who it was even before I opened it. I stepped aside as I let Yanni inside. She headed straight towards the kitchen to pour her a drink.

"I'm sorry to come over here, I know you and Jon had made plans to spend the night together."

"Boo, don't worry about any of that, you are way more important, you always have been there for me so you know I'm going to be here for you when you need me."

I watched as Yanni took a long gulp of vodka and juice and waited for her to tell me what had really gone down with Quan and her. She had given me some details over the phone, but she told me the full story needed to be told in person.

I fixed me a drink as well and took a few sips of it. I was just about to head out to the patio where Yanni and I could talk and get some fresh air when I spotted Jon coming down the stairs.

"Jon, can you roll us a blunt?"

"Okay bae," he replied as he headed back up the stairs to our bedroom where he kept the weed.

After we had made it outside, we took a seat in the fold-out chairs and sipped on our drinks.

"I wish I would have listened to you when you tried to tell me about Quan a while ago. I just didn't want to believe it. I just couldn't believe that he was fucking off on me," Yanni said angrily.

"Yanni you ain't gotta explain shit to me, I understand that's why I ain't pressure you or keep on telling you shit about what he was doing. Eventually, I knew you were going to wake up and see Quan for who he truly was."

"It took me to come home at the right time to find KeKe in my fucking house."

"Dammmnnnn," I replied as I took a sip of my drink.

"Did you beat that bitch's ass? I wish you would have called me I owe that hoe an ass whooping. You know I don't ever forget shit, that bitch sucked my boyfriend dick in high school."

Yanni and I busted out laughing.

"Bihhh, stop it!" Yanni yelled out.

"Shit, these are facts. She sucked my nigga dick in the eleventh grade, I owe her that ass whooping that she never got. That's why I wished you would have called me, I'm down to lay hands on that nasty little hoe."

"Taea, I laid that bitch out. I beat her ass for you and me both. As long as Quan and I have been together never had he invited anybody over to his house, but today this hoe of all people was over, he talking about he sold her some pills."

"Tuhhh, I bet he did," I replied as I rolled my eyes.

"He sold her some dick instead," Yanni muttered heatedly.

"After I stomped the bitch out, she started spilling major tea that she had fucked him, and he was everybody's nigga. Anyway, he denied the shit, so I told him to let me smell his dick and bam that's when I found out that he fucked that hoe in my damn house like she had claimed.

"Quan just ain't giving a fuck," I told her.

"Nope," Yanni replied.

When Jon came to hand us our blunts, he lit them for us as well.

"You going to be okay sis?" he asked Yanni with concern in his voice

"I'm going to be Gucci, what you need to be worried about is if your homeboy going to be okay."

I took a puff of the blunt that Jon had rolled for me and blew smoke from my mouth.

"Quan done fucked up, he has activated beast mode in Yanni, it's no turning that shit down once activated."

"What you mean?" Jon asked me in a confused voice.

I chuckled.

"Oh Quan about to be hurting very soon, he going to be crying like a little bitch when Yanni gets through with his ass, he done fucked over the wrong bitch today," I told Jon in a serious voice.

"What you plan on doing?" Jon asked Yanni.

Yanni smirked.

"I'm going to plead the fifth. I'm far from dumb, I'm not saying shit because I already know who you loyal to at the end of the day," Yanni told Jon with a little attitude.

"Look, Quan my homie, but I told him plenty of times that I didn't agree with what he was doing to you. You can ask Taea she will vouch for me on that shit." Jon told Yanni truthfully.

Yanni looked over at me to see if I was down with what Jon was saying to her. I nodded my head to let her know that what Jon was saying was facts. Whenever Quan would hit Jon up with some new bitch he had smashed, Jon always told him that he was fucking up, but Quan being the type of nigga he was, he didn't give a fuck.

Yanni looked over at Jon and blew out some smoke.

"Okay Jon, I know Taea wouldn't lie to me, so I'm just going to tell you this. I'm going to do that nigga just like he did me. All that love and respect I had for him it's gone down the fucking drain. That nigga broke my heart, he had me out here looking stupid as hell, I was riding hard for this nigga, fussing with bitches about my damn man that they claimed they were fucking, and the whole time he was playing me like a bitch, he is going to fucking pay for it," Yanni spat in a rage.

Jon stared at me as he was in deep thought.

"I'm not going to get involved, but I hope you and Quan try to work things out. He really do love you Yanni."

"Sometimes, love just isn't enough," Yanni muttered under her breath.

Yanni and I talked for a good hour after Jon had left, I listened and wiped her tears as she let all the hurt and anger that she was feeling inside out.

After he had made it back into the house, Yanni grabbed her keys to leave.

"Nah, sis you ain't gotta go, you can stay as long as you want," Jon told Yanni as she headed to the door.

"Nall, I'm going to gone and head out," I've intruded enough.

Yanni was just about to speak when a loud knock sounded.

"Who is it!" I yelled out.

"It's Tay, open up."

My whole vibe changed with a blink of a switch.

"What you doing here? I asked him with an attitude.

"Damn, Taea, why all the hostility? I brought weed and liquor."

"I don't give a damn what you brought. You know I don't like you popping up over here uninvited. You might as well go hop your ass back into your F150 and go find you some little hoe to play with because ain't shit popping up in here tonight." I said hostilely.

"Bae calm all that shit down, I invited him over since Yanni over here. We ain't doing the Netflix and chill, so I thought we might as well have a lil party just so Yanni can take her mind off things," Jon replied.

I bit down on my tongue and closed my eyes as I tried to get myself together. I had to try to calm myself down because if I didn't, I swear tonight I was bound to hurt a nigga's feelings.

I wished that Jon would have told me that he was going to invite Tay over because I would have shot that shit right on down. I didn't want that nigga to my house period, and I didn't give a fuck that he was Jon's homie.

"Tay bring your ass on up in here and don't be on no bullshit," I told him as I slammed the door behind him.

I swear when it came to Jon and his homeboyz, I didn't like any of them niggas. I didn't even like Quan, but I dealt with him because that was Yanni's boo. All the rest of the niggas who Jon dealt with on the regular I couldn't stand. I had my reasons why I didn't fuck with them, and it all came down to none of them wasn't hitting on shit. See what they didn't know was that I had my nigga password to his phone and I knew all his fucking personal information just so I could keep on top of his ass.

There was no way in hell I was about to let Jon start slipping. My man was a good provider, and I wasn't about to let none of his little homies try to boost his head up to think it was okay to cheat or creep on me.

Jon and I both had iPhones, what he didn't know was that I linked our phones together when he gave me some money to get the iPhone X. What he didn't know wasn't going to hurt him though. I saw what Yanni was going through and what she was dealing with, I never wanted to be in her situation, so I was only doing what was needed to be done.

Jon didn't have any privacy when it came to me, and if he ever found out what I had done and tried to check me, baby, it was going to be a war that he was never going to win. Either he was going to let me spy on him in peace, or he was going to catch these hands. I knew everything just by linking my phone to his, whenever someone texted his phone, I got that message to my phone. I knew where the drugs were being dropped off and who was in charge of making the runs and all that shit, I knew the names and the locations of when the drug deals were being done.

I was a dangerous ass bitch and was willing to use all this information to my benefit if he ever thought about fucking me over. The love we had was real, but the love that the rest of these niggas had for their main hoes was some fake puppy love.

They didn't love the girls they were with; they were just telling them lies and playing with their hearts. What they didn't know was playing with a bitch's heart was bound to get a nigga murked these days. These hoes weren't playing with these niggas.

I pulled Yanni by the arm and pulled her into the hallway just so we could talk in private.

"Don't even think about walking out of this house and leaving me in here with these fools," I hissed at her.

Yanni's eyes sparkled with laughter, but whether she knew it or not, I was dead ass serious. When she saw that I wasn't laughing with her, that's when shit started getting real.

"Damn, Taea what the fuck wrong with you?"

"Shid, a lot of shit is wrong with me, first off, I don't like none of Jon's little homies he brings up in this house. I don't want Tay here, but since Jon invited him over, it ain't shit I can do about it."

I turned around and spotted Tay and Jon rolling them a blunt, and I shook my head in disgust.

"Yeah, I saw how you looked at Tay, you must really don't like the nigga."

"Bitch, I despise that fuck nigga."

If I had anything to do with it, I would have told his ass to turn around at the fucking door. I didn't want any of that hoe energy rubbing off on my baby.

"I got some shit that I need to show you, this will help you understand the reason why I don't like any of his lil homies. Ain't none of them hitting on shit."

I pulled out my phone and handed it to Yanni so she could see exactly what I was talking about.

Yanni's mouth dropped open in disbelief as she read some of the messages that Tay had sent Jon. "What in the hell did I just read?" Yanni asked in confusion.

"Some messages that Tay sent Jon a few days ago."

"How in the hell you got these messages in the first place?" Yanni whispered to me.

"I got our iPhones linked up. Whatever comes to his phone comes to mine as well."

"Girlllll, I see why you don't like that nigga."

"Now, you understand why I acted that way with him, that nigga sent Jon a picture of a naked ass bitch and had the fucking nerve to ask him if he wanted to smash her with him."

"Now do you see what these niggas be on?" I told her crossly.

"No telling what all Quan was up to that I didn't know

about. I only know small details, but now I want to know everything, I don't want anything sugarcoated, I want it raw and uncut."

I squinted my eyes at Yanni.

"If you want to know the truth all you gotta do is ask."

Yanni rubbed her hands over her face.

"I can't believe I'm about to ask you this but here goes, do you have any messages with him and Quan?

"I thought that this day would never come. Yanni, I got a shit load of messages for you to read, but I advise that you head on in the living room and take a seat. You going to want to pour you another drink to and roll you a blunt. The shit he was telling Jon is going to blow your mind. Are you sure you ready for this?"

Yanni nodded her head at me as I passed my phone to her.

"Bitch I stay ready."

That was all I needed to hear as I followed her into my living room.

YANNI

If Quan thought for one minute that I was going to let him get away with playing me, then he had another thing coming. This nigga had played me the entire time that we had been together. He had fucked over the wrong bitch. I wasn't going to stop until that nigga felt every ounce of pain that I was feeling at the current moment. I found it crazy how a bitch can give a nigga her all, cater to his ass, treat him like a fucking king only for him to fuck her over and give his all to another bitch. He always claimed I had his heart, but did I really have this nigga's heart? Seemed to me the only people he was loyal to was himself and the streets because he damn sure wasn't loyal to my ass.

Whether he knew it or not so many niggas wanted to fuck on me, but I always turned them niggas down because I knew in my heart that Quan was the only nigga I wanted to be with. Not to mention, Quan was crazy as fuck. He was a hood nigga and didn't mind murking anybody who even thought they could take me from him. He felt like I belonged to only him, but whether he knew it or not, I didn't belong to his ass any longer, I was about to be everybody's bitch. I was going to pop this pussy on every nigga that I would have fucked if Quan wasn't in my life.

This nigga had activated the hoe in me, and I gave no fucks. I was down to fuck his homies and his family members, he had started a war, and I was going to finish the shit with me coming out on top and smelling like peaches and roses.

I pulled my phone from out of my shorts when I felt it vibrating against my thigh. When I saw that it was Quan, I quickly sent his ass to voicemail. If he thought I was about to let him come back that easy, then he had me fucked up. I wasn't ready to talk to him, whenever we talked it was going to be on my terms, right now I wasn't ready, so I put his ass on my blocked list. I slid my phone back into my shorts pocket and flopped down on Taea's couch.

"Damn, Yanni, what up with that ugly ass face you just made?" Tay asked me as he stared me down.

I rolled my eyes at him and huffed.

"I don't know what the hell you talking about," I told him.

I grabbed the drink that Taea had mixed for me and took a sip. I started coughing because the shit was strong as fuck.

"Damn bitch you trying to kill me."

"Never that, but if you drinking with us tonight, you gotta come harder than what you were sipping on earlier."

I picked up the phone that I had taken from her earlier and nearly passed out as I began to read through some of the messages that Jon and Quan had sent one another. I had only gotten to the tenth message when I felt like I was ready to take a murder charge.

When the blunt passed around to me, I held that bitch in my hand and took a deep puff. I started coughing which made Tay and Jon laugh at my ass.

"Yanni, you can't just take long ass puffs like that, I brought some good shit over here," Tay joked me.

My mind was so focused on Taea's phone that I didn't even laugh back.

"Damn, ya'll hoes acting funny tonight," Tay said.

I quickly put my phone down because when Tay said that shit, I knew it was going to be some shit that popped off. The fact that Taea already didn't like his ass was just the fuse to the flame for her to show her ass tonight.

Just when Taea started to pop off at the mouth, I tried to intervene, but it was no stopping Taea when she was lit. The bitch was sort of tipsy and high, the fact she already disliked Tay only made the shit worse.

I grabbed Taea by the arm and tried to pull her into the kitchen, but she wouldn't budge off the couch.

Jon didn't seem to realize right off what was really going on until it was too late.

"Who in the fuck are you calling a damn hoe?" Taea spat with venom towards Tay.

"Whhoaa, baby calm down," he was only joking," Jon told Taea.

"Tay apologize to Taea," Jon told him.

I could tell how Jon was looking that all he wanted to do was get high and chill. He wasn't prepared for any of the drama that was about to go down.

Just when Tay was about to say he was sorry for calling her out her name, that's when Taea jumped from off her couch and walked over to where Tay was sitting.

Smack was all I heard.

I looked in horror as Taea slapped fire from Tay's ass.

Tay sat there for a good second before he realized what had happened. I guess the fact that he was high and she had slapped his ass back to reality was what really set the shit off. Next thing you know Tay pushed her ass slam on the damn floor.

Taea fell down but got her ass right on back up, and she

wasn't backing down for shit. At this point in time, I felt like shit was moving in slow motion, no matter how hard I tried to get to her it seemed like it wasn't fast enough. I was tipsy already and the fact that I had mixed it with some weed, I felt like I was paralyzed.

Next thing you now Taea smashed a vase over this nigga head which made him fall down to his knees. Once Taea had him on the floor, she started hitting his ass. The licks were so hard I could hear them bitches from across the room.

Jon was so fucking high, his reactions was slower than usual, but he did manage to grab Taea and snatch her off Tay. By this time Taea had scratched this nigga face up, and he was rocking bite marks on his cheeks.

Tay was about to give Taea them hands when Jon pulled him away from her. I grabbed Taea and tried to calm her down. Even though she had gotten her some good licks off of Tay without him hitting her back, it was like her body was still filled with so much rage. I tried to pull her towards the kitchen, but the bitch pushed me off her.

When she pushed me, she was headed straight to Tay, but I was lucky to catch her in time. In order for her to stay still and not attack Tay was to slam her against the wall.

I have never gotten physical with Taea, but it was necessary in this case, she was about to fuck Tay ass up, and Jon knew that shit.

"What the fuck wrong with you!?" Tay yelled out at her.

"You is what wrong with me. Nigga I don't fucking like you. I want you to get your shit and get the fuck out of my house, that's what I want you to do."

"Baby, what in the hell going on?" Jon asked Taea as he tried to make sense of what set her off.

I was just about to speak when Taea hushed me.

"Don't say shit Yanni, I will tell Jon my fucking self."

Instead of opening my mouth I closed that bitch and went

back to sit on the couch. I wasn't about to get in their business because at the end of the day it was Taea and Jon's relationship, not mine. I sat my ass down on the couch and continued to watch how everything played out.

We had Tay on one side by himself looking like a bruised ninja turtle. He was a tall ass nigga but he was muscular and looked like he went to the gym a lot, he was a dread head that rocked a gold grill on the top and bottom of his mouth. Apparently, he had hoes, but I don't see how it had to be because of the money he had because he damn sure wasn't fine. The nigga looked like a mosquito in the face, he wasn't cute, but this nigga could pull hoes.

When I saw the message with him asking Jon to fuck a bitch with him, I understood why the bitch probably wasn't going to let him smash on his own. I bet the hoe pussy couldn't even get wet for him, but hey I could've been wrong, but to me, this nigga wasn't my type, and he wasn't someone I would want to be seen with, I didn't care how much money he had.

His face was already ugly, and now he had cuts and shit on it from where Taea had clawed his ass up. His dreads were flying all out of his rubber band, and his shirt had been ripped.

He stood there with his hands balled up, talking shit about Taea and how he was going to break the bitch jaw.

By now, he was making me angry because there was no way I was going to let that nigga get even five hundred feet to my cousin. I was ready to throw them hands right along with her.

Jon quickly began to get pissed when Tay started talking shit about Taea.

That's when shit really started getting real. A whole lot of shit started coming out, I was in the open, and all I could do was sit back and watch it go down.

"Do you want to know why I don't like your ugly ass Tay!?" Taea yelled.

Tay stared at her ass like she was crazy.

"Bitch I want to know why you attacked me," Tay responded.

"Look nigga stop calling her out her name," Jon told Tay angrily.

When Jon reached for his pistol off the bookshelf, I knew Tay had only one more time to disrespect Taea, and it was going to be a wrap. The only reason why I believed that Jon hasn't already shot his ass was because they were homies, but shid homies didn't matter these days, they could be murked if need be.

"Nigga, you going to defend her when you see she attacked me like she a damn wild animal! I don't see why you fuck with her ass anyway she damn crazy!" Tay shouted at Jon.

Next thing you know, Taea grabbed a kitchen knife and pointed it at Tay.

"You ain't seen crazy yet. What I want you to do is get your shit and get the fuck up out this damn house, don't bring your ugly ass back here. I don't care what kind of business you got going on with Jon ya'll handle that shit out in the streets, but don't come back here. But before you go, I want you to know this, just because you feel like it's okay to smash all these nasty ass bitches around here, don't mean you suppose to persuade Jon to do it. You know that's my nigga, he is committed to me, and he's going to stay that way. Don't you ever let me find a text message of you asking my nigga to come smash a bitch again.

"What the fuck?" Tay asked with a shocked expression on his face.

He looked like he ain't know what in the hell Taea was talking about and if it weren't for the screenshots that I had read earlier, I would have thought she was tripping on some shit.

"Yeah, you thought I ain't know. Nigga, I know everything about my fucking nigga. I'm not going to tell you how I actually found out but trust and believe I saw every message you sent my nigga. My nigga will not be smashing no other bitch but me, and if I find out otherwise, I will cut his dick off and feed it to my neighbor's pit-bull. The only reason why Jon ain't get his ass beat was because he was man enough to turn your offer down when the other niggas in ya'll circle would have gone along with you and smashed that nasty thot," Taea spat.

The house was so quiet that you could hear a pin drop. No one said shit, it was like everyone was trying to register in their brains what was really going down and why Taea had let loose like she had.

But just when I thought Tay was about to leave that's when he said some shit that blew us all.

"Since you won't to get your bitch in line then I will do it for you," Tay told Jon nastily.

"Look, little bitch, I've never liked your illiterate ass. For some reason, Jon loves the fucking ground you walk on and loves your crazy ass, but I don't see what he sees in you. You ain't shit. What do you do every day? Nothing, but sit here and try to find out what your nigga doing behind your back. You love saying your nigga ain't crazy enough to cheat, shid, that statement alone is funny to me. Before you go running your mouth and talking about what you found on his phone then first you need to know who the fuck you laying with every night. That nigga you so call obsessing over and trying to watch every chance you get still played your ass right in your face, but your ass was too dumb to see the shit.

Just when Tay was about to say more, Jon grabbed him and slammed his ass on the floor.

"Shit!" I yelled as Tay grabbed Jon and threw him through the coffee table that we were sitting in front of me. I got my ass up and headed to the other side of the room as they continued to punch and slam one another. When Jon got Tay in the choke hold, we already knew it was game over. Tay had come over here only to get his ass beat twice, one by a bitch and once again by his so-called homie. Damn, it made no sense that this nigga had all this mouth but didn't know how to protect himself. All he knew how to do was pop off at a nigga. When Tay tried to reach for his gun, I did what any bitch would have done in that situation I grabbed the gun out of his reach and sat it down on the leather couch where he couldn't retrieve it. He wanted to talk shit then I wanted him to be man enough to take that ass whooping that Jon was giving him.

When Jon released him from the choke hold, Tay laid stretched out on the floor as he tried to catch his breath. Taea and I only stared at his ass as Jon headed towards the front door to open it.

"Get your shit and get the fuck out of my house," Jon told Tay angrily.

For the first time that night, Jon had actually beat Tay ass, when he was supposed to have done that shit from the jump when Taea smacked his ass. Something just wasn't adding up, if Tay was about to tell some of Jon's secrets that could explain why Jon was so focused on Tay getting the fuck up out his crib.

"Nigga, you was my homie, I would do anything for you. I would even lie for your ass, but since you let your little bitch disrespect me the way she did I'm going to let all this shit out in the open tonight," Tay muttered as he grabbed his weed off the floor and stood up.

I watched him as he limped over towards the couch that had been pushed back to the far wall and grabbed his phone.

Just when he was about to walk out the house that's when Tay said some shit that really floored me.

"For the record, you ain't the only bitch Jon fucking with Taea, he got a shorty on the Westside that he used to like in high school. Word on the street the hoe pregnant. Oh, and if you think I'm lying, then I want you to know I'm not. See your ass so fucking smart, but I bet you ain't know that nigga had a second phone that he kept hidden from your nosey ass. He keeps it in his car in the back of his trunk, and before I go, I guess I should go on and tell you that word on the street is that the baby is his."

The slamming of the door was what sealed the deal. My heart felt like it had been smashed and crushed into pieces. No this couldn't be real; this just didn't happen. Tears rolled down my cheeks as Taea screamed to the top of her lungs. I watched in agony as my cousin fell to the floor in pain.

QUAN

Even though I had just caught me a good nut, I still found myself lying in bed an hour later still unfilled. Aisha's pussy was straight fire, but at the end of the day, she wasn't Yanni. I had the urge to call my baby just so I could hear her voice before I closed my eyes and actually fell to sleep. This was going to be the first time that we have gotten into an argument to the point where she put me out and wouldn't reach out to me. I felt so lost as I laid there in the dark. I grabbed my iPhone off my charger and finally got up the nerve to call Yanni.

I called, but the voicemail was all I got. I couldn't even leave her a voicemail because her inbox was full. I always use to fuss with her about that shit, she didn't ever delete shit and would wait until her voicemail got full before she attempted to actually go through her messages and clean them out.

I had the urge to call her back but decided to just send her a text message instead.

Quan: Please forgive me, Yanni, I want to come home. I

know I fucked up and broke your heart, but you the one I want to be with.

After sending the message, I placed my phone back on the nightstand and closed my eyes. I was hoping that sleep would find me, but it never seemed to come. I tossed and turned throughout the night before I decided to get my ass up.

I grabbed my phone and noticed it was four in the morning. I was anxious and decided to try to see if I could call Yanni one more time. I already knew she was sleep, but I just couldn't go without hearing her voice. Just as I put the phone to my ear, I heard the operator talking about my call wasn't able to go through. I sat my phone down, and my heart felt like it had been snatched out my chest. I had to have heard incorrectly, but deep down in my heart, I knew that Yanni had really blocked my ass.

Yanni and I had too much love and history together for her to just up and block a nigga out of her life. If she thought for one second that I was going to let her forget me and I wasn't going to fight for us, then she was going to find out otherwise. Instead of harping on her blocking my number, I closed my eyes because I was beginning to finally get sleepy. The plan was to get my ass up in the morning and head over to my crib so we could talk face to face. Whether she knew it or not, she couldn't just delete me from her life, we shared a crib together.

As sleep found me, I began to dream.

When her lips met mine, my dick automatically stood at attention. Aisha pulled away from me and smirked as she slid on top of me. She pushed my hands over the top of my head and erotically whispered in my ear to not move or touch her. I obeyed her commands and stared at her in awe as she pulled up her orange sundress. She blocked the sun from my eyes when she leaned down towards me and slid her tongue into my mouth. We were outside in a field with a whole bunch of flowers. The bees buzzed in my ear, and the birds chirped in the distance.

"I want you," she whispered to me.

Just hearing her say some shit like that really had me rock hard for her. I was eager to slide deep into her guts, but she wanted to take her time, she didn't want to fuck, she wanted to take things slow. She stood up from straddling me and unzipped my pants. She pulled out my dick and was just about to place my rod into her mouth when someone called out my name.

I froze in place because I knew all too well who that voice belonged to. I tried to hurry up and put my dick back into my pants, but it was too late, there stood Yanni just a few feet away, watching me with tears in her pretty eyes.

I hurried to dress and left Aisha sitting there looking dumbfounded as I tried to run after my girl.

No matter how hard I tried to run, I could never seem to catch up with Yanni. Every time I thought I was going to catch her; she would slip through my fingers.

I woke up in a cold sweat and looked over at the clock that was located above the flat screen TV. It was seven in the morning, and I felt like I didn't get an ounce of sleep. When I did manage to fall asleep, I ended up having a nightmare about not being able to catch Yanni to apologize for what she had seen. I knew this dream was only my subconscious playing tricks on me, I was still aching inside about Yanni finding out about me cheating on her.

I pulled the covers from over my body and headed to the bathroom so I could take care of my hygiene. After brushing my teeth, I hopped in the shower. I stood there for the longest time and let the hot water splash against my body. Thoughts of Yanni and how I was going to win her back began to play in my mind. This wasn't a game; I was going to have to come with something major to grab her attention.

After washing myself clean, I stepped out of the shower

and hurried to put on some clothes. If I left early enough, I was going to be able to see her before she left and went to work. I put on my diamond gold earrings, my two gold chains, and my favorite gold Gucci watch. I sprayed on me a little cologne and was getting ready to head out the door when my phone began to ring. When I saw that it was Jon calling, I hurried to answer.

"Morning bro, what up? I asked him curiously

"I fucked up bruh."

"What are you talking about?" I asked Jon in a confused voice.

"Tay came over last night, I decided to invite him over since Taea had Yanni over here.

I should have known that Yanni wasn't going to sit at the house by herself after I left. She had been pissed so going to her cousin house was going to be the first place she went when she needed to get a lot of shit off her mind. Yanni didn't have female friends that she fucked with, the only bitch she fucked with on a personal level was her cousin Taea. That was the only one she trusted with her life. Thoughts of Yanni came to an abrupt halt when he started talking about Taea and Tay.

"Taea and Tay got to damn fighting last night," Jon said into the phone.

"What you mean they got to fighting?" I asked curiously.

"Bruh the shit got out of hand. Taea beat the fuck out of Tay, and he got pissed at me because I ain't defend his ass. But that's beside the point. I'm calling you because Tay went and broke the fucking code."

"What code did he break?" I asked Jon anxiously.

"The code was to never say shit about what we do when we not around our bitch. This nigga told Taea that I was cheating on her."

"Hold the fuck up, that nigga went and lied on you to your bitch and said you were cheating?" I asked in confusion.

The shit wasn't making any damn sense. Jon wasn't like me Tay or the others. We all had bitches that we fucked with on the side, even if we did have a main bitch.

"He wasn't lying," Jon replied.

"Huh?"

There was no way I had just hard this nigga correctly.

"He didn't lie to her. Nigga your ass talking in fucking circles. You ain't a cheater since I've known your ass you ain't never stepped out on Taea crazy ass," I told him.

"Look, it's a lot I didn't tell you because I just didn't want to put myself out there like that and the fact you with her cousin, was part of the reason."

"Jon, we go way back, you know you can tell me whatever bruh. We don't keep secrets over this way. Now I've been rocking with your ass for a long ass time, these other niggas on the team ain't got the type of history that we have. So, I expect for you to feel like you can tell me shit."

"You know how these females are. They always trying to plot and see what we do. I wasn't trusting telling you anything about what I was doing behind Taea's back because I didn't want Yanni to ever catch a whiff of it."

I shook my head because this nigga just needed to admit that when it came to him stepping out, he didn't want no one to know his moves. I understood that shit when you were doing the fuck shit, the fewer people that knew was, the better.

"Taea ain't too crazy because your ass lived to see today," I told Jon.

"Nigga I'm about to pull up at the hotel, this shit goes really deep. Last night could have been my last night for either myself or Tay."

"Where you at bruh?" I asked Jon as I grabbed my keys to

walk out the door so I could see if I could go find me something to eat for breakfast.

"A nigga woke up hungry as hell, I ain't ate shit since yesterday when I fucked around and ate that KFC. After I put something on my stomach, I was planning on heading over to see if I could see Yanni."

"I'm down the road from your hotel, I had to get away from Taea. She almost killed me last night after Yanni left."

"How Yanni be doing?" I asked him curiously.

I was dying to know how my baby was holding up. It wasn't like I could ask her myself since she had blocked a nigga. The only ones who knew how Yanni was doing were Jon and his bitch Taea. I already knew calling Taea and trying to ask her wasn't going to get me anywhere. The bitch didn't care for me too much.

"Taea calmed her down finally, but I'm going to gone and warn your ass. Watch your back Yanni ain't playing with your ass."

"I ain't heard shit from her, she blocked me, that's why I'm asking you what up with her."

"She going to come back just give her some time, but she ain't gonna be the same bitch you took for granted," Jon assured me

"Fuck all that shit, I just want her to come back so we can get through this shit."

"Would you have cheated on Yanni if you knew you could get away with it?" Jon asked me.

"I'm not going to lie, I would have cheated, but I would have been more careful to make sure she wouldn't have ever found out."

I have always been a real ass nigga. I wasn't going to lie to myself and say that I wouldn't have ever cheated because I know myself, but I can say that I would have been better at hiding the shit.

"Look, I'm pulling up at the hotel. What's your number to the room?"

I told him my room number and told him that I was waiting for him to come up so we could talk.

A few moments later Jon was knocking at my door. I stepped aside to let him in and closed the door behind him. We dapped each other up just before he took a seat.

"Damn nigga, all that shit I used to talk about you being too scared to cheat and you beating down a bitch without me knowing. Shit, I still can't believe the shit."

"Believe it," Jon told me.

"Who the little bitch you fucking with?"

"She lives on the west side, her name Carissa. My shit is just all fucked up, bruh."

"Hold the fuck up, you mean Carissa the one who used to go to school with us? That bitch was bad as hell back in the day. Everybody wanted to smash that lil' Mexican bitch, but she wouldn't give nobody the pussy."

"Yep, that's her, every nigga wanted to tap that ass because she was a virgin. Turns out her father and the rest of her family was deep into the church. They didn't play that shit," Jon replied.

"Now I see why you ain't want nobody to know. I ain't seen her ass in a long time though so I don't really know how she looks now."

"She still looks the same but she way badder.

"Well damnnnn nigga, you over there trying to hide her from everybody, I ain't even mad at ya partna."

"No one knew she was my lil baby. Taea didn't suspect anything on my end. I just feel like shit because Taea might not take my ass back from this shit."

"Nah, this your first-time cheating, Taea gonna take you back, believe that shit. I hate your ass told Tay's loud mouth ass, I wouldn't trust him with no personal shit, he good to do business with but that's about it. You know I wouldn't have ever said shit about whatever you do to nobody."

"I didn't tell that nigga either, I took shorty to the mall when we first started kicking it about three months ago and he just happened to be with one of his bitches, and he spotted me. He knew I wasn't with Taea, so he pulled me to the side and told me that he was gonna keep his mouth shut about what he had seen.

"He knows he wrong for that shit, that was a punk ass move, how he gonna throw you under the bus like that?"

"That little nigga acted like a little bitch, he got big mad because I didn't defend him when Taea was going in on his ass. What I look like? I live with my bitch, I want to stay in good graces with her, but she beat that nigga ass last night, and that's when he told her everything."

"Oh, hell nall, that's a bitch ass move, we need to sit down and have a fucking meeting for real, this is a fucking brotherhood, we all need to have each other's back when it comes to our bitches."

"I agree, but I ain't got shit to say to that nigga, I don't even want to see his ass because if I do, I swear I might shoot his bitch ass."

"Just calm down bruh, I'm going to handle everything okay."

"Just get him off the fucking team altogether, I don't wanna be nowhere near his bitch ass."

"Is that what you want?" I asked him.

"Damn right, he got me all the way fucked up. I know we were all fucked up last night, but even when Taea jumped on him, he should have taken his bitch ass home like we both told him to."

"Why Taea crazy ass jumped on him though?"

"He was joking around with her, and she went off, it was unexpected. She went through my damn phone apparently and saw that he had sent me some messages about fucking some little bitch on the Northside. Never do Tay ever send me shit like that, but shid, now that he knew I'm not the faithful nigga he thought I was, he felt like we could fuck hoes together."

I shook my head and grabbed a cigarette from off the bed. I lit the bitch and inhaled.

"But the shit goes deeper than that bruh, turn out I might have a baby on the way, Tay told Taea that shit too."

I wasn't prepared for the shit he had just told me; I was in the middle of exhaling when I started choking on my cigarette smoke.

"Oh, shit nigga, you wasn't wrapping your dick up?"

"Fuccckkkkk," Jon groaned as he rubbed his hand over his face.

"The little bitch told me she was on birth control."

"And you believed her ass? Bruh, you still supposed to wrap your dick up regardless."

"At the time I believed her, I knew she wasn't lying about being on the pill because she showed me the pill packs."

"Rightt, but you know with them pills, all she gotta do is not take them bitches and bam she knocked up. I'm guessing the little bitch caught feelings and decided she wanted more than what you were willing to give her. Getting knocked up is something these females do to secure a bag from a dope boy and also try to pull a nigga that she wants. I just wished you would have trusted me before you started fucking with Carissa's ass. I would have put you up on game. I know bitches and how they think. I have been doing this shit for years. I'm not a rookie, but you are. You ain't the cheating type bruh."

I could see the tears in Jon's eyes, I knew he was hurting, I didn't look at him as being weak. I was the hardest nigga in the streets in Warner Robins, but if I even thought for one second that Yanni and I were never going to be together again, then I would be crying like a little bitch too. Getting your side bitch pregnant was something that you didn't do, most likely if you fucked around and got a baby on your main bitch, you were going to find yourself single. Now I understood why he felt like Taea wasn't going to take him back, maybe she would have taken him back if he had just cheated, even though it wasn't going to be easy, but he had a better chance to win her back. Now that he had a baby on the way, that was a wrap on that shit.

"Jon, I'm going to be real with your ass, you done fucked yourself up bad, but if Taea really loves you like I think she does then believe with time; you may win her back. Ya'll have so much history together but getting Carissa pregnant is something that is going to be hard to get over," I told him truthfully.

I wasn't about to sugar coat shit, this nigga needed to know exactly what he had done.

"You already know Taea don't like my ass like that either, but I can try to do whatever I can to help you out bruh. What you need just let me know."

"The only thing I want you to do is to handle Tay's ass, handle it or I will. This nigga ruined my damn life."

"I understand bruh. The plan is to call a meeting. Look I'm going to get on that shit right now."

I grabbed my phone and sent a message to the squad to meet up with me at the warehouse off North Davis Drive in an hour, I didn't give a fuck what they were doing. I wanted everyone present. A few moments later everyone started to respond to confirm that they were going to be pulling up.

Jon stood up and dapped me up before he told me he was heading out. He said he wanted to clear his mind. I understood he needed space to think about what he was going to do next about his relationship.

After he walked out of my room, I stayed back and tried to call Yanni yet again. My heart sunk once again when I saw that I was still blocked. I hurried and placed my phone in my pocket as I headed out the door. Even though I was starving, I hopped in my whip and sped over to my crib. Yanni's car wasn't parked in the driveway, which let me know that I had just missed her, and she was probably on her way to work.

Instead of going into the house to get some more clothes and personal items, I decided to take the chance and head over to her job so we could discuss our relationship. I didn't give a fuck that she was at work if she didn't want to talk to me over the phone, then the only option I had was to talk to her at work, that was the only place I knew she couldn't hide from my ass or dodge me.

I pulled up at The Lodge Nursing Home ten minutes later and parked next to Yanni's car. I stepped out and headed to the main desk and asked for Yanni Brown. One of the nurses who was sitting behind the main desk was an older woman who I had never seen before. She looked to be in her late fifties but didn't have a funky attitude like most of the other workers did. The only reason why I think the young nurses were rude towards me because I had turned every last one of them hoes down who tried to fuck on me. That was something that I wasn't going to do, I wasn't about to fuck no bitch that Yanni had to work with. I knew how messy bitches could be when shit went sour. They would be quick to try to expose a nigga and fuck up their happy home all because you wanted to cut them off.

I took a seat in the waiting room that was diagonal from the front desk and waited for Yanni to come out from the back. I sat there it seemed like forever before I finally spotted Yanni's fine ass step out from the back. She was dressed in a pair of black scrubs with her weave pulled back in a ponytail. She wore little makeup, and she seemed to be glowing until she spotted me, the smile she wore on her face quickly disappeared.

"Nigga, what the fuck do you want? Why, you here?" Yanni asked with a nasty attitude.

"Baby..."

"Nall don't baby me, nigga, I ain't your fucking baby. You better call one of them other hoes you fucking with, because I'm not the one to fuck with."

"Yanni, please just hear me out."

"What the fuck you have to say to me nigga. Huh?" Yanni asked loudly.

The nurses who were walking past us looked over at us which made Yanni furious.

"Damn, can I get some privacy?" Yanni asked them angrily.

The nurses turnt their heads and kept on walking.

"You probably done fucked one of them bitches too," Yanni told me nastily.

"Hell no, there is no way in hell I would ever fuck around with a bitch I know you have to work with every day. I don't want none of these hoes, I just want to be with you."

Yanni rolled her eyes at my statement of truce.

I grabbed Yanni and pulled her ass out the double doors so we could have some privacy.

"Nigga don't fucking touch me," Yanni said as she snatched her arm away from me. After we made it outside, Yanni started popping off at the mouth.

"I don't know why you coming to my damn job, anything that you have to say you can say that shit over the phone."

"Well damn, I would have called, but shid you blocked my ass."

"Oh, my bad, I blocked you. Well damn, what does that tell your stupid ass then?" Yanni asked.

"Look, I'm not about to stand here and let you disrespect me."

"Well damn. You in your feelings about me disrespecting you, but it's okay to have me out here in these streets looking dumb as hell."

"I know I fucked up baby, but please let me come back home so we can work this shit out."

"Why don't you go stay with one of them hoes you were cheating on me with."

I rubbed my temples with my fingers because she was stressing me the fuck out.

"If you thought you were going to pull up in here and make me change my mind on how I feel about shit then boo, you got me all the way fucked up. You fucked over the wrong bitch, you brought out my beast mode, you going to feel this shit, you going to feel all the pain that your ass put me through."

"Sweetie, I love you with all my heart, I don't want anyone else," I pleaded.

"I don't believe the shit you telling me nigga."

"What can I do to prove to you that you the only one I want?"

Yanni stared at me for the longest time.

"It's nothing you can do. Just leave me alone and watch me do me," Yanni replied before heading inside the nursing home.

I stood there and watched her as she walked away from me. There was nothing that I could say or do to change her mind. She was being stubborn, but she had her reasons to be. I was the one who had fucked up but watching her do her wasn't going to be an option. She had lost her fucking mind if she thought I was going to let her be with some nigga other than me.

I jogged to my car and started it. I sat in there for a few

moments as I gathered my thoughts to myself. Losing Yanni wasn't an option. She can be mad all she wanted, but I wasn't going to go anywhere.

I grabbed my phone from off the passenger seat, so I could see if I had any missed messages. Sure enough, I had about two text messages from Jon stating that he was about to pull up at the warehouse in ten minutes. I pulled into traffic a few moments later and headed towards the warehouse that I had purchased when I was only eighteen years old. Back then I was just getting deep into the game and thought it was a good idea to get a building that I could meet my squad at without anyone knowing our location.

It was a good fifteen-minute drive because traffic was hectic as fuck, as soon as I pulled up at the warehouse, I was met by Jon who was sitting in his car rolling a blunt.

I knocked on his window to get his attention. He placed his blunt on his dashboard and stepped out the car to dap me up.

"Let me handle everything, let me do all the talking, I don't want you coming in here and showing your ass today."

"I got you, as long as that bitch ass nigga don't come near me then I'ma be cool," Jon replied as he headed inside the warehouse behind me.

All four of my niggas was chilling, some were playing pool and the Xbox one when I stepped inside. Everyone stopped what they were doing when they spotted me. I dapped each one of them up including Tay. Tay looked like he didn't have a care in the fucking world. I was itching to kick his ass but decided to do shit the right way.

I should have known that Tay was going to cause issues eventually. He was a risk taker and never thought shit through. The only reason why he was still included in this squad was because I was cool with his older brother JoJo. His older brother was the complete opposite of Tay.

JoJo was a type of nigga who showed nothing but loyalty from the moment we started slangin dope on the block. He always looked out for me, and in return, I made sure to look out for him. When JoJo fucked around and got killed in a car crash, I took it upon myself to look out for his little brother Tay, but Tay didn't have the same qualities as his older brother.

Tay, on the other hand, was one of them bitch ass niggas who was always looking for a way to one-up a nigga. I believed the only reason that Tay had targeted Jon was because he wanted Jon's position on the camp. It was only a few months ago Tay had hit me up talking about he wanted to discuss some business with me. When I found out that Tay was interested in being my right-hand man I was in disbelief because I wasn't expecting him to step to me with some shit like that. I told him that I already had the nigga who was my right hand and I wasn't looking for another one. I never told Jon because I didn't want to have him paranoid, but if I had known what I know now, I would have told him to watch out because Tay probably was going to come for him when he least expected it.

I had known Jon the longest; we went way back. There was no way I was about trust anyone other than Jon when it came to the drug business. Jon and I had been through a lot of shit, but he never folded. Tay and I didn't have this type of history, and I always found myself getting a vibe that just didn't sit right with me when it came to Tay.

It was something about him that just wasn't right, and now I finally realized exactly what it was. This nigga wasn't a real nigga. Instead, he was a pussy ass nigga who was willing to destroy anyone who got in the way of getting him what he wanted.

As I took a look at Tay, I noticed a few cuts and scrapes on his face.

Damn, Taea had put some hands on his ass, I thought to myself as I made my way up to the front.

I cleared my throat just so I could get everyone's attention.

"Do ya'll know why ya'll here today?"

Everyone looked around and shook their heads.

I paced the floor as I gathered my thoughts. I wanted to make this shit clear, so we didn't have this fucking problem ever again. I spotted Tay standing over by Richie Boy with a blunt in his mouth. When he saw me looking at him, he broke eye contact with me.

I already knew then that everything that Jon had told me was true. Jon was never the type of nigga to lie, but I wanted to make sure that I wasn't biased either. The fact that Tay didn't want to look at me let me knew right then, that he knew exactly what he had done.

"When I started this team, I started it as a brotherhood. We are supposed to protect one another and be there for each other, no matter what. I called this meeting because one of you have fucked over one of your partnas. We don't do this shit here, we don't snitch on one another, I don't care how pissed that other nigga has made you, we all got dirt, nobody's dirt better than the next nigga's dirt."

Everyone started looking around at one another as they tried to figure out who I was referring to, but it didn't take long before Tay spoke up. The last thing I wanted to do was to kick this nigga's ass, but the way he came at me was disrespectful as hell. I was already going through shit, the last thing I wanted to hear was that one of my niggas was trying to get smart with me.

"You love preaching about we brothers and how we need to stick up for one another, but let's be real, ain't nobody really for one another, fuck everybody in this room. All ya'll some pussy ass niggas who will sell the next one out if they had the fucking chance. You always talking about we need to look out for one another, but what happens if you looking out for a nigga who a pussy and fake as hell. What do you suppose we do then boss man?" Tay asked me nastily.

I swear this nigga had caught me on the wrong fucking day. What I hated the most was when I spoke some real shit and a nigga had the audacity to question me. I was the leader of this squad. Nobody had a right to question my ass period. I wanted nothing more to silence his ass, but Jon beat me to it.

"Ain't nobody in this bitch a pussy ass nigga but you. You had no fucking right to come to my fucking house and tell anything that you knew about me to my fucking bitch, what I do is my fucking business," Jon snapped.

"Fuck you Jon, you a pussy. You got these niggas in here thinking you better than them, but you out here getting your dick wet and fucking another bitch too. You ain't loyal to your bitch either!" Tay yelled out.

The whole warehouse looked back and forth from the two men and waited to see just how things were going to play out.

"Jon!" I yelled out, but it was too late.

Jon had lost it and it was no stopping it. When Jon slammed Tay's ass against the floor, I knew that someone was going to end up dying that day. One thing I knew about Jon was when he was mad; you wanted to stay out of his way. He was cool as hell but once you pissed him off it was a fucking wrap. Jon was stressing about his girl and was fearful of losing the one person who he loved with all his heart. Tay was going to pay. I just prayed it wasn't going to be with his life.

As Tay and Jon fought everyone stepped out of the way and watched as Jon beat the brakes off of Tay.

Once Tay was laying on the ground groaning in pain, Jon

looked down at him and told him some shit that I would never forget.

"You fucked up when you came to my house and told my girl all that shit about me. One thing you never do is fuck with another nigga's family. I will never forgive your ass for that shit," Jon spat before pulling his pistol out and aiming it at Tay's head.

Pop, pop.

Blood pooled around Tay's body and all the other niggas stared in disbelief. Never had anyone killed one of our own, but today was a first for everything. Jon put his pistol back on his waist and stared at the other niggas who was standing there frozen into place.

"Look at this as a lesson, everyone has their own fucking life to live. Stay out each other's business. If you ain't down for the next nigga beside you, that's cool, but don't go out your way to fuck up whatever he got going on. Do ya'll fucking understand?" Jon asked them crossly.

Everyone nodded their heads in agreement as they stared back at Tay's lifeless body.

"Clean this shit up," Jon muttered as he headed out the warehouse.

I followed behind his ass and caught him before he got inside his car.

"Damn, Jon, I mean did you really have to murk his ass though?" I asked him.

"Fuck that pussy ass nigga, we don't need no nigga on our team who will try to rat someone out. If he could snitch on me and fuck up what I had at home, just imagine him snitching and trying to fuck up our money and drug business. Nigga what I did was necessary and it was beneficial to our future."

Now as I thought about it, Jon was right, if a nigga couldn't be trusted then he had to be eliminated. He snitched on Jon, just imagine what he probably would have done if he had gotten mad with me. The nigga would probably go and tell all our business to our enemies.

Jon made sense, so I let that shit go. I mean I wasn't mad about him killing Tay, I would have done the same damn thing if he had done that shit to me. Yanni and I were already having issues, if she knew how many bitches, I had really fucked around on her with, it would blow her damn mind.

Jon was right when he told everyone to keep their business to themselves, you never knew when you had an enemy in your own crew who was waiting on your downfall.

"I don't think we going to have any more problems with anyone else. You just showed them what will happen if they get stupid."

Jon nodded his head and slid inside his midnight blue Camaro.

"Gone home and see what you can do to make shit right with Taea, I will get shit cleant up here," I told him.

"Thanks, bruh," Jon replied before pulling off.

JON

Temptation was a bitch at times and I had fallen prey to it. I now found myself in a situation that I had no clue how I was going to get out of it. Taea and I had a love that was going to last forever, but I fucked all that shit up when I ran into Carissa, three months ago. I had always wanted to fuck on her, but I never got the opportunity in high school to make that happen. She was so fine back in the day and had all the niggas crushing on her. Back then Carissa wasn't giving any of us niggas any play. I was the only one she would talk to, but like I said it didn't go anywhere because we were young and her parents didn't allow her to date.

In a way, I didn't see that as a bad thing, so many bitches were getting knocked up and her parents didn't want her to have that type of life. She was untouched, and she was beautiful in every way. Instead of pursuing anything with Carissa, I moved on and started fucking around with Taea and fell in love with her.

Honestly, I thought the desire to fuck other bitches didn't excite me. So many of the crew had their main bitches and had side bitches they were fucking on as well, but I was different. I was never tempted to cheat on Taea with no other hoe, but when my eyes laid on Carissa,, all the feelings that I had for her back in high school began to come crashing back right before my eyes.

Running back into my past was something I wasn't expecting, but that was what happened. Life had a way of making you do shit that you never thought you would do. I never thought I would break Taea's heart, but I had managed to do just that. Not only did I cheat on her but I had fucked around and gotten Carissa pregnant. I already knew the baby was mine, there wasn't any doubt in my mind that she was carrying my child.

I had been fucking her ra, and she carried herself the same way that she had in high school. Back then she didn't entertain any nigga, and to this day she didn't entertain no one. If she did the bitch was sneaky as hell and hid it well.

I had always been the type of nigga who could read people, and I never got a bad vibe from Carissa. When she told me, she wasn't fucking anyone but me, I believed her. I had no reason not to, never had she lied to me, but like I said, if she was lying, she was a good liar because nobody could get over on me.

When Carissa first told me three weeks ago that she was pregnant with my baby, I almost passed out. She knew that I was with Taea, but still, Carissa was determined to keep me in her life. She didn't want to let me go, and she didn't give a fuck about the history that Taea had with me.

When Quan told me that Carissa had gotten pregnant on purpose, I already knew in my soul she had as well. When she started talking about us being together and me leaving Taea, I knew I had fucked her mind up. She wanted to be with me, but there was no way that could ever happen.

I hated in a way that I had fucked her, I should have been

strong and told her ass no, but the temptation was just too great.

My loyalty was to my bitch Taea, but even that had waived, if I was loyal, there was no way I would have fucked around with Carissa on that level, no matter how hard I wanted to.

Sex was sex, but it was so amazing when you were fucking someone who knew how to please you. Carissa was everything I had dreamed about. She knew how to snatch my soul and made sure to do this every chance that she got.

The pussy was so fucking good that it was no way in hell I could stand to wrap up my dick. I wanted to feel all of her. I wanted to see her cum on my dick every chance she got. Fucking around with Carissa had me all the way fucked up. My love for Taea was strong as hell, but my lust for Carissa was just as strong, if not stronger. No matter how hard I tried, I could never get her out of my head. Just thinking about her brought me back to the moment when we ran into each other.

I was heading out of the mall when someone called out my name. I turned around, and there stood Carissa. She was leaning beside a purple Honda smoking a cigarette.

I jogged over to her, and that's when I finally got the chance to make out her features. My heart was pounding, and my breathing began to get heavy as I got closer to her. She still looked the same, but the bitch was way finer. She was thicker, and her skin seemed to glow. She was dressed in a pair of blue jeans with a black designed shirt that said Queen on it. She was rocking a pair of black flip flops that showed her perfectly polished toes. Her long nails were wrapped around a Newport as she took a long puff. Her hair stopped at her ass and a pair of silver hooped earrings dangled from her ear. She didn't wear any makeup; all I noticed was the dark purple lipstick that was painted on her lips.

We briefly talked for a while and just when she told me she was about to head out, I stopped her and asked for her number since then we had been kicking it and fucking every chance we got.

When I first hit her up, she told me she had some nigga on the Westside that she was fucking around with. At first, I ain't know who she was talking about until she finally told me his name.

I almost threw up when she told me she was fucking around with Ken's lame ass. Ken and the crew went way back because he was the nigga that was beefing with Quan when we started making serious money on the streets. He eventually left the Northside and started hustling on the Westside but shid, he wasn't pulling in the type of money that Quan and I were making.

Once I dropped some dick up in her, she got rid of that lame ass nigga really quick. I already know Ken pussy ass was super pissed when he found out Carissa didn't want to fuck with him anymore. But if he wanted beef or ever got in my face about Carissa, I was willing to lay that nigga out.

He couldn't give her what I could, and she knew that shit, that's why she didn't hesitate to fuck with me. Even though I cared about Carissa, I didn't have the type of love for her like I had for Taea. Three years of being with Taea wasn't something that I wanted to just throw away. Most niggas would have not bothered or stressed over any of it, instead, they would have gone straight to their side piece after their girl put them out and made a whole relationship, but that wasn't who I was. I had made a mistake, I had taken shit way too far, and I was willing to do anything to make things right with the one bitch who had my heart.

The dinging of my phone let me knew that I had a text message. I picked up my phone, and that's when I saw that Carissa had texted me over three times. The last text message she was pressing the issue of me coming to see her. As I sat in my car, I debated on what I needed to do, should I go see Carissa or should I go back to Taea and try to talk things out with her.

I picked up my phone and tried to call Taea, but it went straight to voicemail. I sighed with irritation because I knew without a doubt Taea was still pissed. She had every right to be, but I just wished she gave me the chance to explain myself.

I found it ironic that Quan and I both had gotten exposed within a day of one another. But that just was part of life, when shit was going well, there was always somebody waiting for it to go to shit and back.

Instead of heading towards Taea's, I decided to go to Carissa's house instead. We had a lot of shit to discuss anyway so I might as well get it over with. Having this conversation wasn't something that I was looking forward to, but I knew it had to be done. As I cruised through the heavy traffic towards the Westside of town, I couldn't stop thinking about Carissa being pregnant, if she kept the baby, Taea was never going to accept it. She was always going to feel hatred towards me, and she had good reasons why she felt that way. I had betrayed her; I had gotten another bitch pregnant that wasn't her. I already knew what had to be done, I only prayed that Carissa didn't make it hard for me.

The only time I came on the Westside was to see Carissa other than that, I stayed far away from that side of town since that's where Ken and his crew hustled at. Living on the ghetto side of Northside use to be rough, but as I headed into the Westside, the struggle looked even much real.

I spotted a few kids on the block hustlin and drove past their young asses. They looked like they were in the 10th grade. These days the streets got the kids early and once they were grown; they already knew the game and how it was played. I had witnessed a few of the niggas from my side of town being kilt or shot for hanging with the wrong motherfuckers. They always found themselves in the wrong place at the wrong fucking time. So many had lost their lives, but I was lucky that I wasn't in that number.

I started hustling when I was in high school. My home life wasn't hitting on shit, and I had to survive. What was so crazy was that my childhood could have been so much better if my parents would have cared about me. They had no excuse because they both had good ass jobs, my pops worked in business, and my mama did hair. The bitch had her a small shop not far from up the road from our three-bedroom house that they raised me in. All the money that they were making and I still found myself hustling on the corner and slangin dope. The money that they made they spent it on themselves. The first thing they would say when I needed something was that I better go get a job, my pops would kill me with that statement.

I can remember when I was on summer break and was heading to the tenth grade, I asked them were they going to buy my school clothes and shoes. They both laughed in my face and told me that I was old enough to get a job if I wanted new clothes or shoes. They both told me that I better work for it like they did every day.

My pops believed in tough love and hard work.

"Ain't' nothing free in this world, Jontavian, it's time you know that," my father would tell me.

I didn't grow up in the projects or come from a background where any of my parents did drugs. I came from a good background but found myself hanging around on the Northside in the projects trying to figure out how to survive because my parents weren't giving me the things, I felt I needed. Selfish was what I always used to call them. I had no hate for my parents, but I'm not going to lie when both of them died in a plane crash on their way to Paris when I was seventeen, at their funeral I didn't shed one tear. I only stared at their coffins and said a silent prayer for them both before taking a seat in the first row of the church.

When they died, I thought things were going to get better for me, but when it was time to read the will, the money that they had left over after their debt had been paid ended up going to a charity that they both had supported when they were alive. Not a drop of money came to me. I was hurt and angry about that shit for a long time.

I didn't have any means of earning enough income to take care of myself. The family wasn't close on either side, but my uncle who was my pop's brother ended up taking me in and letting me live with him until I got my own little crib. My uncle wasn't any better than my parents. He didn't give me shit either, and that's when I knew it was time for me to get out. I continued to hustle until I had saved enough money to move and fix up my one-bedroom apartment.

When I moved away from my uncle, I cut his ass off as well. I didn't have a family; all my family was dead to me. Now at the age of twenty-seven, I was making shit happen for myself. Thinking about the past was something that I barely do. I was just grateful to be doing better for myself.

I was just about to pull into Carissa's driveway when I spotted a nigga coming from out her apartment. I squinted my eyes as the nigga made it towards the curb, he waited until traffic had cleared to jog across the street.

Only then did I recognize who this nigga was. I wasn't expecting to see Ken anywhere near Carissa's apartment, so I automatically went on high alert trying to figure out why all of a sudden, he had come by.

Carissa never told me nothing about this nigga was still coming over, I gripped the steering wheel rather tightly as I tried to calm myself down. I never wanted to think the worse of anyone I fucked with because hat only proved to me that I didn't know the people whom I let enter into my life.

But as I began to think, everything began to finally make sense. Carissa was from the Westside, and Ken was living on the Westside slangin his dope. She told me out her own mouth that they used to fuck around, but swore that she had cut him off once me and her started fucking around, but if that was true, why in the fuck was this nigga coming out her crib?

Something wasn't adding up, and I was beginning to think that Carissa was trying to play me. Whether she knew it or not she was fucking with the wrong nigga. She had a nigga thinking that I had a baby on the way, but shid that probably was a lie too.

If she was pregnant, I was beginning to think that it was a high chance that the baby wasn't even mine and the only reason why I was saying that was because a nigga just came out of her apartment, it was the same nigga she claimed she had cut off.

If that bitch could lie about cutting a nigga off, I was beginning to wonder what else she was lying about. The only way for me to find out where Carissa and I stood was to confront her ass about the shit. There was no way in hell I was going to lose Taea over a lie that wasn't true.

Yeah, I cheated, but did I really have a baby on the way? I needed to know the truth, and I was going to find that shit out today, one thing I didn't wanna do was smash a bitch who was fucking around with a nigga who I didn't fuck with.

I didn't give a fuck if Carissa was fucking with someone, if she was, she could at least let a nigga know. I already had a bitch that I told her I was never going to leave, so she was down to fuck who she wanted, but if she wanted to continue to fuck on Ken, then we were going to be done because me and the squad had beef with his pussy ass.

I pulled up at her crib and stepped out the car a few moments later. I took in my surroundings which I did each time that I came over to her apartment.

I walked up to her door and knocked a few times before she opened it. She opened the door with a surprised look on her face, but she did step aside to welcome me in.

"I thought you had forgotten about me; I been blowing up your phone. You never did respond that you were going to pull up."

"I got a lot of shit going on that's all. You must have made other plans? I can dip if you have."

"No, don't go. I don't have no plans," she told me as she pulled me inside.

I caught her peeping outside like she was looking for someone. I guess she was wondering if Ken had disappeared since I pulled up the during the time he was dipping out. I already knew she ain't want me to spot his ass but it was too late, I had already seen him coming out her crib.

She tried to lean in to give me a kiss, but I pushed her away from me.

"Damn Jon, what the fuck is wrong with you? I've barely heard from you, and then you have the nerve to come over here with a fucked up attitude!"

I lost it for a quick minute. I don't know if it was the anger I had built up about Taea, or if I was just fed up with all the bullshit and lies. I know what I saw, and I didn't like the shit at all. Suspicions were weighing heavy on my mind.

I snatched her ass up by her slender throat and pushed her up against the wall. She was trying to shove me off of her, but I was way stronger than her. She was gasping for air, but I acted like I didn't care. I looked deep into her eyes before I asked her a serious question.

"Is that my baby you carrying inside you mine?"

She tried to speak, but no words came out. I removed my hand from her throat which made her drop to her knees as she gasped for air.

"Get the fuck out!" Carissa yelled at me in a hoarse voice.

If she thought I was about to leave this crib without getting the information I needed then the bitch had lost her damn mind. I leaned down beside her, so we were face to face.

"I'm not leaving until I know the damn truth."

"Why are you doing this to me?" she cried out in agony.

"I hate a lying ass bitch. You told me that you had stopped fucking with that pussy ass nigga Ken, but explain to me why I just spotted the nigga leaving out your crib?"

Carissa didn't say shit, she just stared at me with her big wide eyes in horror.

I laughed at her ass because the shit was hilarious.

"You were the one begging me to come over, so when I pull up to see you, you have the fucking nerve to have another nigga coming up out this bitch, and it ain't just any nigga, it's a nigga I don't fuck with."

She bit down on her bottom lip as she stood up from off the floor.

"I don't have anything going on with him I swear."

I stared at her for the longest time and that's when I noticed for the first time that Carissa wasn't shit, she was standing here in my fucking face and lying to me like I was some dumb ass nigga she was fucking with on the block.

I took a few steps back and rested my hand on my gun, I had the urge to pull it out, just to scare her because the only way I was going to get some answers was if she thought her life was in danger. Instead of pulling my weapon out I decided to try to calm myself down so I could try to get what I wanted to know from her.

I took a deep breath before I turned back to her. Her tank top clung to her body as sweat began to fall down her chest. Her booty shorts hugged her body as she stood perfectly still. I turnt my head away from her for a brief moment because I didn't want to get distracted. Even though I knew Carissa wasn't shit, her body still made my dick get on hard. There was not going to be no fucking done today until I knew the fucking truth. Either she was going to give it to me, or she was going to take an ass whooping. My life and my relationship were at stake, and I was ready to fuck a bitch up if need be.

I watched a Carissa rubbed her hands through her long weave.

She wouldn't even look at me. There were either two reasons why she couldn't look at me directly. Either she knew she was guilty and couldn't lie to me in my face, or she was in utter disbelief that I had just roughed her up. If she thought me choking her out was bad, she hadn't seen nothing yet.

Carissa had fucked around with nothing but dope boys, she knew the game, and she knew what to do and what not to do. Lying was something that you didn't do unless you wanted to get beat down or worse killed.

The apartment was so quiet that you could hear a pin drop.

"I have two questions that I need the answer to. Don't lie to me either because I don't mind choking your ass out again."

Carissa nodded her head at me.

"Are you still fucking with Ken on the low?"

"No," she told me emotionally.

"Why the fuck was he over here then?"

She couldn't look at me which pissed me off. I was just about to smack her ass, but that's when she finally answered me.

"He came over to tell me that his sister KeKe told him that Quan beat her up. He was pissed off, and he needed someone to talk to. He said when he saw Quan, he was gonna fuck him up for putting his hands on his sister.

I took a seat on her couch because it all was coming together. There was no way that Carissa was lying because I never told Carissa about KeKe and Quan. I never told her ass shit because it wasn't her business. I knew to never trust a bitch with no personal information because that's what always seemed to get a nigga fucked up. Pillow talking could be deadly.

This shit was getting out of hand, and someone was bound to get hurt. If KeKe told Ken that Quan had beat her ass, I already knew Ken wanted to confront Quan. Even though Ken was a pussy ass nigga, he was a fool when it came to his thot ass sister. I had the urge to pull out my phone to shoot Quan a message to warn him about Ken, but I got distracted with trying to get as much information out of Carissa while she was willing to talk.

"What else Ken told you?" I asked her calmly.

"He wanted to know was I still fucking with you. He wanted us to start back fucking round."

"What you told him?" I asked her curiously.

"I told him the truth, I told him that I wasn't going back to him and I was with you."

"What happened next?"

"He got mad at me and told me that he could make you disappear along with your homeboy Quan if I didn't leave you alone."

Just knowing this nigga had threatened my life really got me heated. I swear if I knew he had said some shit like that about me when I spotted him coming out her crib, I swear I wouldn't have thought twice about murking his ass right in the middle of the street. This nigga wasn't ready for these problems, but apparently, this nigga was ready to die. Anger consumed my body, and I was ready to get the fuck up out her crib so I could hit Quan up to let him know what was up.

Carissa must have noticed my whole vibe changed because she immediately got silent. She started fidgeting, and I could tell she wanted to be anywhere but there.

"I GOT one last question for you, and I want you to answer it truthfully."

I didn't want to hear any lies, because this question was something that could change my life forever.

"What is it?" Carissa asked cautiously.

"Are you sure that baby you carrying is mine?

"Of course, it's yours, you the only nigga I been fucking, I swear to you."

I walked over to her and pushed her up against the wall. Her breathing was heavy, and I saw fear in her eyes. I never wanted her to fear me, but it was gonna be needed from here on out. The fact her ex nigga had an issue with Quan and me made her my enemy. If he told her that much that meant he still trusted her.

"I want you to do something for me," I spoke to her roughly.

"What?" she asked timidly.

"I need for you to get rid of that baby inside you."

The second I said that Carissa was no longer scared. Instead, she had toughened up very quickly. It was as if a light switch had been flipped.

"What the fuck? Hell no, I'm not killing my child."

"Look, my relationship is on the fucking line. Taea has cut

my ass off because of this shit. I'm not about to lose her because you wanna keep this baby. I told you up front that I wasn't gonna leave my bitch for you. You told me you were on birth control, and now all of a sudden you pregnant. Get rid of it," I demanded her coldly.

"I'm not killing my baby just because you don't wanna leave your bitch. It's good that Taea knows about this baby because I was gonna tell her ass myself if I needed to."

I swear I was about to snap on this bitch.

"Carissa, I'm not about to stand here and repeat myself. After today, you won't be seeing me no more. I'm cutting your ass off."

Carissa laughed.

"As long as I got this baby I'ma always be in your life, and it ain't shit you, or that ugly bitch Taea can do about it."

Smack.

Carissa fell to the ground as I smacked her across her cheek.

I stared down at her.

"Don't fuck with me Carissa, I will kill your ass if I need to."

Tears fell down her cheeks as she stared up at me.

"You gonna regret this shit. You may be a dope boy with a lot of money, but I know people who can take your ass up out of here. I don't give a fuck what you say, I'm not killing this baby nigga. If you're smart, you better leave that ugly hoe you with and make a family with me."

I shook my head at her.

"Bitch, I will never be yours," I hissed at her before I walked out her crib.

I slammed the door behind me and hopped in my car. If this bitch thought I was scared about who she knew, then she had another thing coming. I stayed ready to pop a nigga. I pulled out my phone as soon as I crank my car up. I connected my phone to my car speaker as I hit Quan up. His phone rung close to four times before I heard his deep voice coming from my car speaker.

"What up bruh you good?" Quan asked

"We got a problem..." I told him seriously.

CHAPTER 8

I have never been the type to fuck with another bitch's man, but when Jon came back into my life I put all of my morals aside and did the one thing that I said I would never do. My parents didn't raise me to be a side chick, but that's the role that I now found myself in. I was sexy as hell and could have any man that my heart desired. I was Mexican, with long black hair that stopped at my ass, I was thick in all the right places with pretty lips and straight white teeth. Even though I knew I could get another man that didn't stop me from wanting Jon and making him mine.

I grew up in a strict household, my parents didn't allow me to date or have any friends in high school. I was sheltered from life and I hated every minute of it. I wanted to be free, but I was trapped until I graduated high school. I didn't go off to college like most in my class, instead I went to the technical college and came home every day. Even though I was grown any in my early twenties my parents still wanted to control me. Their smothering behavior that they had drove me away from the both. Even though I had little money I was lucky enough to find a low-income apartment and get the hell n from my controlling parents. The fact that both of my parents were lawyers and I was their child I believed was some of the reason they was so demanding and wanted to control my life.

Moving out of my parents' house gave me peace of mind that I was longing for and gave me the freedom I needed to date. The first man I met when I move out from my parents was a dope boy named Ken. He lived around the block from my apartment. We bumped into each other one day and I was instantly attracted to him. I always had a weakness for a fine light skinned nigga. He introduced himself and told me if I ever needed anything to let him know. Moving into my own crib struggling wasn't something I wanted to do but I managed it. Living on my school checks was what I was doing to keep myself a float because asking my parents for help was out of the question. They would have quickly come to my house and dragged me back home with them.

Ken and I became close by smoking weed together. We chilled for the first few weeks but things quickly turned sexual one night when I had had too much to drink. We ended up fucking and after that first session neither one of us wanted to let the other go. I was so in love and felt Ken was all I needed. I ended up flunking out of school and basically letting Ken take over with helping me out. I felt like all I needed was Ken and no one else but all of this changed when my high school crush, Jon walked back into my life. I thought I was over him and had moved on but when I saw him at the mall I nearly passed out. I had always had a crush on Jon, but back then neither one of us was able to do anything about it. Now ten years later, we were fully grown and could do exactly what we wanted. When he told me he had a girl already my heart was crushed, but I wasn't going to let that shit stop me from making Jon mine.

Breaking Ken's heart and falling in love with Jon was

reckless, but Jon was someone I always wanted and I wasn't about to let anything stand in my way. Ken swore up and down that I left him because Jon had more money than him, but that wasn't why I had left. Yes, Jon had more money and could give me anything that I wanted but money wasn't what I was after. I wanted to be Jon's main bitch and the woman who had his heart.

Breaking it off with Ken knowing how much he hated Jon really hurt Ken and he made that shit clear on a few occasions, but honestly, I didn't give a fuck when I did it. I only cared about myself and what I wanted.

But now I was beginning to feel as if I had fucked around and fell in love with a nigga who didn't feel for me like I felt for him. Just thinking about how Jon had gone off on me and told me he didn't want me really had me in my feelings. I understood he was mad about Ken coming by, but Ken and I were over with, but Jon thought otherwise. Ken wasn't trying to fuck me he really did come over to tell me about his sister KeKe. After Ken filled me in with KeKe and Quan situation he turned the conversation on me and Jon. He didn't sugar coat shit and told me straight up that Jon wasn't going to leave his bitch for me. He wanted me to help him bring Jon down but I told me to get out of my house with the fuck shit. I didn't give a fuck what he did to Quan, Quan wasn't my nigga but I didn't want him touching Jon at all.

Thinking back to Ken's conversation only made me think hard about what I was going to do next about Jon. If Ken went for Quan, I knew he was going to have to go for Jon to. Ken had his own personal reasons why he wanted Quan and Jon gone. After how Jon went off on me today, I now knew where he stood with me. I was going to give him one more chance to get his shit together and realize what he was doing. If he didn't leave Taea I knew all bets were off and I was going to take Ken up on his offer. My pregnancy confession was all just a test. I was testing his ass and he didn't even know it. I wasn't pregnant with his baby, but he thought I was, and I was going to keep it that way. I was clearly beginning to see that this nigga didn't give a damn about me. After the reaction I received today it broke my heart to know that he wasn't shit.

TAEA

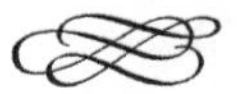

TWO DAYS LATER...

I was beyond hurt; I was heartbroken. Tears fell down my cheeks, and Yanni hurried to wipe them away.

"Shhh, don't cry Taea," I'm here for you sis.

I moved away from her and covered my face in my pillow. I didn't want her to comfort me, I just wanted to be alone. Anger shook my entire body, I wanted nothing more than to grab a gun and blow Jon's brains out. How could he do me like this? How could he betray me the way he had? Not only did he cheat on me, but he even got the bitch pregnant. There was no coming back from that shit, there was no way I was going to be able to get over any of this. Yanni pulled the pillow from off me and demanded that I get my ass up.

"Taea, you gotta get up, you been laying in this bed for two days. I'm not about to let you sit here another day crying over Jon's ass. Get your ass up, I just got paid I'm taking you shopping."

"I don't wanna go anywhere," I mumbled.

"Well, you going somewhere to damn day. I'm not doing shit that you ain't never done for me. You always been my bitch and always looked out for me. So now it's my turn."

I already knew arguing with Yanni wasn't going to get me anywhere. I groaned as I slid out of bed. Yanni was already dressed, she was wearing a pair of skin-tight blue jeans, a pair of black and white Nike sandals, with a white tank top. Her milk chocolate skin seemed to glow even though she was still depressed over Quan's cheating. Her hair was pulled back in a low ponytail, and her silver diamond studs sparkled in the sunlight that was coming from my bedroom window. She stared into my face, and only then did I notice the sadness in her eyes. I could tell that she had been crying because of the bags under her eyes.

"Go wash your ass and I will find you something to wear for today," Yanni instructed me.

I headed towards the bathroom so I could shower and brush my teeth. As the hot water splashed across my body, I stood there not able to move for the longest time. I never thought Jon could hurt me, but he had. He had crushed my whole soul. Could I forgive him? Would I forgive him? I didn't know any of the answers to the two questions. I have never been the type of bitch who cries about anything but going through a heartbreak from a man you had given your all to would make any bitch break down and cry.

As I washed my body the hurt that I was feeling turned to rage and anger. I wanted to hurt him like he had hurt me. To know that the man I had trusted had been cheating and lying to me began to make me wonder if I ever knew him at all. Here I was thinking I knew my man's every move, and he had a whole another phone that he was talking to another bitch on. Here I was believing that Yanni had a fucked up ass boyfriend, and mine wasn't any better.

I finished washing my body clean and stepped out the shower. I brushed my teeth and pulled my weave into a messy bun before I stepped out of the bathroom. As soon as I had stepped back into the bedroom, I spotted my clothes already laid out on the bed. I guess Yanni had taken it upon herself to find me something to wear. I slid on a pair of red shorts with a black tank top. I slid my feet into my favorite black and red Nike sandals and placed a dab of lip chap on my lips.

I stared at myself in the mirror and felt disgusted with myself. How could I sit here and let myself get so emotional that I could barely get out of bed? I never wanted a nigga to have that much control of me, but I was giving that nigga just that. I had stopped living my life because of some shit that he had done.

I put a little mascara under my eye so it could hide the bags that was under them. I didn't bother by putting any makeup on, instead, I stared at myself for the longest moment in the mirror trying to figure out what I was going to do with myself and how I was going to get back to the Taea that I knew. I needed the Taea who didn't give a fuck, I needed her ass to jump back into my body and make this emotional Taea take a backseat.

Yanni stepped back into my bedroom and walked over to me.

"You actually look like someone today. I have never seen you let yourself go like you did these past two days."

"Don't worry, it will never happen again," I said sternly.

"If I got anything to do with it, it will never ever come to this."

"Are you ready to go to the mall and shop your ass off?"

I shook my head at her to let her know that I wasn't interested in shopping.

"Well, what you wanna do then?"

"I stared at myself in the mirror and smiled evilly. I think it's time for us to let our niggas know they fucked with the wrong bitches."

"I think it's about that time too," Yanni agreed.

Let me unblock Quan's dumb ass and call him to see if we can link up for tonight. I been avoiding him like the plague, but you know Quan, he ain't going to let me cut him off. He came up to my job trying to talk with me because I had blocked his ass. For the first time in two days, I finally had the urge to laugh. Yanni made that shit possible because the bitch didn't have no fucking sense. When she started going into detail about her conversation with Quan on her job, she had crying laughing at her crazy ass. When she told me she was cold as ice to him, I believed every word of it.

We came from the same blood, and neither one of us gave a fuck when someone fucked us over, we could be some cold ass bitches if someone wronged us.

"What you gonna do to Quan?" I asked her.

"Oh, I got something up my sleeve that you and I both can do to these lying ass niggas. When I get done with Quan, he gonna wish he never fucked with me."

I watched as Yanni pulled her phone out and dialed Quan's number. I took a seat on the edge of my bed as I listened as Yanni spoke sweetly into the phone to him. She wanted him to believe everything was okay and persuaded him to come back home later that night. As I had expected he agreed that he was ready to come home and talk everything out. Yanni hung up the phone with a smile on her face.

"This is going to be so fucking easy, they ain't even going to see this shit coming," Yanni said with excitement in her voice.

Yanni slid her phone into her pocket and grabbed her purse from off my bed.

"We need to head to the grocery store. I have the perfect dish that I'm going to cook for Quan, and the dessert is going to be to die for. All you have to do is find something that you know Jon will love to eat for tonight, whip it up and make sure to find him a desert as well because that's gonna be the most important part of the dinner. We gonna cook their favorite meal and once they think everything is good that's when they're gonna learn the awful truth, nothing is good, at least not yet. We gotta make them suffer, bring them to their knees, and make their ass cry."

I looked over at her and giggled. I was always down for the fuck shit.

We pulled up at Kroger's on Watson Blvd and stepped out the car. It was so hot outside that sweat was dripping from my brow, and I wasn't even outside two minutes good.

"Shit it's hotter than a pregnant bitch's pussy," I complained as I followed Yanni inside the grocery store.

"It damn sure is, I feel like I'm going to pass out if I don't hurry up and get some air."

We were lucky that Yanni had air in her damn car because it was no way I was going to get in the car with her on this hot ass day to ride in a hot ass car. Once we stepped foot into the grocery store, we both grabbed a shopping cart and headed towards the meat department.

"What you thinking about cooking for Jon?" Yanni asked as she pushed her shopping cart alongside mine.

"I'm thinking about something Italian; he loves lasagna.

"What you going to do for dessert?"

I smiled evilly.

"I'm thinking about mixing up some brownies."

"Sounds perfect," Yanni replied as she grabbed some cube steak and some instant mashed potatoes.

"What are you cooking for Quan?"

Yanni smirked.

"Oh, I'm cooking cube steak, mashed potatoes, green beans, and rolls, I'm cooking chocolate cream pie for dessert."

"Damn bitch, I need to come eat with you."

"No bitch, you don't, because what we about to do, you ain't gonna want to eat this shit."

Even though Yanni didn't tell me what the plan was, but I was beginning to piece shit together. We were cousins, and we thought alike. People always said the way to a man's heart was through his stomach, and this was definitely the case. We headed over to the medicine aisle of Kroger's, and that's when I had found the courage to pull out my phone to call Jon to see if he could pull up at the house later on that night.

"Taea are you ok?" Jon asked desperately into the phone.

I held the anger that I was feeling inside at bay, and politely told him I was good.

Even though I wanted to rip his eyes out his head, there was no way in hell I was going to show signs that I had snapped towards another level. When he did what he did, he brought out a side of me that he didn't want to ever see, but he was going to see that bitch tonight. No more crying about what he had done, it was time for him to suffer the consequences of his actions.

"Look we need to talk, come by the house later tonight."

"I'm so glad you're ready to talk, I know I have a lot of explaining to do, and I'm willing to tell you everything."

I rolled my eyes at his comment instead of continuing to listen to him yap in my ear, I hung up the phone while he was mid-sentence of telling me how sorry he was. I didn't call to hear his apology; I called just so I could get him to pull up later tonight, that was all I cared about. I shot him a text message to let him know to be at the house at eight. He shot a message back agreeing on the time and asked me why I hung up on him. I shook my head at his text and placed my phone back in my pocket.

Yanni and I went from aisle to aisle as we searched for the perfect laxative for Jon and Quan. After twenty minutes of reading different brands, we finally decided on one.

"This chocolate covered laxatives will do the fucking trick," Yanni told me as she passed me two boxes.

"How much do we suppose to use?" I hissed at her.

Yanni shrugged her shoulders.

"I'm using the whole box for Quan's stupid ass."

"Ain't that too much?" I asked.

"Nope, he got a lot of shit he needs to get out of his system, maybe he will shit some of that hoeness out, while he on the toilet tonight, Yanni joked."

I couldn't help but laugh which drew attention to us.

"Damn, what the fuck y'all looking at?" I asked an old white couple that had their eyes squinted at us like they had a problem or some shit. The woman's thin lips pressed together as she looked at us in a disapproving manner. She looked every bit of eighty. She clutched her hand to an old ass man who looked to be around the same age as her. The smell of Bengay filled my nose which made me feel like I wanted to pass out. They both were rocking a back brace and was hunched over as they slowly walked to their destination. They both tooted their nose up at Yanni and I and kept on walking down the aisle to be checked out I assumed.

Yanni must have known I was pissed because she quickly told me to calm down.

"Leave them old white folks alone. It looks like they have about one more year on this Earth before they croke and die," Yanni whispered into my ear.

I clutched my two small boxes of laxatives in my hand as we headed to the self-checkout line. I wasn't about to sit there all day waiting to be rung out. As usual, Kroger was busy as hell. I was becoming agitated because I was ready to hurry my ass home and get right for tonight. Yanni and I headed straight towards the self-checkout line. As soon as we had rung ourselves out, I grabbed my shopping bag with a smile on my face. I was on a mission to blow Jon's whole asshole up. He was lucky that I wasn't a killer because this shit I was about to do was child's play. It would have been easier to stab or shoot him, but I wasn't stupid. I knew deep down in my heart I still loved my man.

Killing him wasn't going to make me feel better because then I was gonna lose him forever. Losing him wasn't an option and losing him to a thot wasn't about to happen neither. Eventually, I was gonna forgive him and try to move on with what he had done, but it was gonna be a long time coming.

As Yanni and I headed towards her car, I noticed that the sky was beginning to get dark and the wind was blowing. My hair whipped across my face as I slid into the passenger seat. Yanni started the engine, and Cardi B started blasting from the speakers.

This was the last thing Yanni, and I needed to hear because Cardi B didn't give a shit and we had that I don't give a fuck attitude already. Twenty minutes later Yanni pulled up at my crib and put her car in park.

"Do you know what to do?" she asked me gently.

"Yes," I told her.

Yanni nodded her head at me before I stepped out.

"Thanks for everything Yanni, you have always looked out for me."

"Don't thank me boo. I'm glad neither one of us is going through this shit alone."

"It's sad that our niggas ain't shit," I muttered.

Yanni laughed.

"When we get through with them, they gonna wish they would have kept their dick in their pants."

I grabbed my bag out the back and waved Yanni off. When she had pulled out of the parking lot, only then did I head inside to start the perfect dinner that was gonna end rather dreadfully for Jon.

DINNER TIME

The kitchen was smelling good as hell, it smelled of my famous lasagna and brownies. My stomach growled as I checked the oven. I had about twenty more minutes on the food and took that time to find me something sexy to wear. I wanted something that was gonna catch Jon's attention. Was I gonna fuck him? Hell no, but I wanted him to see exactly what he was going to be missing if he kept fucking around with these hoes in the streets.

I took the time to flat iron my shoulder length hair as Trina blasted from the speakers in my bedroom. After my hair was flat ironed, I hurried back to the kitchen so I could cut off the food. I checked the clock that was on the stove and noticed that I didn't have long before Jon was going to be pulling up. I hurried back to my bedroom and decided on wearing a red see-through tank top with no bra, a pair of white lace shorts, with a red pair of Nike and white sandals. I put on some red lipstick that made my lips pop and fluffed my hair one last time before heading back to the living room. I turned on the TV and was just about to find a horror movie on Netflix when my phone dinged. I grabbed my phone from beside me and smiled to myself once I noticed that it was Jon telling me that he was outside.

I hopped off the couch and headed towards the front door. I took a deep breath before I came face to face with the man I thought I was going to spend the rest of my life with. As our eyes connected, I took in his features. He was dressed in a pair of all black jean shorts, a pair of lime green and black Jordan's with a lime green shirt to match. He was rocking a lime green snapback cap with his diamond cut earrings. Even though he was looking sexy as hell, I could see the pain that was behind his eyes. Just knowing he was hurting made me feel just a little bit better. I highly doubted that he was feeling the type of pain that I was experiencing. He was going through the pain of probably getting caught up in his lies. I immediately stepped aside to let him in.

"Damn, it smells so good in here," Jon said as he headed towards the living room to take a seat.

"Thanks," I replied back rather lightly.

I couldn't show just how I actually felt around him. I didn't want him to know that I still loved him so deeply. I wanted him to suffer just by knowing that everything wasn't okay. Once he noticed that I wasn't going to sit down next to him, he stood up and walk over to me.

"Baby…"

"Don't... I don't want to discuss this shit right now. The food is ready, let's eat before it gets cold."

Jon didn't press the issue he only nodded his head at my request and followed me to the kitchen. He took a seat at the kitchen table as I busied myself fixing his plate.

I cooked your favorite, lasagna, green beans, and rolls. For dessert, I decided to cook some brownies.

"It smells delicious, I already know it's going to be good."

I smiled a fake smile and handed him his plate.

I made sure to grab him a beer out the fridge and popped it open for him.

I watched him as he took a few sips of his Bud Light and started digging into his food.

I fixed me a small plate as well and took a few bites before putting down my fork. Eating was the last thing on my mind. I wanted answers, that was why I had invited him over, I wanted to know why he had done what he had done. He stopped what he was doing, and also put his fork down when he noticed I wasn't eating.

"Are you ready to talk?" he asked me gently.

"The talking is over with; I just want you to answer a few questions."

"Okay," Jon replied tensely.

I took a deep breath before staring in his pretty brown eyes.

"Is it really true?"

"Is what true love?" Jon asked as if he was confused.

This was beginning to irritate me because he knew damn well what I was talking about.

He must have noticed the irritation in my voice and told me that he wanted me to explain further.

I rolled my eyes and took another deep breath. Just talking about this shit brought pain to my heart. It was like an open wound that was sensitive to the touch.

"Is it true what Tay said the other night?"

Jon didn't answer at first, but when he did my heart instantly sank. I guess deep down inside, I wanted him to say that what Tay had told me was a mistake and that he was just pissed about me hitting him. I wanted in my heart for this to be a big misunderstanding, but I knew subconsciously that what Tay had so horridly told me had to be nothing but the truth.

I stared down at the plate as my brain began to register what he had just admitted.

When did you meet the bitch? When did you start fucking her? I want to know every fucking thing, and you better not leave shit out," I told him calmly.

He didn't speak at first, I guess he was wondering if he should say or admit anything because I was acting so calmly. By now I guess he expected me to be nutting up and trying to kill him, but that wasn't going to solve anything, but it would lead me to serving a life sentence in prison.

Her name is Carissa, she was somebody in high school that I used to have a crush on. Back then we never went farther than being just friends. I was focused on getting money, and her parents were super strict on her. I met her about three months ago when I was coming out of the mall, she spotted me, and we started talking about old times and shit. I got her number just so we could stay in touch, and we ended up fucking around. Everything else that was said after he met and fucked her went straight out my ear. Tears were bound to fall very soon if I didn't get away from him at that very moment.

I stood up just so I could try to get myself together. I grabbed the brownies from out the oven and cut off the warmer. I cut him a big slice and made sure to serve it with a scoop of vanilla ice cream. Everything in my soul wanted me to grab the knife that I was holding and slit his throat, but I refrained. I was going to stick to the plan that Yanni and I both agreed on.

I passed him his brownies and ice cream as he continued to apologize for his actions. After I sat his desert in front of him, he grabbed me by my arm.

"Please, Taea. Please forgive me."

"Maybe one day I will," I told him truthfully.

"Eat up, I cooked all this food just for you. I worked hard on these brownies."

"Of course," he replied as he took a big bite of the gooey dessert.

I let him eat in peace because I wanted him to eat as many of the brownies as he possibly could. I wanted to see if the chocolate laxatives were going to work. It said it would take up to six hours which meant that in order for me to witness it, he was going to have to stay over. It was only eight, so him staying over was the only option.

After he had eaten three brownies and two more servings of Lasagna only then did I feel like it was ready to try to talk about our relationship. I gave him a fake smile as he continued to compliment me on the meal that I had cooked especially for him. I watched him as he ate. I tapped my fingers on the hardwood table as I gathered up the courage to ask him the one question that was going to change both of our lives forever.

"Is she pregnant with your baby?"

Jon stopped chewing and stared at me.

I looked him in the eye coldly and asked him yet again.

"Baby, you ain't gotta worry about nothing, I've already taken care of everything, it's in the process now."

I don't want to hear that shit Jon; I want to know the fucking truth. I'm not working shit out with you until I know the fucking truth about you and this bitch you been cheating on me with."

"I'm going to tell you the truth," Jon promised.

"Don't hold shit back," I demanded him.

Jon took a deep breath and then begun with his story.

"Before I started fucking with Carissa, she told me that she was fucking around with a nigga named Ken who live on the Westside as well. You know Ken he's KeKe brother."

"I know who Ken and KeKe are what this got to do with anything?" I asked irritably.

Jon sighed.

"Well, Carissa was fucking around with him but cut him off when she started fucking around with me. I asked her was the baby mine she told me it was. But honestly, I don't know. I sort of believe that she still fucking around with Ken on the low because when I went over there to talk with her about the so-called pregnancy, I saw Ken coming out of her house.

My heart was racing, and I felt as if I was going to be dizzy.

"So basically, the bitch you fucking was fucking you and Ken, and now you don't know if the baby yours or not? So that only means one thing, you were fucking that hoe raw, knowing you coming home to me every fucking day. What would have happened if you would have given me something?" I asked him furiously.

"I know baby, it was so stupid of me, I just want us to get through this. I just want us to try to start back over."

I shook my head at him as I stood up and pointed my finger at him.

"There is no getting over this shit. You really fucked up by cheating on me with another bitch for the last three months. I mean damn, you must was really planning on being with this bitch, she just wasn't a fucking nut to you, apparently, the hoe meant something."

"No, she don't mean nothing to me, I broke it off with her."

I laughed evilly, "you only broke it off with her because Tay ran his mouth and told everything, you probably would still be fucking that bitch right now."

I saw the tears in Jon's eyes, but I didn't give a fuck, I had cried for over two days. I felt like crying now, but I had to remain strong.

"You won't ever have to worry about the baby Taea," I told you I handled that shit.

"How did you fucking handle it!?" I screamed at him loudly.

"I went to her and told her to get rid of it, that was the point of me going back to her crib, so we could both talk about her getting the abortion. I didn't want her to bring a baby here. I know I was never going to leave you for her and she knew that shit too. She wanted me to leave, but I never planned on leaving you baby," I swear.

I shook my head at him in bewilderment.

"Is she going to get rid of the baby? I'm a bitch, I know how they think, that hoe isn't going to get rid of that fucking baby if she really wanna be with you. That baby is all she has of you, she's going to do whatever she can to keep it and use that shit against you," I told him furiously.

"I'm never going to be happy with you ever again, so we might as well call the shit quits," I told him emotionally.

"Fuck that shit, if the baby mine I'ma do my part, but I'm never leaving you."

I huffed.

"Jon wake the fuck up, you ain't gotta leave because I'm leaving your pathetic ass. You betrayed me. You fucked another bitch without a rubber and got her pregnant. It's no coming back from that."

I grabbed his dessert plate and placed it in the kitchen sink and started busying myself in cleaning up the kitchen. I had to do something just so I wouldn't lose it. He grabbed me by my arm, and I snatched away from him. He got down on his knees with tears in his eyes and started begging for me to take him back.

Jon has always been the type of nigga who was tough and

didn't show emotions on the regular. Yes, he would show me affection but never had I ever seen a hood nigga cry. I took a few steps back as he pleaded for me to forgive him. Every time I thought I felt some sympathy towards him it was later replaced with anger and rage.

"Get the fuck off the floor Jon, I don't care how hard you beg me, things are never going to be the same with us ever again. I'm never going to be able to trust you," I told him angrily.

"I will do whatever I need to to win your trust back, I'm not going to pressure you to get back with me now, but at least think about it. Let's at least try to work this shit out. I don't want to live my life without you."

I laughed at him.

"Damn, I sure wished you would have thought that way before you stuck your dick into that hoe."

Jon stood up off his knees and took a seat back in the kitchen table.

He was quiet for a long time before I finally asked him for the keys to his car.

He looked at me with wide eyes as if he wasn't expecting me to ask him something like that.

"Give me the fucking keys to your car Jon," I want to check something out.

Jon fished the keys from out his pocket and handed them to me. My hands closed around them tightly, and I headed out the door.

I popped the trunk as soon as my feet touched the ground.

Jon was right behind me, I guess to see what I was trying to do. I hurried to the trunk of his car and began to dig inside. Tay had claimed Jon had a phone in the back of the trunk I wanted to see that fucking phone. That was going to be what I needed just to see how serious him and that hoe was. Text messages never lied.

As soon as my hand found the phone and its charger, I slammed the trunk down and ran back towards the house. Jon closed the door behind me as I took a seat on the living room couch.

"Taea..." he said.

I gave him that look that told him to shut the fuck up.

He didn't sit beside me instead he sat across from me. I powered up the Samsung Galaxy with shaky hands.

"Baby, I love you," Jon said.

"I bet you do," I muttered back to him.

As soon as his phone had powered up, I first went to his photos and noticed a few pictures of the bitch who I assumed was Carissa. I didn't know the hoe, but I was going to make it my business to find out everything about her. The fact that this bitch knew that Jon already had someone and she still wanted my nigga was grounds for an ass whooping. I didn't give a fuck if the bitch was pregnant, I was ready to stomp that baby right up out of her.

I flipped through almost forty pictures of pussy shots and ass shots. There were only a few face shots, but that was all I needed when I ran up on that hoe. After I was done looking at the pictures, I went to his messages. I skimmed through a few of them and got instantly upset when she started talking about them being together and how much she loved him.

I read his response before I sat the phone down on my coffee table.

I stared at him as anger seethed inside me.

" You know what Jon you better be glad you all the way over there and I'm all the way over here because if I could, I would kill you right now," I told him furiously.

Never had I ever been this angry, so Jon knew to stay away

from me. I stood up and smashed the Samsung Galaxy phone that he had been talking to the bitch on. I made sure that when I was done stomping on it that there was nothing left of it.

Jon didn't dare speak; he didn't even say sorry.

The rage that I was feeling was the type that murderers have when they had lost all of their senses.

You know what I hate the most then a cheating ass nigga, I despise a lying ass nigga.

"You told me that what you had with her ain't mean shit, but them text messages says something so fucking different. Every time this hoe said she loved you and wanted to be with you, you always told her that you cared for her, and would have been with her if you would have never me. When you told that hoe that, that was everything she needed to plot to get knocked by you and you were dumb enough to be fucking her without a rubber."

"She told me she was on birth control," Jon stated.

I laughed.

"You a hood nigga, you know bitches lie."

"I've always been with you Taea, you act like I've come in contact with a bunch of hoes."

"You should have talked with Quan before you stuck that bitch, that nigga always cheating but never has he ever got a bitch knocked up on Yanni."

"I'm going to fix this shit Taea," I promise.

"You better fix it, because if you don't, you going to lose me forever."

Jon walked over to me and kissed me lightly on the cheek. I wanted to push him away but decided against it. The smell of his cologne filled my nose and made my panties wet. My body wanted him even though my mind told me to get away from him.

He pulled away from me a few moments later before pulling out his phone.

"It's getting late, I'm not going to keep you up, I know you got to head to Taco Bell to open in the morning," he told me as he embraced me in a tight hug.

I bit down on my bottom lip because I didn't know how I was going to get him to stay over without seeming like I was begging him. I had my reasons why I wanted him to stay. I had given him them chocolate laxative in his brownies, and I wanted to see them bitches work. I wanted to see the look on his damn face.

"Stay," I told him softly.

He looked at me with a shocked expression on his face. I knew he wasn't expecting that shit.

"Sleep on the couch, I don't want you sleeping with me, it ain't about to be no fucking around here."

"I know that much Taea, it's going to take time and I'm willing to wait as long as I got to."

"Yeah," I muttered as I headed towards the linens closet and pulled out some blankets.

I went to my bedroom and pulled one of his pillows off and went back into the living room to find him pacing the floor. He spotted me and quickly stopped.

"Here to you go," I told him as I passed him everything he needed to sleep on the couch.

"Thanks, baby."

"Your welcome," I told him.

He flopped down on the couch grabbed the remote and flipped on the TV. Instead of sticking around in the living room with him, I felt the best thing to do was put a little distance between us.

I headed towards my bedroom and closed the door gently behind me.

SIX HOURS LATER...

I woke up to the sound of footsteps. I laid in bed for a few moments as I listened.

"Shit," I heard John say as he headed toward the bathroom closing the door slowly behind him.

I slid out of bed and opened my bedroom room door. The laxatives had begun working and I was up to witness it all. A smile appeared on my face as I tiptoed to the bathroom and lightly tapped on it.

"Jon are you okay in there?"

Silence.

"Jon are you good in there?" I asked him again.

"I'm okay, but my stomach tore up, I'm cramping and got to shit," he said in a muffled tone.

I snickered lightly as I stood by the door. Ten minutes later he came out and ran into me.

"Sorry baby, I ain't see you there," he replied.

"Are you going to be okay?" I asked with fake concern.

He was just about to respond when he told me he had to go back to the bathroom yet again.

I headed back to my bedroom and retrieved my phone.

SIX HOURS LATER...

I shot Yanni a text and waited for her to respond.

Taea: The laxatives are working boo....

Yanni: Really? Quan started an hour ago, he over here on the toilet bending over in pain. I almost feel sorry for him, not, lol.

Taea: I can't believe it actually worked.

Yanni: I told you it would.

Yanni and I texted for a little while longer before I threw my phone on the bed and went back in the hallway as Jon continued to struggle on the toilet.

I headed towards the hallway closet and grabbed a can of air freshener and started to spray my whole house down. After I was done spraying, I headed back down the hallway only to hear him throwing up.

"What the fuck did you put in that damn food?" Jon cried out in pain.

I debated on if I should tell him or not. I finally decided it wasn't no point in doing any of this if I wasn't planning on telling him why I was doing it.

"I didn't do nothing to the food sweetie, but I did do something to the brownies you ate," I replied in a sweet tone.

The door opened a few moments later and out stepped Jon.

"What you mean you put something in the brownies?" he asked me in a confused voice.

I put some laxatives in the brownies. Let me rephrase that, I chopped up a whole box of laxatives and put them on top of your brownies.

"What the fuck? Why would you do that shit."

I stared at him and noticed I saw a spark of rage on his face. I couldn't help but laugh.

"The same reason you fucked that bitch, is the same reason I put laxatives in your dessert. You cheated for the thrill of it and for your own satisfaction, and I am getting the satisfaction to see your ass suffer. Now you know that I'm not the one to fuck with. I wanted to kill your ass for having me out here looking stupid, but I'm not a killa. Blowing your ass hole out seemed so much better. Next time you think about sticking your dick in another bitch's pussy you will always remember the consequences."

Jon was just about to let loose on my ass, but thought better of it, instead he ran back in the bathroom and slammed the door behind him.

I chuckled as I took my happy ass back to my bedroom. I closed the door behind myself and slid back under my covers. It wasn't long before I dozed off to the horrible sounds of him groaning in pain.

JON

Damn, my little baby Taea had really fucked my ass up. If I knew she was going to do what she had done I would have stayed my black ass away from her. I stayed up most of the damn night throwing up and shitting. I groaned as I slid off the couch and headed towards the kitchen. I opened the fridge and was lucky enough to find a pack of Gatorade that hadn't been opened. I dug out one Gatorade and popped it open. As the cool liquid washed down my throat, I heard the footsteps of Taea. I turned my head to where the footsteps were coming from and spotted her standing in the doorway with her uniform already on.

"I'm about to head to work, I expect for you to be gone when I get back."

I almost choked on my drink because she had to have bumped her damn head.

"Taea, have you lost your fucking mind? You could have really killed me."

Taea rolled her eyes at me like she wasn't the least bit concerned.

"Stop whining, you weren't going to die, if I wanted you

dead, I could have killed you after I found out what you had done. I spared your life only because I care more about mine."

Taea turned around and was just about to leave when I grabbed her and pulled her towards me.

"I was wrong for what I did. I guess I deserved what you did last night."

Taea snickered.

"It was funny as hell to me, but we both know that the betrayal you done to me, you deserve death. Now like I said earlier, be gone when I get home."

I stared at Taea in amusement as she hurried out of the house and hopped in her car that I had brought her for our third anniversary. This bitch was really acting different because she never would drive the car when I was living with her, I shook my head because she was driving that bitch today. Lawwddd, please be with her ass because I swear Taea wasn't the best driver. I hoped she didn't run into no damn body.

I flopped back down on the couch and closed my eyes.

I wasn't expecting to go to sleep but that was exactly what had happened. I had stayed up most part of the night sick as hell, so sleep was what I needed.

I didn't know how long I had been sleeping before the vibration of my phone woke me, I grabbed my phone from off the floor just to see who was messaging me. I wiped the sleep from my eyes when I notice that it was Quan. I pushed the covers off of me and read the text more than three times before everything began to register.

Quan: morning bruh, I fucked around and came to see Yanni last night and that little bitch fucked my ass up, she put something in the damn food, she had me shitting and sick all fucking night. She thinks the shit funny but I wanted to choke her ass out last night. You good over there bruh?

Jon: Nigga, you went through the same shit I went through last night, I swear Yanni and Taea was scheming together to fuck our asses up. Taea said she gave me some laxatives, so I assume Yanni probably did the same thing.

Quan: I'm not going to lie, I'm pissed as hell, but I know I can't step to her on no hoe shit because I did fuck her over and hurt her, I'ma let her do whatever she feel like she got to do to make her feel better as long as she plan on staying with a nigga and not dipping... I'ma just have to take whatever she throw at me.

Jon: I feel the same way bruh, we both fucked up, but damn I don't think I can take anything else Taea throw my damn way. I love her ass to the moon and back... just hate I fucked her over the way I did. I'm still trying to figure out how I'm going to make this shit right.

Quan: Give it time bruh, we soon going to have both of our bitches back with us where they belong.

Jon: I hope so, my life is going to be worthless without her... we need to meet up asap, we got some shit to discuss.

Quan; Drop the location and I will meet ya.

Jon: Shid meet a nigga at Arby's at noon. I'm hungry as hell.

Quan: Cool, I will be there... don't eat shit else that Taea give yo if you don't cook it or pour it yourself then don't even fuck with it.

Jon: Say no more... she talking about when she gets home, she wants me out of her house. I ain't going no damn where. That bitch could have killed my ass last night.

Quan: Awww shit, you still over there??

Jon: Hell Yeah, I'm about to shower and get ready to meet you. I ain't about to go back to no fucking hotel when I pay bills in this damn bitch.

I hopped off the couch and made my way into the bedroom that Taea and I shared. I opened the side of my closet and wasted no time finding me something to wear. I grabbed my Red Aeropostale shirt with a pair of khaki shorts, with my favorite red Nikes. I grabbed my boxers and my socks out my sock drawer and was just about to close it when I spotted something hidden beneath my underwear. I pushed my boxers aside and pulled out a vibrator. I looked at it for a while and almost dropped it when it started vibrating in my hand. I found the off switch and hurried to turn it off.

I was a little relieved about seeing the dildo. I mean I felt nothing but relief to seeing a toy than to find out she was fucking with some other nigga. I swear that shit would have killed me to know she was giving my pussy away. Taea belonged to me, and I wasn't going to allow her to fuck no other nigga but me. I know I had fucked up on her, but I wasn't ever going to do that dumb shit again.

I headed into the bathroom and adjusted the water to the temperature that I wanted it to be. After stepping into my own shower for the first time in almost three days, I was beginning to feel relief. Showering at the hotel still had me feeling grimy, and I guess it was because it wasn't my own shower.

As I washed myself clean, I knew without a doubt that I had a chance to win my baby back. Yeah, she probably was going to hate me for a very long time, and it probably was going to be a minute before she forgave me, but I had faith. Eventually, I was going to make Taea mine again. I was the only nigga who had her heart, and I wanted it to stay that way.

After taking my shower, I stepped out and dried my body off. I stared at myself in the mirror for a while, and that's when I noticed just how tired I looked. I had been stressing so much about my relationship with Taea, that a nigga was barely sleeping or eating like I should. That just goes to show you just how much she really meant to me. I didn't want to lose her and was going to do whatever I could to keep her.

I took care of my hygiene before stepping back into the bedroom. I took my time as I got dressed for the day. I sprayed on a little cologne, stuck my phone in my pocket, and went into the living room. I grabbed my keys and stepped out the door. The bright sun tried to blind my ass as I jogged towards the car and hopped inside.

I still had another hour before it was time to meet up with Quan at Arby's. I pulled my car into traffic and headed to the Hilton Inn so I could check out. I had been laying low there until Taea cooled off. Instead of waiting around for her to give me the signal when I could come back, I decided that it was time for my ass to come back home.

I was not about to keep paying for a room when I had a three-bedroom home and enough space to just go into the other room and not even be in her way until she was ready to forgive me. I parked my car next to this raggedy ass Altima that had their back window busted out. I shook my head once I spotted that all the tires were slit but one.

I could tell instantly just by looking at this car that some crazy ass bitch had gotten mad and had done the shit. I couldn't tell if the car belonged to a nigga or a bitch, but by looking at the size of the rims and the color of it, I figured that it was a nigga that owned this damn car. It was going to be a minute before his ass would be driving again.

Instead of heading straight to the office, I went to my room so I could gather my things. I popped the trunk of my car, and shoved my clothes inside before making my way towards the office to turn my key in. As soon as I stepped inside Hilton Inn, I was met with the breeze of cold air. Even though it was hot as hell outside walking into some air really felt good. I wiped the sweat that had started to form from my eyebrow and made my way over towards the lady who was in charge of running the front desk.

She looked like she was in her early twenties, and she was

fine as hell. I looked and admired, and that was it. She had a low cut and had her hair dyed like a honey blonde. She was the color of caramel with pretty full lips. I didn't want to stare too long because I didn't want her to think I wanted to fuck her. I had already gotten myself into a situation that I had no clue how I was going to get my ass out of.

She was polite and flashed me a smile when I told her that I was ready to check out.

"Do you have all your belongings out of the room before I send someone to clean up?"

"Yes, I have everything out."

I handed her the room key, and she brushed her hand up against mine. She looked up at me, and I saw nothing but lust in her eyes.

I smiled back at her but that was about it.

I wasn't trying to get myself caught up, even though she was attractive, I just couldn't risk it.

"Did you enjoy your stay here?"

"Yes, I did."

"Well, I hope you will be coming back soon."

"Thanks," I told her and walked out.

As soon as I hopped back into my car, I turned my speakers on and started blasting some Migos. My car shook as the bass began to drop. I rolled my a blunt as I nodded my head to the music. I checked my phone and noticed that Quan had text me to let me know that he was on his way to meet up with me at Arby's. I lit my blunt and merged my way into the busy traffic. Soon as I pulled up at the red light that's when my phone started going off. I put my blunt out and grabbed my phone off the passenger seat.

I groaned when I noticed that it was Carissa calling me.

I debated on if I should pick up the call or not. I wasn't in the mood to fuss with Carissa. But I was curious to know what she was going to get rid of the baby or not. The last time she told me that she wasn't going to do it. Hopefully she had changed her mind and had decided to terminate the pregnancy. If she was trying to keep this baby just so she could be with me, then she was going to have some hurt feelings. I wasn't about to be with her only because she had my baby.

Just because she had a baby by me didn't mean this was going to keep me as her man. This was what some bitches failed to realize. They thought if they trapped him, he would be forced to man up and be with them and leave the bitch he with, but I wasn't one of them type of niggas. Yeah, I wanted Carissa at one point of time, I wanted to fuck on her for a while, but I wasn't trying to make her my main bitch. Taea had that title and was always going to have it.

I hated that shit had to go down this way, but it wasn't shit that I could do to change anything. I felt like if I sat down and talked to Carissa about the baby maybe then she would see things my way. I just felt like she was having this baby for all the wrong reasons. She went from being on birth control to not taking them so she could get a baby by me, but she was going to learn that her happily ever after that she wanted wasn't about to happen with me.

I picked up the call just to see what she was talking about. "What up?"

"I just wanted to call so we could talk," Carissa spoke softly into the phone.

"What you want to talk about?" I asked her.

"Us..."

"Carissa, I already told you, there isn't no us. I thought I made that shit clear when we saw each other last time."

"I know what you told me, but I don't want that shit Jon, you fucked up when you fucked me and had me thinking that it could one day be an us."

"Carissa, I never made you think that you and I could be

more than what we were. You made that conclusion your own self. Look I'ma pull up in a few, I got to handle some business first."

"Cool."

I disconnected the call before I lost my cool with her over the phone.

I was really beginning to get frustrated with this whole situation. While she was up here trying to make me be with her ass, she needed to be worried about what she was going to do about the baby that she was carrying inside her. I never once made Carissa feel that she could ever be my main bitch. All I ever did was drop dick up in her and treated her to a nice time every now and then. Yeah, I had told her once that if I wouldn't have met Taea that I would have made her mine but Taea was in my life now, and I wasn't about to let her go for a high school fantasy.

Instead of letting Carissa put me in a bad mood, I quickly cleared my mind because I had bigger problems then a bitch who was doing whatever she could to be with me. I pulled up at Arby's a few moments later and waited inside my car until I spotted Quan pull up alongside me.

I put out my blunt, hopped out my car, and slid into the passenger seat of his whip.

"What up bruh?" he asked as he dapped me up.

"Shit, partna...we got a situation that you and I need to damn talk about."

"Gone ahead and talk bruh," Quan said as he started to roll him a blunt.

"I learned some shit the other day when I went over to Carissa's house to talk to her about the baby."

"What you learned?" Quan asked as he licked his blunt and lit it.

"Carissa told me that Ken told her that you were responsible for beating his sister's ass. KeKe is going around and lying on you bro, she telling people that you jumped on her."

"What the fuck? Hold the fuck up, so you telling me this bitch actually went and told her pussy ass brother that I beat her ass? I ain't even touch that hoe, Yanni beat that bitch ass because she was popping off at the mouth like she always does. I ain't have no reason to hit her ass, even though I wanted to. She's the reason why Yanni put a nigga out. She ain't nothing but a hating ass bitch. I swear."

"I know you ain't hit that bitch, it was fucked up how bitches can lie on you, but Carissa also told me that Ken's gonna handle it. Ken told her when he saw you, he was gonna fuck you up. Shid, that ain't even the half of it. Ken wants Carissa to get back with him. I'm not upset about that shit, they can have each other, I don't want that Mexican bitch no more, but she told me that he was gonna make me disappear just like he's gonna do you if I don't leave Carissa alone.

Quan blew out a cloud of smoke but didn't say nothing for the longest moment. When he passed me the blunt that's when he finally spoke.

"You already know what we got to do," he told me.

I nodded my head.

"We gotta get their punk asses before they get us. You got your burner on you? Quan asked.

"Yeah, I always stay strapped."

"Make sure you take that bitch every fucking where we never know when he may pull up and try some stupid shit over a lie that his sister told. If I kilt bitches, I would blow her brains out.

"I know you would bruh."

"Now what we can do, is head on over to the Westside and go find his ass, but I'm gonna leave that shit alone because I don't know if Carissa telling the whole truth. I ain't seen Ken or his crew on the Northside, but we gotta let the team know if they see his ass shoot his ass on sight," I told Quan.

"I got you. Imma make sure to alert the team that we gonna have a meeting later today," Quan said.

"Carissa a lying ass bitch, I can't trust her, she says the baby mine but nigga I don't even know because when I pulled up at her crib the other day Ken bitch ass was coming out. He ain't see me but I asked her ass about his visit, and she said that he came over there to confide in her about his sister."

"Right, don't trust that bitch, Jon. Matter a fact I don't even want you around that hoe period. You stay far away from her ass until all this shit blows over."

"I gotta stop by and see her so we can finish discussing this pregnancy. She trying to pin this baby on me and I ain't liking that shit. I know it's a possibility that the baby could be mine because I was fucking her raw, but something in my heart telling me that she was fucking Ken on the low too."

"I put nothing pass none of these hoes, she probably was fucking him on the low. Look if you got to go over there just let me know and I will ride over there with you bro. I ain't trusting you going on the Westside by yourself after all this shit done went down."

"Thank, bruh."

"You're welcome."

I passed the blunt back to Quan and hopped out his whip.

"What you about to do?" Quan asked.

"About to go inside and order me some damn food, I'm hungry as hell."

"Cool, I'ma be out here when you get back then. You going to Carissa's house after?"

"Yeah, I want to get the shit over with."

"Say no mo," Quan replied before rolling his window back up.

I headed inside and took my time as I decided to figure out what I actually wanted to eat. Some people behind me started muttering and complaining for me to hurry the fuck up. I looked back at their asses with a mean look on my face. They all got silent as I continued to think.

After a few moments of thinking, I finally placed my order and stood aside to let the others behind me get their orders taken. I stood there a good ten minutes before my order number was called. I grabbed my bag and was heading out the door when I spotted my high school science teacher. The bitch had failed me, and after failing, I refused to take the class back over, selling dope seemed to be the best option anyway.

Mrs. Peesly was her name. She was one of them old shriveled up black women, who looked seventy but was probably in her early sixties. She still looked the same but older.

At first, I thought she wasn't going to recognize me, but she shocked me when she spoke to me. I couldn't believe that the bitch had even remembered my name.

"Jontavian is that you?" Mrs. Peesly asked.

"Yeah, it's me."

I gave her a fake smile. As she assessed me, I already knew what was running through her mind. She thought that I wasn't going to be hitting on shit and homeless all because I said fuck school and didn't get an education, but I was pushing a damn Camaro and was dripping with swag.

"You look like you doing good for yourself," she said

"Yeah, I'm doing good Mrs. Peesly. What about you?"

"I'm doing well, just making it. I just wanted to speak, I thought it was you, but I wasn't sure."

"Yep, you still remembered me."

"I can never forget you Jontavian, you had so much

potential in high school, but that's the past as long as you doing okay that's all that matters today."

"Right, well take care of yourself," I told her before heading out of Arby's.

I walked out with a smile on my face, all them teachers who used to think that I wasn't shit was getting a taste of their own medicine. A nigga was balling, and I did all of it without a high school diploma.

I hopped back into the car with Quan and began to dig into my food.

"Guess who I just saw," I told Quan with a mouth full of food.

"Damn, nigga you act like you ain't ate in days."

"Everything I ate for the last few days I shitted out when Taea fucked around and gave me them damn laxatives. She fucked my damn stomach."

Quan laughed.

"Who did you see though?" Quan asked curiously.

"My science teacher from 11th grade, Mrs. Peesly ass."

"Awww man I remember that old ass lady, she used to give your ass hell."

"Hell yeah, I was shocked her ass remembered me."

"Nigga, all the teachers remember our asses."

I took a sip of my sweet tea and nodded my head.

"We were savages back in the day."

"Shid, we still are."

"She swore that I wasn't' going to be shit because I didn't pass her class. She saw me today, and the bitch was speechless. I'm making more money than she will ever make."

"That's right, and I'm loving it," Quan replied.

"Follow me to Carissa's house," I told Quan before starting my car and pulling into traffic.

Fifteen minutes later we were pulling up at Carissa's crib. Quan stepped out when I stepped out.

"I'ma stay on the porch and wait on you," Quan told me as I knocked on Carissa's door.

Carissa opened the door and squinted up her face when she spotted Quan sitting in a chair on her porch.

"What's he doing here?" Carissa asked with an attitude.

"He here just in case Ken pops up. He wants us to disappear right? So, we ready for his ass," I told her bluntly.

"Tell that nigga when you see him again that I'm waiting on him to jump stupid. No talking we gonna shoot on sight if he even step on the Northside," Quan told Carissa seriously.

"Look, I'm not about to tell him shit, don't throw me in the middle of ya'll beef, I don't want no parts of it," Carissa told him angrily.

"You already involved since you pregnant by my partna," Quan told Carissa.

I snorted.

Carissa looked like she wanted to slap my ass. But I didn't give a fuck, I wasn't about to start claiming no baby that I wasn't sure was mine.

"Jon, we need to talk in private."

"Cool," I told her as I followed her inside her crib.

I closed the door behind her, and that's when I noticed the tears falling down her cheeks.

"This is your baby; I don't know why you don't believe me."

I was becoming frustrated because I understood what she was telling me, but my gut was telling me that the bitch was lying. After seeing Ken coming out of her house, I was beginning to believe she was hiding way more shit then she wanted to tell. Trusting her and what she said wasn't about to happen.

"Look, Carissa, if the baby mine like you claim then you already know what I want you to do."

"You have lost your fucking mind. I'm not doing that shit."

I pulled out my wallet and handed her the money that she needed to get the shit taken care of.

"Here is the damn money, you can't say you don't have the money, I just gave it to you."

Carissa looked at me and rolled her eyes. She wouldn't take the money, so I threw it on the coffee table.

"I don't want any kids right now, what I look like bringing a kid in this world with you and I don't even have a kid by Taea yet, and she is the one I'm in a relationship with."

"You one selfish ass nigga, how can you tell me to kill your fucking baby, that we created all because you want to save your relationship with Taea and give her your first child. It's too late nigga, you got me pregnant first."

I was very close to smacking the shit out of Carissa but decided to just leave the bitch alone.

"Have the baby if you wanna, but I'm not going to be in its life, stay away from me your ass is dead to me bitch," I replied nastily.

Carissa stared at me in utter disbelief. She looked like I had smacked her ass even though I haven't, I guess the saying was true, words could kill a bitch, it could be toxic and really hurt worse than a smack in the face."

I watched as Carissa walked away from me and headed to the back of her apartment. I heard her crying from where I stood. I figured she was going in the bathroom to clean herself up, if I would have known what was about to happen, I would have dipped the fuck out.

"Carissa I'm about to dip!" I yelled out to her.

I was met with utter silence.

I walked down her hallway and came to her bedroom to find it empty. I turned towards the left and noticed that the bathroom door was closed and the light was on inside. I knocked on the door a few times but got no answer.

I began to panic and knocked the door down to find Carissa sitting on the toilet staring into space.

"Carissa you ain't hear me calling your damn name?" I asked her irritably.

"All I ever wanted was for you and me to be together. I thought we were going to have this happy ever after. I didn't give a damn that you were in a relationship with Taea, I thought you were going to at least leave her and be with me. I was your high school crush. I thought you were going to at least give me a chance, but all you wanted to do was fuck on me for a while and fulfill your sexual fantasy. You get me pregnant and want me to kill our baby all because you don't want to leave Taea, but ask yourself, if you loved that bitch so much then why even fuck me raw and get me knocked up?"

I was silent. I didn't speak for a while.

The bathroom was so quiet that the dripping of the faucet was all you heard.

Men are going to be men Carissa, they going to cheat sometimes, it doesn't mean they don't love their girlfriends any less.

"This will be the last time that you hurt me, Jon. I don't give a fuck what you say. I'm going to have this baby; this is my first baby who didn't ask to be here. I'm not going to let you take that shit away from me. But I also won't allow you to leave me either. If I can't have you, then Taea will have to bury you."

It took me a minute for what she had said to register in my brain. I was just about to respond when I heard some shots being fired.

I left Carissa in the bathroom on the toilet and pulled out my pistol. I ran straight to the door and was about to run out that bitch to check on Quan when Ken busted in.

Pow, Pow, Pow, Pow, Pow.

I fell to the floor as pain penetrated my body. I tried to speak, but no words seemed to leave my mouth.

The whole room seemed to spin, and I could barely make out what was really going on around me. I felt helpless and felt as if I couldn't breathe. I stared at Carissa as she stood over me with tears in her eyes.

"None of this would have happened if you would have chosen me, I could have stopped Ken but you made your choice, and I made mine."

I wanted nothing more than to strangle the dumb hoe. I hated that I had ever fucked her, but I had no one to blame but myself. I had everything, and I threw it all away to fuck someone who wasn't even my bitch.

As I laid there on the cold floor, my life began to flash before my eyes. The thought of Taea crossed my mind. I didn't want to die, I had so much shit that I wanted to do, I didn't want to leave this world with Taea hating my ass. I wanted to settle down, make Taea mine, and have all my kids by her, but I didn't know if any of this was going to ever happen. I heard the sirens in the distance and silently began to pray until everything went black.

YANNI

EARLIER THAT MORNING

I woke up not in the mood to go to work. Two days ago, the supervisor added a few women to my rounds. There was one woman that I had to take care that was working my last nerve. She was in her late seventies, and she was close to three hundred pounds, she was a big ass bitch and always had some smart shit to say to me. Let her tell it I was never doing in my job correctly. She was never satisfied with my work ethic. I swear if I didn't need the job, I was at I would have slapped the old bitch. The reason why she was now my patient because she had been moved around the nursing home so much and every CNA just couldn't handle her attitude. Now I understood why. She was too fucking much to handle and was going to be the reason why someone would lose their job.

Honestly, I don't know who was responsible for putting her in the nursing home, but I bet it was because they couldn't deal with her ass either. She was dark skinned in complexion, with long hair that stopped at her shoulders. I had tried plenty of times to comb her hair for her because the shit be nappy as hell. All that long hair and he wouldn't let nobody mess with it. She would holler and scream if I said something about touching her hair. She couldn't comb her own hair due to her claiming her hands and fingers be hurting, but when I offered to help, I got a tongue lashing. There was no way I was going to allow her to run over me. The first time I let her ass get away with it because I didn't want any problems but today wasn't the day for the bitch to get wrong with me. These two days felt like it had been a month, but some type of way I was going to get through it.

Dealing with my love life and dealing with work was becoming too much. I didn't know if I was coming or going. I was still bitter about Quan's disloyalty and his cheating, but it was time that I got over the shit and moved on with my life. I knew I loved him and I wanted him to be in my life. I was never the type of bitch to play games with nobody I wasn't about to start now. I had to urge to get even with him, maybe fuck one of his partnas just so I could make him look stupid in these streets, but I knew fucking one of his partnas was going to end with them dead. There was no way I wanted someone blood on my hands. I doubted any of his partna's would go for that shit anyway. They didn't want that type of heat coming from Quan. One thing I knew about my man was that he wasn't with that dumb shit, he was quick to pop a nigga about some fuck shit. He didn't play about me. I can remember the time that he and I had first started fucking around, some nigga was looking way too hard at me when he had taken me to the movies. Quan straight up threatened the nigga. He had that nigga scared as fuck and had made it clear once we had gotten in the movies that he would murk a nigga about me. Getting someone involved in this love complication that I had with Quan wasn't something that I wanted to do.

I thought I would never have to worry about Quan cheating because he wasn't about to let me cheat on his ass or even look at another nigga, but I guess I had been wrong. I understood niggas made mistakes and with my love for him, I knew that I was going to eventually take him back. After seeing him the other night, I knew there was no way that I could let him go even if I wanted to. I loved that nigga with all my heart and soul, and I wasn't going to give up on us or what we had. I couldn't throw away three years of the love that I had for him. I didn't give a fuck about no other bitch, but I was going to make sure that no matter what that he knew that the next time he cheated, I was going to bury his ass. The only way I was going to let him move back in was if he promised me that he was going to leave them hoes alone. I wanted him to change his number and get rid of all the hoes that he was fucking around with. It was going to take time for me to trust him again but time was all we had, we both knew that I wasn't going to go anywhere.

After sliding off my bed, I dragged myself to my closet and slowly opened it up. I grabbed the first scrub outfit that I found and closed the door behind me. I went in the bathroom that was connected to the bedroom and hopped in the shower so I could take care of my hygiene. As the water splashed over my tired body, I couldn't help but think about Quan. I wondered what he was doing at the current moment, my body was in need of some dick I knew his was the only one I wanted. I already knew I ain't have enough time to catch me a nut before work, so I finished washing my body and stepped out the shower. I brushed my hand through my hair as I stared at myself in the bathroom mirror. My body was on point, and I could pull any nigga that I wanted but none of them niggas could fuck me like Quan did.

He knew exactly how to touch me to set my body on fire. I had never experienced this type of passion with anyone but him. His dick game was a beast, and I loved when he was inside of me.

After taking care of my hygiene, I pulled my weave up in a messy bun and began to get dressed for that day. When I was fully dressed, I grabbed my phone and was just about to text Quan when Taea name popped up on my phone.

"What up boo?" I asked her as I answered the phone.

"You headed to work?"

"Yeah, I'm about to walk out of the house now."

"Damn bitch you sound like you in one of your moods."

"You have no idea; the supervisor added this patient who is giving me a hard time. I almost walked off my job yesterday."

"Whatttttt? I can't believe that shit, as much as you like your job."

"Some patients can be hard to handle. The patient name Ms. Cromer, she about seventy. She a black ass fat bitch who always got some smart shit to say."

"Oh, hell nall, I would have smacked that bitch."

"I know, I wanted to so bad yesterday, but I had to walk away to calm myself down."

"This lady has been with every CNA, and everyone has complained about her and asked to have her removed from their roster. I'm the last one left."

"Damn."

"I know, I'm just going to make the best of it, but if she gets wrong with me one more time, I swear I'm going to hurt her feelings. Either they move her out of this nursing home, or I'm leaving and finding someone where else to go, I ain't about to go to work to let no bitch who can barely walk and shitting on herself disrespect me."

Taea laughed so hard into the phone that I couldn't help but laugh my own self.

"Bitch, I can't with you."

I laughed.

"I'm so serious boo, she doing way too fucking much, but enough about that bitch, what you got going on over there?"

"Shit, I just left to head to work, Jon stayed over, but I told his ass to be up out my house by the time I get home from work."

"Ummmmm, you need to stop lying to yourself. You know you want that nigga to still be there when you get off."

Tea sighed.

"I love that nigga; I can't just let him go even though I know I should."

"I understand Taea, shid you and I both love our niggas, but I hope they love us as much as we love them."

Taea agreed.

I grabbed my keys and headed out the door towards my car. I slid into the car still on the phone with Taea.

"Are you going to let Jon move back in?" I asked her as I snapped my seat belt in and put my car in drive.

"I want to, but I don't know, I feel like it still too soon. I don't want to take him back to fast, and he ends up fucking me over again, plus this nigga may have gotten this bitch pregnant, I just don't know what I'm going to do."

"Don't rush it if you ain't ready, you got a lot of shit that you need to think about. If this baby is his are you going to stay?" I asked her.

Taea became quiet.

"Taea?"

"Yeah, I'm still here. Yanni I'm going to be real with you, I don't know if I can be with him if he got that bitch pregnant. We always talked about us having kids but I never thought that it was going to happen like this we were supposed to have our first baby, and it ain't happen."

I felt the pain in her heart, and my heart broke for her. Taea and I talked until I pulled up at my job fifteen minutes later.

"Wish me luck; hopefully I won't lose my job today."

"You want, if you need me, call me boo. I fight kids and old people; I don't care about knocking Ms. Cromer old ass out. Remember I don't work there, so I can't get fired for hitting her ass."

I got off the phone with Taea and couldn't help but laugh at her ass. If it came to that, I was definitely willing to hit her ass up to take care of Ms. Cromer old ass. I stepped into the nursing home and had just clocked in when I heard some loud screaming down the hallway. I ran to see what was going on and came to a halt when I spotted Ms. Cromer lying in her bed. Her hair was scattered over her head, it needed to be done, and the room reeked of pee.

"Why the hell are you just standing there little stupid girl? I been covered in this damn pee for an hour straight, nobody wouldn't come and change me. When I get the chance, I will be calling my niece to let her know what has been going on in this nursing home. Y'all ain't doing ya'll job and need to be shut down. Look at me crazy all you want to; your young ass will soon be without a damn job if you don't get this shit together."

All the professionalism that I thought I had gone out of the window, the savage in me came out, and I didn't give a fuck what my mouth said. I wanted to choke her fat ass but decided my tongue was more lethal and could do damage.

"Maybe if you stop being so fucking rude to people, maybe then people would have changed your pissy ass. What I want to know is where your fucking niece at? You been in this nursing home for how many months? I ain't seen nobody walk up in here to see your old ass. Your niece must've got tired of your ass and threw you in here for us to handle. I highly doubt your niece gives a fuck about you Ms. Cromer. My job is to see about your ass, but I swear you make that shit so fucking hard. No one will be losing their job up in this bitch. The only person who is going to be out the door is your fat ass. You have been with every CNA that this nursing home and no one can deal with you. Either you let me do my job, or I will talk to the supervisor about getting you removed from my roster as well. Since you so fucking smart do you know what will happen then? You will be shipped to some other nursing home, and I promise you, you won't like that one. This is the best nursing home in Warner Robins, you don't want to get on my bad side because I will have you going to a nursing home where your ass can piss and shit on yourself all day, and nan bitch will lift a finger to change your stank ass," I spat at her.

Ms. Cromer looked at me with her mouth wide open. I guess she had never had someone talk to her like that because for the first time in two days she hushed her mouth and let me did my job.

I slid three soaking pads from under her and got her up off the bed with her help. Normally she had me trying to help her ass to the shower by myself, but today it was different. I waited until she had gotten herself in the wheelchair and rolled her to the shower where I bathed her. I brushed the little teeth that she had left in her mouth and cut on the TV to let her watch something while I changed her bed sheets. They smelled of pee, and I had to get them washed and cleaned.

The only reason why Ms. Cromer had such a hard time getting what she needed was because all she did was talk shit to everyone. No one was going to lift a finger to help her ass out, I was the one who was responsible for her since she was now on my roster. I shook my head as I stripped her bed and put some clean sheets on them.

"Are you ready to get back in the bed?" I asked her.

"No, I'm fine," she muttered.

I looked down at her, and for the first time, I saw tears in her eyes.

I wanted to ask her what was wrong with her but decided the best thing to do was to leave her alone. Sometimes we all needed a reality check, and today Ms. Cromer finally had gotten hers. I was just about head out the door to check on the rest of my patients when Ms. Cromer grabbed me by my hand.

I looked down at her just to make sure that she was okay because never had she ever touched me for any reason.

"Before you go, can you comb my hair for me?"

I was shocked as hell because every time I offered to try to comb her hair, she always told me to leave her head alone. I'm sure if she looked at herself in the mirror, she would see just how crazy she looked with her hair scattered out.

I grabbed her combed out of her nightstand and began to comb out her hair before I started to braid it for her. When I was done, she thanked me.

"You're welcome."

I was about to head out the door when she called out my name.

"I just want to say sorry for mistreating you."

I stared at her, and for the first time, I saw the hurt in her eyes.

"I hate it here, I just want to go home," she cried.

I walked over to her and wiped her tears from her eyes.

"I understand you would rather be in your own home, but this is your home now. I'm here to help Ms. Cromer. I'm not your enemy."

"My niece doesn't' want me there, she just got married and told me that I was in the way of her living her life. I don't want to be a burden on anyone but how could she dump me in here and never come here to visit really tore me up inside."

I listened to her as she cried and wept about her life before she came to The Lodge.

"Stop crying Ms. Cromer, I promise that I'm not going to leave you, you have no reason to be nasty and mean to anyone."

She nodded her head at me and once again told me how sorry she was.

I walked out of her room with some sort of satisfaction. Finally, Ms. Cromer and I had come to some sort of understanding. I now understood what she was going through emotionally. I found some relief to know that from now on she wasn't going to make my job hard for me.

Rarely did we ever get a patient like Ms. Cromer, but when we did it was hard on the nurses to get anything down, and it made the job so stressful. I said a silent prayer to the man above for looking out for me. I knew it had to be him to reach in her heart and to make her see just how she was affecting everyone in the nursing home. Some people just don't know how brutal they were until they were told. I guess me telling her about herself opened her eyes to the realization that I was all she had. I breezed through the rest of my patients and was just about to take me a lunch break when I was buzzed to the front because I had a call. I hurried to the front desk just to see who had called for me.

"You got a call on line three from the hospital," Jannie told me.

I grabbed the phone from he, and as I put the phone to my ear, I knew something just wasn't right. My heart felt like it was about to fall out my chest and I began to feel sick to my stomach. Something had happened but to who I didn't know.

"Hello," I muttered into the phone.

"Is this Ms. Yanni Brown?"

"Yes," I said desperately into the phone.

"This is Houston County Medical Center calling you to inform you that Quantavious Johnson is here."

"What... I said with panic in my voice.

"What happened?" I asked into the phone.

I felt as if I couldn't breathe, I prayed that he was okay.

"I can't give out any information on the phone but please get up here as quick as you can."

I hung up the phone and didn't waste any time clocking out.

"Is everything okay?" Jannie asked with concern on her face.

"No, I told her. I got to go."

"What do you want me to tell Mrs. Cater," Jannie asked.

"Just tell her I had an emergency and I had to go," I told the Jannie who was the first desk nurse.

I grabbed my keys and was just about to run out the door when my supervisor yelled out my name.

"Where are you running off to?"

"Mrs. Carter, I got to go. The hospital just called me. It's a family emergency."

"Okay, do you know when you will be back?"

"I don't know, but I know for a fact it won't be today."

I didn't give Mrs. Carter time to respond before I ran out the door and hopped into my car.

Tears fell from my eyes and blurred my vision as I sped through the Warner Robins rush hour traffic. I needed to get my ass to the hospital, and I wanted to get there as soon as I could. I didn't know what I was walking into, but my anxiety levels were at an all-time high by the time I pulled up at the Houston County Medical Center ten minutes later. I hopped out my car and ran into the front entrance towards the front desk.

"I'm here to see Quantavious Johnson."

The lady seemed to take forever as she searched the

computer for his name. I already know I probably looked like a crazy woman standing before her. My eyeliner was probably smeared from all the crying I did in the car driving over here.

"I don't see anyone by that name in our system but let me get in touch with the Emergency room maybe they can tell me something."

I began to pace as I waited for her to give me some type of information about Quan. A few moments later I finally got the answer I was desperate to hear.

"I just talked to the emergency staff he is on the emergency side still.

I rushed out of the main hospital and practically ran towards the emergency room that was alongside the hospital. I ran through the double doors towards the nurse I spotted at the front desk.

"I'm looking for Quintavious Johnson. Someone called and told me that he was here."

The nurse stood up from her desk, walked over to her clipboard, and nodded her head and confirmed that he was there.

"Take a sea, and someone will get with you."

Taking a seat was the last thing that I wanted to damn do, but instead of pacing like I was some crazy bitch I took a seat and pulled out my phone.

I first dialed Taea to fill her in on what was going on with Quan. Taea phone rung one time before I heard her loud breathing over the phone.

"Taea you okay?"

I could barely hear anything that Taea was saying because of her crying.

I instantly began to panic because never did Taea ever damn cry, so I knew something had to have happened.

"Taea, calm down, what's going on?" I asked her.

"Jon, he's been shot, I'm outside in the parking lot at the emergency room," I just made it here.

My heart seemed to stop beating because if Jon had been shot that only meant that Jon and Quan were together when this shit went down.

"Taea, I will be outside to walk you in. I got a call to come here because Quan had been brought in."

I didn't give Taea time to respond before I headed out the door to find her car. She was the first car that was parked next to the handicapped. I jogged over to her car and knocked on her door. She opened it slowly and slid out. We wrapped each other in a tight embrace as she and I both began to cry for our men.

"I was at work when I got the call, I swear my whole life seemed to stop when I got that call." Taea cried.

"I know what you mean. I was at work as well. I flew out the door and came over here immediately."

I wiped the tears that had fell from my eyes and held her as we headed back inside the emergency room. I walked Taea up to the front so she could let them know that she was here for Jontavian after the nurse told her that the doctor was going to be with her as soon as he could, we both took a seat in the waiting room as we both waited for someone to tell us something.

Taea continued to cry on my shoulder as I sat there with a blank expression on my face. All the tears that I wanted to let out I just couldn't. I had to stay strong. I wanted to think nothing but positive shit, I said a silent prayer as I closed my eyes. I prayed that Quan and Jon both pulled through. I wanted him to pull through, I needed him to. I didn't see no life for myself if he wasn't here with me. He was the love of my life, we didn't have any kids, so he left me. I wouldn't have nothing or no one to keep his memory, only my own. If I could get one more chance, I was going to shove the anger aside for the fuck-ups that he had done and love his ass until I couldn't love him anymore. I never thought that I could ever lose Quan and here I was trying to keep my emotions together because the fear of losing him was just too great. If only God spared his life this once I swore that I was never going to leave him ever again. Working things out was the only option that I had. So many days that we had gone without speaking, kissing, hugging, and fucking, so much time wasted, and here he was now fighting for his life.

I already know that Taea was feeling the same way that I was.

"It's all my fucking fault," she cried to me.

"No, don't say that."

"It is my fault; I was such a bitch to him this morning. He spent the night and the first thing I told him when I saw him this morning was that I wanted him out of the house by the time that I got back home from work. I told him I didn't want him there, maybe if I wouldn't have said that shit, he wouldn't have never left. He would have been home when I got there today, but I was so angry at what he had done that I couldn't stand the sight of him."

Taea wiped the snot that had fallen from her nose as she continued to cry.

I understood the pain that she felt because I had been as equally cold to Quan.

"Let's not blame ourselves Taea, let's just pray that they both pull through."

Jontavian didn't have any family that Taea could call, his parents had died when he was younger, but as I sat there Quan's mama began to weigh heavily on my mind. Should I call her? I thought to myself. Rarely did Quan ever talk to his mama, but not telling her what was going on with her only son would have been too cold. I pulled out my phone and found her number that I had saved in my phone a few months prior. My heart began to pump erratically as I pressed my phone up to my ear.

She picked up after three rings.

I took a deep breath before I told her that she needed to get to the emergency room because Quan had been hurt. When she told me that she was on her way only then did I hang up. I had done the right thing by getting his mama involved, she needed to know what was going on with her son, it was only right. Twenty minutes later the emergency room door swooshed open and there stood Quan's mama.

She was dressed in a white sundress with black sandals. Her hair hung freely down her shoulders. I waved her over to where Taea and I were sitting still waiting for someone to tell us something. Quan's mama was beautiful in every way, so I understood what Quan meant when he told me that his mom had been a little thot back when he was growing up. She had the looks and the body for it. She was in her fifties, but the bitch was in good shape and could have easily passed as being her in late thirties.

She pulled her shades from her eyes and took a seat by me.

"Have either one of you heard anything about Quan?" she asked us.

Taea didn't respond. Instead she buried her face in her hand.

"No, we ain't heard nothing I told her, he and Jon are both here."

Quan's mama gasped as she clutched her chest.

"You don't know what happened?"

"No, I don't know anything," I muttered to her.

"Don't worry baby, Quan's a fighter he going to pull through and far as Jon he ain't about to go anywhere either. Those two are like brothers from different mamas, so I know both of them are going to get through this. Don't cry and don't stress ya'll pretty little minds.

I nodded my head, but Taea still continued to cry and whine. I tried my best to comfort her as well as try to comfort my own self. Twenty minutes later we spotted a doctor who was a black man with a balding head walking towards us. He looked to be in his early sixties, he was thin and tall. He introduced himself as Doctor Harvard.

"I'm looking for the family of Quantavious Johnson."

I hopped up to let him know I was there for Quan. His mama also stood up and held my hand in hers.

Doctor Harvard cleared his throat.

"When Quantavious came in he had lost a lot of blood. He had two gunshot wounds one was in his left jaw, and one was in his stomach. We had to operate immediately on him when he made it here. We lost him for only a brief moment, but we revived him thankfully. He is finally stable, but it's going to be a long recovery for him."

Tears fell down my face as I took a seat on shaky feet.

His mama rubbed my back as she continued to talk to the doctor about her son. I was so out of it that I didn't hear anything that the doctor told me after he told me that Quan was going to have a long recovery ahead of him, but it also depended on the individual.

My whole body shook as I cried to the man above for saving his life when he could have taken his very soul today. Losing Quan would have been the end of me, to know that he was going to live brought joy to my heart, but to know that it a gong to take time for him to recover was what hurt me the most. I was going to have to be the one to take care of him. Quan has always been the one to look out for it but for the first time the tables were beginning to turn, it was going to be me because I was all he had. I didn't mind by doing any of this. I was willing to do whatever I had to do, to take care of man for however long it took. For the past three years even though I was able to do for myself Quan was always there to give me a hand if I needed him to.

"Thank you, God, for not taking him. I promise I will keep my word and look after him the best of my abilities," I whispered in my head.

"Quan is going to be fine sweetie the doctor just said that they going to put him in a room in a little bit so we can see him." Quan's mama told me gently.

I nodded my head and looked over at Taea.

For the first time, I saw that Taea wasn't crying. She embraced me in a hug and whispered in my ear, "I'm so glad that Quan is going to go be okay."

"Me too," I told her emotionally.

We pulled away from each other when another doctor who looked like he was in his forties walked over to us. He had come from the back and spoke to one of the nurses for a brief moment before she pointed to Taea.

My heart began to race as I grabbed Taea.

"Excuse me, my name if Doctor Coleman. I'm looking for someone who I can talk with about Jontavian Harris."

"I'm the only family he has, I'm his girlfriend," Taea said anxiously.

The doctor wasted no time as he gave Taea the rundown on Jon and didn't suga coat not a damn thing.

"Jon came in with multiple shots to his chest. He had over three bullets that had hit his chest area. One in specific punctured his right lung."

Taea started crying and I took it from there. I knew there was no way that Taea was able to get the details that she needed with her being so emotional. Today I was the strong one for the both of us when normally it was Taea who always held my ass down whenever I needed her. There were questions that needed to be asked, and they were going to be hard to ask, but it was a must.

"Doctor Coleman, will he survive?" I asked emotionally.

Doctor Coleman didn't answer right off, it was as if he had to think about how he was going to respond to this simple question.

"He is stable for right now, he lost a lot of blood, but we did get a chance to get a chest tube inside his lung and hooked it up to suction. With this, we can keep the air and blood out of his lungs.

"How long will he have to wear the tube?"

"It depends, it can be a week, a month or even three months. We just have to keep a check on his progress. I'm not saying he won't survive this, but he has a good chance of surviving since he made it out of the surgery alive. All we can do is keep him monitored and hope that everything heals up with no infections. The other wounds that were also located in his chest area may cause severe scarring when they do heal up."

"Can I see him?" Taea finally asked weakly.

"Only one can go in the room for right now, but yes you can go see him. The time with him will be limited. We need him to rest as much as he can so his body can heal properly."

Taea tore away from me and followed Doctor Coleman into the back.

Me and Quan's mama sat back down in our seats without speaking a word to one another. We were deep in thought about what could have happened to cause this shit.

"All I ever wanted was for my son to leave this street life alone, but he wouldn't listen to me anytime I begged him to give up that life. I blame myself because I wasn't there when he needed me. I was out living life and wasn't ready to settle down to be a mama. I was a selfish bitch back in the day.

After his father died everything changed. Quan left, and he never came back."

I listened as she emotionally spilled what had happened in Quan's childhood, I already knew most of it from what had told me, but it was always helpful to listen to her side of the story as well.

"I have never been on drugs, but the only drug that I had was fucking other men. I loved Quan's father with all my heart, but he couldn't give me the life that I wanted. I cheated and hurt him every chance I got. If I could go back and change the shit, I wouldn't have been doing any of it, and maybe his daddy would be here to teach him the right path. When his daddy found out that I was cheating on him he lost it, he couldn't even give Quan the guidance that he needed. Quan needed someone stable, a loving father and mama and we failed him. He wouldn't be laying up in this hospital if I would have been a better mama," Quan's mama cried.

I have never been the type of bitch to judge anyone, and I wasn't about to start now. We all made mistakes because no one was perfect. It wasn't Quan's mama's fault that he turned to the streets. Quan chose that life because he felt that was what he wanted to do, my baby was smart, he could have gone to college and got him a good ass job, but he chose to hustle for his, he didn't want to slave for the white man, and selling dope was what he felt like he wanted to do for easy cash. It was a risk he took. Every morning he woke up, it was always a chance that he could end up dead or in prison, but so far neither one had happened.

I was becoming impatient and wanted to know when I was going to be able to see Quan. I pulled out my phone and noticed it had been almost thirty minutes, no way it took them nurses that long to move Quan to a room. I was just about to get my ass up and talk to the front desk nurse when

I spotted Quan's Doctor Harvard approaching us. I jumped out my chair and Quan's mama did the same.

"Is everything ok?" I asked him in a panicked voice.

"Yes, everything is okay, it just took time to find an available room on the floor of ICU. Follow me, and I can take you both to see him."

It seemed like the longest walk ever. When we came to the double doors that separated the emergency room from the main wing hospital, my heart felt as if it was about to fall out of my chest. The closer I got to seeing Quan the more my stomach did somersaults. When we finally made it to his room, the doctor told Quan's mama and me that we couldn't stay too long.

"Is he up?" I asked him.

"Yes, he was up when we first brought him in, but he is going in and out of sleep. He can't talk right now, he got his jaw wired shut he may be a little woozy and be going in and out of sleep due to him just getting out of surgery, that's why I said y'all can't stay long, he needs his rest."

"We understand," his mama told him before pushing open Quan's door.

"Thank you, Doctor Harvard, for all you did," I told him softly before I went inside Quan's room. His mama had pulled a chair up to his right side and was holding his hand. I noticed she had fresh tears running down her face as she softly spoke to him. I stood by the door and decided to let her have her alone time with Quan first. I understood their relationship had always been rocky, but this was no time to be selfish and think only of myself. His mama had a point to prove, she had been nonexistent, but today she was here, and I saw nothing but genuine concern for her only son.

She sat there and talked with him for over fifteen minutes before I heard her phone jingling in her purse. She pulled away from Quan and spoke softly into her phone before ending the call by telling the person who she was on the phone with that she was going to be home soon. I already knew that it was probably some nigga who she was dating that was calling just to see where she was at. She stood up after ending her call and placed a kiss on Quan's forehead before walking over to where I was standing by the door.

"If anything changes, let me know. Please call me."

"Are you leaving?" I asked her.

"Yes, I got to get back home, Tyrone and I had made plans for later tonight."

I watched her as she fluffed her shoulder-length hair and headed out the door.

"Bitch," I muttered under my breath after she had left.

Just when I thought I could feel an ounce of sympathy for her, all that shit flew out the window. Your son was laid up in the hospital trying to fight for his life, and she was leaving him because of a nigga. Some bitches never change I thought to myself. Maybe I was being judgmental and harsh but, I just felt that today it should've been all about Quan and what he needed. She had been absent out of Quan's life, and here she was being given another chance to be a mama and what does she do? She leaves because she and Tyrone had plans for later that night.

I stared up at the clock that was hung not far from the forty-inch flat screen TV and noticed that it was only two in the afternoon. I slowly walked over to him and took a seat in the very chair that his mama was just sitting in. I wrapped my hand around his and held it tightly as I cried on his bed. When I looked at him, his eyes were closed. He seemed as if he was in a peaceful sleep. I didn't want to wake him, but I wanted to talk to him so badly.

"Baby, I know that you and me been going through some things, but please pull through, I need you baby. I don't know if I'm going to be able to make it without you here. Please, if you can hear me just let me know," I cried to him.

Tears blurred my vision, but when his hand squeezed mine, I felt as if the whole world stood still. Even though his left jaw was patched up and bandaged, he still looked so damn fine. His long black dreads fell down his shoulders, and I gently rubbed them with my hands. His eyes fluttered, and then they opened. He looked into my eyes, and I saw nothing but love radiating from them.

"I love you," I whispered to him.

I knew he wanted to say it back but couldn't, but I didn't give a damn about any of that. I was just glad that he acknowledged that I was there in his presence.

I wet my lips before telling him about his mama.

I called your mama. I didn't know your status, but I felt like she needed to be here. I knew she would be really hurt if I didn't reach out to her. She was genuinely concerned about you. She came and waited in the waiting room with Taea and me until they finally let us see you. Even though I was pissed that she had left the way she did, I wasn't about to say anything to him about it, I didn't want to say or do anything that I thought would cause him stress. With the type of relationship that they had, I didn't want to be the reason that he had a setback with his recovery. I knew if he was able to talk that he would have easily told me that he didn't care if she showed up or not to check on him, the one person who he cared about and wanted to be here was me.

I stood up and placed a kiss on his lips, and that's when I saw tears running down his face. I gently wiped him away as I stared down at him.

"We going to get through this baby, I promise, no matter what happens I'm always going to be here for you, I'm never leaving your side. I put my life on that," I whispered into his ear.

QUAN

I woke up to the sound of machines beeping with a bright light shining down on me. I groaned in pain as I tried to move.

"Sir try not to move," someone told me gently as they pushed me back down.

"Give your eyes enough time to adjust to the light. Do you know where you're at?" Someone asked me.

I couldn't see that well so I couldn't see who this bitch was talking to me and asking me all these questions. I tried to speak, but no words but the words just wouldn't leave my mouth.

After not being able to respond, the nurse told me that I was in the Houston County Medical center.

I tried to swallow, but I felt nothing but pain shoot down my throat.

I wanted to scream, but for some reason, I knew if I screamed, I would cause myself a shit load of pain.

"You were brought in here a few hours earlier, you were shot in your left jaw and your stomach," the woman told me as she stared down at me.

It wasn't long after I woke up that my vision finally began to clear and I could see. The bitch wasn't lying; I was definitely in the hospital.

I tried pulling the white sheets from off of me but found that my arms and my hands felt like rubber.

The woman who was writing something on her clipboard glanced down at me.

"Sir, I would advise you to try not to move."

She was dressed in blue scrubs with her hair pulled back in a low ponytail, she was white and pale, and looked like she was suffering from an eating disorder, the bitch was just that skinny. Here she was trying to check on me but the bitch needed to be more concerned about her own health.

She sat her clipboard down after she was done writing and walked out of the room. She came back in a few moments later with a bald-headed man who I assumed was the doctor.

"My name is Doctor Harvard. How are you feeling?"

Just when I tried to speak, the pain shot down my body so bad it brought tears to my eyes.

Doctor Harvard walked closer to me and asked if I was in any pain.

I nodded my head yes. I needed to take something, the pain that I was experiencing was something that felt like I was dying even though I knew I wasn't.

"Jody, can you come in here and give him a little bit more morphine?"

I watched in agony as the skinny heifer walked over towards my IV bag and administered me the pain medicine.

"You are lucky to be alive if you would have been rushed to the ER any later than when you came you wouldn't have made it. The shot in your stomach caused a lot of bleeding which sent your whole body into shock. We lost you for a few moments during the surgery, but thankfully we got your heart back to pumping. When the bullet hit your jaw, it didn't shatter it, but it did some damage, but it will heal, and you will be able to speak again."

I nodded my head slowly to let him know that I understood what he was saying to me.

"Give the morphine a few moments, and you will be feeling somewhat better, you have a long recovery ahead of you, but I believe you will get through it. If you got through the surgery, then I know you will get through the recovery process. The surgery was the hardest because you had already lost so much blood when you came in."

I was lucky to be alive, but the only thing that I could think about was Yanni. I watched him as he handed me a black marker. I grabbed the marker with shaky hands, and that's when he passed me a small whiteboard with a mini eraser attached to it.

"This is what I want you to use until your mouth heals. I don't want you talking at all. Not a word, this is going to be your only way to communicate with anyone. We need to keep your jaw bandaged and also keep your dressing changed, so it won't lead to any infection."

I popped open the black marker that he had just given me and wrote only one sentence. There was only one thing that I was concerned about more than my health, and that was Yanni.

Is Yanni here? I wrote on the whiteboard.

"Yes, she was the only one I called. If I'm not mistaken, I believe she is sitting out front."

Can I see her? I wrote slowly on the board. I held it up so he could see that I had written him another message.

"Yes, you can see her, but first we have to find you a room. Rest your eyes and let the morphine do its job," Doctor Howard instructed me.

I waited patiently for him to leave out of my room so I

could finally have my thoughts to myself with no interruptions. The sound of the machines beeping in the distance didn't seem to bother me. Instead, they seemed to keep me calm. I wanted nothing more than to walk my ass up out of this hospital butt ass naked with my gown still on and put a bullet in Ken's head. The nigga thought he had gotten away with trying to take my ass out, but he made one motherfucking mistake, he shot at me, but the dumb ass nigga didn't kill me, he left me to choke on my own blood, but I didn't fucking die, instead I lived, and I was already plotting for my revenge.

Once he knew that I wasn't dead, I only prayed his bitch ass got the hell out of Warner Robins because if he didn't, I swear I was aiming to shoot that nigga on sight. I wasn't about to get no law involved. I was ready to do my own justice. I had spared this nigga all these years, but I should have been murked his ass because I knew that eventually, it was soon going to come to this. Even though I didn't believe in killing bitches, I wanted to murk KeKe. I wanted to see her brains get splattered as well. If that hoe was smart, she would get the fuck out of town, but the bitch was dumb as hell, so I knew as soon as I got out of here, she was still going to be in town doing what she does the best, which was being a hoe.

KeKe had gone to the extreme, so she deserved to fucking die. Right now, I didn't know what the point of her doing any of this shit. I mean damn, she was that upset that Yanni beat her ass and that I didn't defend her that she was willing to go that fucking far. The bitch was crazy, and all I wanted to do was to take that miserable hoe up out of here as soon as I was discharged out this damn hospital.

As the morphine began to kick in, my whole body began to relax which caused me to close my eyes. As my eyes began to close, I began to dream about Ken and how he had even gotten the opportunity to shoot my ass.

I was sitting my ass in Carissa's porch playing with my phone. Jon had just stepped inside the house with Carissa. I heard them fussing, and then shit went silent. I wasn't trying to eavesdrop on what they had going on because it wasn't my damn business. I had the urge to text Yanni and was so deep in thought about her that I didn't hear Ken when he walked up on me from the side. If this nigga would have made his ass known by coming to me head on, I would have spotted his ass and popped him before he popped my ass, but like I said this nigga came up from the left side and started blasting at my ass. I didn't even have time to even get my hands on my Glock to even aim at his pussy ass.

The first shot hit me in the left side of my face which made me fall out of the chair. I tried reaching for my gun, but the nigga stood over me and held me down and started telling me about his sister.

"Nigga, you hit the wrong fucking bitch, hitting my sister wasn't even worth losing your life? Oh well, see your ass in hell bitch", Ken spat at me before aiming his pistol at me and popping me right in my damn stomach.

I tried yelling to warn Jon, but that was impossible for me to do. I was coughing up blood, and as I laid there on that fucking porch, I began to wonder was I really going to die by the hands of some pussy ass nigga. I prayed and asked the man above to look over Yanni if he decided to take me. The sound of some gunshots really sealed the deal. I didn't know if Jon had survived or if he had been killed. When I spotted Ken jumping off the porch, I knew that Jon had probably been done in as well. Tears fell from my eyes as the sirens blasted in the distance.

"Please hurry up and get here," I cried out in my head.

I didn't want to die, I still wanted to at least make shit right with Yanni first. I didn't want to leave this Earth with her hating me, but I couldn't decide my fate only the man upstairs could. I muttered a prayer that I had learned when I was a kid and tried to stay awake, but eventually, I was met with darkness.

I don't know how long I was sleep, but when I woke up, I was in a new room. I was falling in and out of sleep but tried to stay awake just so I could be able to see Yanni when she came in to see me. I sat there; it seemed forever before the door swung open. I didn't turn to move to see who was there, but I eventually found out the answer when her hand touched mine. I opened my eyes and there stood my mama. To be honest, I wasn't even expecting to see her here. Even though she and I was on good terms, I didn't fuck with her like that. The only way that my mama had known what was going on with me was if Yanni had called and told her.

I saw the tears in her eyes as she caressed my hand and told me just how much she loved me. I listened and felt nothing but love radiating from her body. I closed my eyes as I basked in her motherly love. Finally, I was getting some of her attention. Growing up my mama only cared about her men. Now that she thought she was going to lose her only son here she stood telling me just how sorry she was on how she treated me as a child. I hated that I was so tired, but I listened with my eyes closed to as much as I could before the ringing of her phone brought me back into reality.

I was upset when I found out that she was leaving, but the fact she did show her face and come by to see me was the only reason why I let her had that shit. She could have not shown up, but the fact she came that was enough to let me know that she did care about me, she just had a sorry way of showing it.

My heart skipped a beat when I felt Yanni's hands on me next. This was the moment that I had been waiting for, and finally, here it was. She spoke to me for a few moments and placed a kiss on my forehead. I stared up at Yanni, and I saw nothing but pain in her face. Tears fell from her eyes as she began to confess her love for me. Listening to her speak brought tears to my eyes as well.

"Who did this shit to you?" Yanni asked in a shaky voice.

I grabbed my whiteboard and marker and slowly wrote down the one name that I was planning on murking.

"Ken…" Yanni read off the clipboard

Yanni placed her hand over her mouth. She already knew exactly what I was thinking and knew exactly what I was planning on doing without her saying a damn thing. Our eyes talked to one another.

"Why Ken?" Yanni asked with confusion in her voice.

I took my time with my shaky hands and wrote a few sentences that summed up everything perfectly.

The day you beat KeKe, she went and told Ken that I beat her, by us already having beef he wanted revenge. But he should have known his sister was lying, but I guess he thinks if he took Jon and me out, he believed he was going to take over Warner Robins. Even if I do die tonight or tomorrow. He could never replace my ass ever.

"Baby, we going to get through this shit, don't think about Ken or what KeKe did period, just focus on getting well."

Focusing on Ken was the only thing I knew I could do just so I could push my body to the point that I could get well. People always said that love fueled the body but so did hate and revenge. I was coming for Ken's head, and I knew once Ken was killed KeKe would disappear on her own, she wouldn't have nobody, and she would die a slow and painful death. I hope Ken was getting ready because I was coming for that nigga's life.

I had no idea how Jon was doing, and I wanted to know. I knew that he wasn't dead because Yanni would have told me when she first saw me. I wrote a sentence on my whiteboard asking her about Jon.

Is Jon doing okay?

Yanni didn't look at me directly so that shit sent me to panic mode.

"He's alive if that's what you asking. Um, I talked to his doctor for Tea because she was really upset about the shit. She thought she was going to lose him. He was shot three times in his chest. One of the bullets hit one of his lungs. He's in bad shape baby, but he pulled through the surgery they got some type of tube in his lung at the moment. They said they are waiting to see how he do before they can take it out. It's some type of tube to keep his breathing regulated to keep the blood from filling up in his lung."

Damn, my partner had been shot three times, and he didn't die, Jon was a fucking fighter, a bullet to the damn lung wasn't nothing to play with. I have never been the type of nigga to cry, but after hearing that shit about Jon, I couldn't help but shed a few tears. I was just glad that he had survived. It could have been so much worse. There was no way in hell I was ever going to get over it if I knew he had been killed by Ken's bitch ass.

I stared at the ceiling as Yanni tried to comfort me. Just having her here with me helped me emotionally. All the anger that Yanni had for me before I nearly lost my life seemed to have evaporated. Instead, she showed my ass nothing but love.

"I always knew I loved you, but I never knew how much until today."

I tried to smile but I couldn't.

When a soft knock came at the door, Yanni yelled out that they could come in.

Doctor Harvard stood at the door with his hand in his pockets.

"I just wanted to come let you know that visitation hours are up for Quantavious. We are trying not to over exceed an hour for a patient who just had surgery. They need their rest, and they won't get it if they have someone in their room that they can talk to."

Yanni looked down at me, and I could tell that she didn't want to leave, but I knew she had to.

"Can I come back tomorrow?" Yanni asked Doctor Harvard without tearing her eyes away from mine.

"Yes, he will have regular visitation hours then. It's just today he isn't allowed to. We have to keep a close eye on him to make sure he stays stable."

Yanni nodded her head at the doctor and bent down and placed a kiss on the good side of my right cheek before whispering she loved me and would be back to see me tomorrow.

I closed my hands around her tightly because I didn't want her to go.

She pulled away from me with tears in her eyes and looked down at me.

"When I come here tomorrow be here, don't fucking die on me. Not now, my heart can't take that shit."

I watched her as she grabbed her purse and walked slowly out the door. She didn't look back at me, but if she would have, she would have seen the tears falling down my face.

THE NEXT MORNING

I slept peacefully last night but woke up in pain. I didn't waste no time by clicking the panic button to let someone know to bring their ass in the room asap. My entire face felt like it was on fire along with my damn stomach. I was in so much pain I didn't even want to move, but a nigga had to pee.

It took close to ten minutes for anyone to bring their ass in the room to see what I wanted. By that time a nigga was ready to box a bitch out.

"How are you doing this morning, Mr. Johnson?" the young nurse asked sweetly.

She was a little dark-skinned ass bitch who looked like she was fresh out of college.

I was far from fucking happy with her ass already. I wanted to slap that hoe because she was taking her fucking time to see about me knowing that I was a gunshot victim and then when she does come to see about me, her ass got a happy ass smile on her face.

I groaned with pain because that was all I could do. She took that as a hint that I must was in pain. She checked the board that was posted beside the flat screen TV and checked her watch.

"Okay, it looks like it's time for us to give you some more morphine."

I scribbled on my whiteboard that I needed to pee, and she read it just before she gave me my dose of medicine.

"Okay, this is what we going to do, I'm going to help you to the bathroom as soon as the morphine kicks in. If I take you now you only going to be hollering about you in pain."

"I will be back to take you to the bathroom," she said to me.

I watched as she scribbled her name, Winter under the date and told me that she was going to be my nurse for a few hours. After she had written her name on the whiteboard, she grabbed her clipboard and walked out of my room.

When the morphine started to kick the nurse walked back into my room and helped me off the bed. It wasn't a far walk to the bathroom, I took care of my business with no help. When I was done the nurse made sure to help me back into the bed. I placed the covers back over my body and flipped on the T.V. I flipped the T.V channels until I found something interesting to watch. Sitting there not able to do anything really fucked with me. I've always been the type of nigga to do everything for myself. Being shot and nearly dying changed all that shit.

I eventually dozed off but woke up when I felt someone touch my hand. I slowly opened my eyes to find Taea staring down at me. Taea has always been slim, but today she looked even thinner and frailer. I knew it had everything to do with what had happened to Jon. Her eyes had bags under them and looked swollen from what I assumed was from her crying. Her hair was pulled back in a messy bun, and her clothes were wrinkled. She looked like she had just hopped out of bed and had come straight to the hospital. Even though Taea and I had our differences, but here she was standing over me trying to make sure that I was good.

"I know you can't talk, but I just wanted to come by to see how you were doing," Taea said emotionally.

I picked up the whiteboard that was next to me and slowly scribbled down a reply to her question.

Taea read it slowly and nodded her head.

"Yanni told me who did this shit and everyone who is involved, just know I'm willing to do whatever I got to, to make that bitch ass nigga pay. Jon is fighting hard, but I don't know how long it going to take him to get well."

I didn't want to cry, but tears instantly began to form in my eyes as I began to scribble on my whiteboard.

I'm so sorry, Jon got to pull through, if he doesn't, I swear I'm going to murk every last one of Ken's crew, his sister, and save Ken bitch ass for last. The whole Westside is going to bleed for what they have done.

"Don't worry about shit, me and Yanni are going to find a way to take care of all this shit, all you and Jon need to do is rest up and get better. I can't lose Jon, he all I have. I just can't imagine my life without him."

Alarms started going off in my head. I could tell how Taea was talking that something wasn't right. Taea was one crazy bitch, and Yanni wasn't far from behind her. Them to together, plotting and scheming against anyone could end deadly. I didn't want either one of them to get involved in any of the shit that Jon and I had going on. Taea was Jon's girl if anything ever happened to her, I knew he was never going to get over the shit. If something ever happened to Yanni, there was no way I was ever going to get over the fact that I was the reason the shit went the way it did. Now I hated that I had told Yanni everything but not telling her was only going to stress and worry more than she already was doing.

I took a deep breath and let it out as I slowly began to

write how I felt about a lot of shit. This was the moment in my life that I hated the most. I wanted so badly to get out of my bed and shake some sense into Taea, but all I could do was scribble down everything that I couldn't voice out loud.

I know you upset and pissed about what happened to Jon, but Please leave that shit alone. Me and Jon is going to take care of that pussy ass nigga as soon as we get out of this bitch. Stay away from Ken, his crew, and his stupid ass sister and make sure that Yanni does as well. I'm not playing with your ass Taea, leave that shit alone. Jon will strangle your ass if he finds out what you trying to plot to do.

After Taea had finished reading what I had written, she looked down at me and shook her head.

"Jon isn't gonna do shit. I already spoke to him, he tried talking me out of it, but I don't care what ya'll say. Nigga, you delusional if you think Yanni and I are about to let this shit ride. He nearly killed both of you. We don't know how long it's going to take for either one of you to get out of this fucking place, so with that being said we gonna do what we gotta do. When you and Jon got with Yanni and I we automatically signed up to ride for ya'll until the very end. It's time that we let both of ya'll know that's it real. We both some smart bitches don't worry we know what to do."

I felt like my chest was tightening up and my heart was beginning to ache. I didn't want this shit to go down this way, but the way that Taea was talking, I knew she wasn't on that fuck shit. She was determined to make Ken pay, and there wasn't shit that Jon or I could do to stop her or Yanni.

"Look, I gotta go."

Just when I thought she was heading out the door that's when she turned around and stared at me briefly.

"Don't be mad; we're only trying to help. No way me or Yanni can sit on our asses and not do nothing. We going to demolish everything and everyone who had something to do with this shit. Rest up Quan, because you going to need it," Taea said softly before walking out of my room.

JON

THE NEXT DAY...

"None of this would have happened if you would have chosen me, I could have stopped Ken but you made your choice, and I made mine."

I swear this shit still haunted me because this was the last thing that I can remember after getting shot.

Fucking around with a stupid bitch was the real reason why I was sitting in this damn hospital. I almost lost my fucking life, but the only reason why I was trying my hardest to pull through was because I couldn't bear the thought of Carissa or Ken being the two who took a nigga up out of here. I should have known not to trust Carissa when I found out she used to fuck around with Ken. For all I know they both could have been setting me up from the jump.

As I sat laid down in the bed, I muted the T.V so I could think in peace. These doctors had my ass so doped up in this bitch, I was praying to the man above that I didn't walk up out this bitch a dope fiend; waiting on my next hit. From the time I opened my eyes up yesterday after surgery, to the time I closed them last night, I was on some type of pain medicine.

The doctors were constantly checking my vitals and making sure my lungs were okay and keeping a check on me.

When I first opened my eyes from surgery the first person, I saw was Taea. She was crying over me and begging me to not die on her. I can remember staring at her, with cracked lips, and a bitter aftertaste in my mouth. She was beautiful in every way, and just seeing her in tears broke my heart. I moved underneath her tight embrace to let her know that I heard everything that she had said. She confessed her love to me and told me that she was never going to leave me. Just knowing that I had a real bitch like Taea in my corner helped me to remain stress-free. I didn't have to worry about my shorty out here in the streets having me looking stupid as fuck while I'm laid up in the hospital fighting for my life. Some females would have dipped out and found them another nigga to fuck on, but Taea wasn't that type of bitch she was so much better than that she was my rider.

When she asked me, what had happened and who had shot me, I told her everything that I fucking knew. I even told her about the part of being going over to Carissa's apartment, and I gave her the address. I wanted her to know everything because I didn't know if I was even going to make it through the night, I was in that much pain. The fear of the unknown is why I told Taea everything she needed to know. I knew she wanted closure and to find out who was responsible for nearly killing me. Holding secrets back from my day one wasn't about to happen.

When she asked me why I had gone over to Carissa's crib, I told her the truth. I told her I had gone over there because she had called and I was still trying to talk to her about getting an abortion if the baby was in fact mine. We got into it and next thing you know Ken was kicking down the door, guns blazing.

Once Taea understood Carissa's role in what had happened to me, that's when I noticed Taea had changed.

No longer was she the crying girlfriend begging me not to leave her alone. She was a savage ass bitch who didn't have a heart. When she told me that she was gonna fuck Carissa up and didn't give a fuck if that baby was mine or not, I knew she wasn't talking about beating that bitch's ass. She was talking about putting that hoe six feet deep. I wanted Carissa dead too, but I didn't want any blood on my girl's hand. I had gotten myself in this situation, and I was going to have to find out how I was going to get out of it by myself.

Taea wasn't having any of that shit. When she told me that she and Yanni were going to take care of Ken, his sister, his crew, and Carissa, I knew Taea wasn't playing; she was dead serious about everything. I tried fussing with her, but I was way too damn weak. They had me so doped up yesterday, that I fell to sleep mid-conversation with Taea talking about the plot to get rid of Ken, his sister, his crew, and Carissa.

If Taea couldn't find Carissa to put a bullet to her head, Carissa better hoped when I got my ass up out of this hospital that she had disappeared because the first mission was to stomp her ass out and put a bullet in her head. She went to damn far when she put my life, and my partna's on the line.

When I woke up this morning Taea was there laying in the chair, in deep thought. I didn't want to disturb her, but she must have heard when I moved because her eyes cut directly towards mine. I knew she was going to come to check on me. She looked tired and looked like she hadn't slept. I understood the stress that she was going through. When I asked her about Quan, she gave me the cutthroat version, she was never the type of bitch to sugar coat shit. When she told me that my nigga was shot in his face and stomach, and couldn't talk, I broke down. I couldn't control my emotions even though I wanted to. Just knowing now that he was going to make it put my mind at ease. She stayed and sat with me for over two hours before she finally left.

After she left, the doctors came in and examined me. They had this gloomy expression on their face, so I already knew what was up. They thought I wasn't going to survive, but I wasn't going to give up fighting. I had too much shit to live for still. Fuck these damn doctors, they didn't have my life planned out. I was strong, and the thought of watching Ken and Carissa drown in their own blood seemed to give me the strength to push on. The entire time that the doctor was talking to me I zoned out and started thinking about Taea.

I was stupid as hell to cheat on her and put myself in this fucked up situation. I was weak, and the thought of finally fucking a bitch that I always wanted was something that I thought I needed, but apparently, I had been wrong and blinded by lust. That bitch wasn't what I needed, who I needed was Taea, she had been riding for me since day one. Our love ran deep, and whenever I came up out of this hospital, I promised myself that no matter what I was always going to remain loyal and faithful to my bitch. After I got myself up out of this hospital, there was no way I was going to even stare at another bitch.

It took me nearly dying to know just how blessed I truly was with the life that I had. I wasn't about to let Ken or Carissa get away with trying to murk my nigga Quan or me. I still didn't know if the baby that Carissa was carrying was mine, and to be honest, I didn't even know if the bitch was really pregnant. I never saw no fucking papers confirming any damn thing. So, for all I know that could have been another lie to try to get me to leave Taea and be with her trifling ass.

I always knew that bitches could be petty but Carissa was just plain crazy as hell, that bitch really had set my ass up to be murked all because I ain't want to be with her little Mexican ass. I mean damn bitch, there was too much dick out here in this world to get obsessed with some other bitch nigga. Even though Carissa swore up and down that she and Ken were no longer fucking, as I sat up in the hospital bed, I knew that bitch had to be lying. She and Ken made the perfect team. She wanted me to be hers, and I ain't want her ass in that way. I didn't want a forever with her, Ken wanted to murk my ass because he felt like I had taken her away from him which I did. I could pull any bitch that I wanted, and at the time Carissa was what I wanted.

If Carissa was pregnant, I figured it had to be Ken's baby, but eventually, the truth was going to come out. I only prayed that I ain't get that crazy bitch pregnant and even if I was the father, that hoe was still on my hit list. I drifted off into a deep sleep and was awaken by Mike Mike, Richie boy, and Gangsta G. The crew had come by to make sure that I was good.

Gangsta G, Mike Mike, and Richie boy had been in my crew for a good minute, and I trusted each one of them niggas to hold shit down when Quan and I couldn't do it.

Gangsta G was a big ass nigga, he stood at least 6'5 with all muscle, he was dark in complexion rocked a silver diamond grill in his mouth, and sort of resembled Rick Ross in the face.

Mike Mike, was average in height brown-skinned, and rocked a low-cut fade, he was the one who had all the crazy ass baby mamas. I swear that nigga had almost six of them bitches and all them hoes stayed trying to fight each other over him.

Richie Boy was a light-skinned ass nigga that rocked dreads that were almost down his back. He was a cool ass nigga, he was quiet and didn't say much, he was the type of nigga you wanted on your team because he was always observing shit even when no one knew he was doing it. He was good at reading between the lines and could spot bullshit from a mile away.

"Have ya'll been to see Quan yet?" I asked them hoarsely.

"Yeah, we went to see him first." He can't even talk, they got him writing shit down on a whiteboard. Boss man ain't liking that shit," Gangsta G, said.

"He told us about Ken, his sister, and that Carissa bitch, so we ready to open fire on their asses when we see them," Mike Mike added angrily.

"Don't. We got everything under control. Leave it to Quan and me. If I need you, I will let you know," I told them with as much force as I could.

One thing about the crew that Quan and I had made, they were some loyal ass niggas. Besides the issue I had with Tay, I never had any issues with any one of them being on no fuck shit. They were always ready to fuck a nigga up whenever they got out of line.

"What you fail to realize Jon is Ken, his sister, his crew, and Carissa are your enemy that makes them our enemy as well," Richie Boy said.

"Just give us the word, and we will make their asses disappear," Richie Boy added.

"All I want you to do is make sure that neither of them comes anywhere near the Northside."

"They would be some dumb motherfuckers if they did, they already know the Northside Squad is going to shoot on sight," Mike Mike proclaimed.

"Shidddd, they dumb as fuck. They sat here and shot at Jon and Quan and knowing damn well it was going to start a war. They all dumb as hell," Gangsta G stated as he looked out the hospital window.

I sat and listened as they all went back and forth on what they needed to do if any one of them showed their face on the Northside. After over thirty minutes of plotting the crew left and told me if I needed anything to let them know.

"There is one thing that I want ya'll to do."

"What is it?" Gangsta G asked.

"I want ya'll to keep an eye on Taea and Yanni. Don't let either one of them out of your sight. Don't let them know that ya'll watching them. You got to be low key with it."

"We got you, we will all take turns watching them," Mike Mike promised.

After they had left only then did, I feel somewhat at peace.

TAEA

If Jon thought for one minute that I was going to sit back and let him do everything, then he had lost his damn mind. He wanted revenge, and I wanted the same thing. I have never been the type of bitch to sit on my ass and let a nigga handle everything. I was a real ass bitch; I knew exactly what I was getting myself in when I gave him my heart three years ago.

Yeah, I know he had hurt me, and most bitches wouldn't lift a finger to help him, but I was cut from a different cloth. I wasn't your average bitch. I was far from dumb, and I wasn't about to let nobody play with me or my feelings. That was going to get someone kilt if they thought they could play me.

What Jon was going through was some serious shit. I knew I loved this nigga and was eventually going to take his ass back. Now knowing my baby had nearly died really changed a lot of shit. No longer was I holding all that anger inside. Instead, I deaded that shit. We all had to die one day and knowing that I was so close to losing the man that I've given my heart to let me knew to put all that petty shit aside. He didn't love the bitch, he didn't leave me for the bitch, but the hardest thing that I hated to think about was if she was carrying his baby.

I wanted to murk the hoe, not because she had slept with my nigga, but because she had given him something that I haven't even had a chance to give him. It wasn't that me and him weren't trying, it just never happened yet. I had been to the doctors numerous of times to find out what was the hold up in us having kids, and each doctor would tell me the same thing, nothing was wrong with my body, maybe it just wasn't the right time.

What the fuck they meant by it just wasn't the right time? Just thinking about the shit put a frown on my face. If nothing wasn't wrong with me, then I should be able to automatically get pregnant, but still, after a whole year of having unprotected sex with Jon, nothing had changed. Now that this bitch claimed that she was having Jon's first baby, this really was sending me over the edge.

I was his ride and die, I was his day one bitch, if anyone should be pregnant it should have been me. The betrayal ran deep in my veins, and my heart felt broken, but I knew I had to push on. I had so much I wanted out of life, and I wanted it all with Jon.

I didn't just want to be his baby mama, but I wanted to be his wifey and the only bitch who had his heart. I had been loyal to my nigga from day one, I wasn't about to let some stupid bitch come and snatch that shit away from me.

The hoe had to die, but before I killed her, there was some info that I wanted to beat out of that bitch. Was the hoe really pregnant and if she was, was it even my nigga's baby? Some hoes will go as far as claiming they were pregnant to try to keep that nigga in their life.

If Carissa got pregnant on purpose to keep Jon in her life, then she was one dumb, stupid hoe. If she wasn't pregnant and only had lied about the shit, she was one desperate ass hoe. If she thought she was winning for getting pregnant and nearly having him killed the bitch had another thing coming.

I couldn't stop thinking of Carissa, but I forced myself to push her to the back of my mind. I had shit that I had to do and going to work on time and trying to be in a good mood was going to take a lot of effort. I didn't want to have all that negativity on my brain because if I did, I was going to snap as soon as I stepped foot into Taco Bell. I didn't even need the piece of shit ass job, but I kept the bitch because it allowed me to go somewhere every day and it was some pocket money for me to keep my hair and nails looking good. Taco Bell was my money to do what I wanted with it. It was money that I didn't have to take from Jon. Even though Jon was always throwing me money, I still worked so I could make money on my own and Jon never minded that.

Soon as I pulled up at Taco Bell, I had the urge to take my ass back to the house. It was only noon, and Taco Bell was suffering from the lunch rush hour. I was an hour late, so I already knew that was going to lead to me being fussed at. I haven't even stepped foot in Taco Bell a whole minute before I was met by Mookie, the bitch that I had just beat last week. She had her arms folded over her big chest which only made her titties look as if they were about to fall from her chest. I could tell by how she was looking at me that the bitch was pissed, but I didn't give a fuck. I wasn't in the mood to be fussing with her fat ass. I swear if this hoe got wrong, I was going to beat that ass again, and this time, I was going to make sure I stomp her head in the damn floor.

I guess she was still mad that everyone had sided with me when she tried to get my ass fired for beating her ass last week, but hell, the bitch, didn't have proof that I did anything. The cameras just happen to not be working that day, which made it even better for me. I had gotten away with beating her ass with no consequences.

"You're late, she spat at me angrily.

"Look, my nigga is in the fucking hospital, he fighting for his life. I had to go see about him, I was not about to break my neck to rush over here when he needed me."

I could see the fire in Mookie's eyes, but me being the bitch that I was I ignored it. I tried walking past her, but she grabbed me by my arm.

"I don't give a fuck about your nigga or why you late, don't let the shit happen again, because if it does, you will find yourself without a job."

I snatched my arm away from her and stared at the bitch like she had lost her fucking mind. The hoe had to have bumped her fucking head. Even though what I was going through at home wasn't her business, she should have shown some type of compassion. If I told her my nigga was in the hospital fighting for his life. It took all the power in me to not smack fire from that bitch.

"Last time I checked; your ass wasn't the general manager. You just the fucking shift leader, get the fuck out of my face bitch, it's rush hour I got a job to do," I hissed at her before walking off to clock in.

No one seemed to even notice that Mookie and I had said some foul words to one another, the restaurant was just that fucking busy. After clocking in, I did my job and kept away from Mookie. The only thing that got me through my shift was the thought of Jon getting out of the hospital and us starting us a family. I wanted the title of his wife, I wanted another house, and I wanted some bad ass fucking kids. I didn't just want one, but I wanted three of them. I wore a smile on my face for the rest of the day just from the thought of having that happily ever after with my man.

* * *

When my six hours were done, I wasted no time getting the hell out of Taco Bell, I shot past two of the others that were getting off as well and headed straight to my car. I slammed my car door and pulled out my phone and hooked it to my speakers. I hit Yanni ass up and waited for her to pick up the phone.

"Bitch, are you ready?"

"I stay fucking ready, what's the plan?" Yanni asked.

"We gonna talk about this shit in a few, I'm headed home to change out of these work clothes and then I'm headed your way."

"Ok cool, see you then."

I pulled up at my house a few moments later and hopped out my car. I groaned when I spotted one of my nosey ass neighbors. I swear the bitch didn't have a life, all she did was stare out her window and watch folks' houses. Today she was outside watering her lawn dressed in some old clothes. Ms. Howell was around eighty years old but she was the neighborhood gossiper; I guess that type of shit was why she was still living.

I slammed my car shut and locked it as I jogged up to my porch. I was almost to my house when I heard her yell out my name.

"How you doing over there Taea? I ain't seen your boyfriend in a while!" she yelled loudly.

I took a look around and noticed that I was just me and her outside.

I gave her a fake smile and told her that Jon as gone visiting family. She was just about to say some more shit, but I cut her off with a quickness.

"Ms. Howell, I'ma have to talk to you later, I'm in a hurry," I told her before jogging into my house and slamming my door.

Time, I stepped into the house I headed towards my bathroom where I undressed and hopped in the shower. I wanted to wash away the smell of Taco Bell from off my skin. After taking me a thirty-minute shower, I stepped out smelling fresh and good. I dried my body clean and headed straight towards my bedroom to find me something to wear. It didn't take me long to find me a pair of dark grey shorts with a lime green and grey shirt, with my lime green Air Forces. After I was dressed, I pulled my shoulder length hair into a ponytail and moisturized my lips with a little strawberry Chapstick. I wasn't in the mood to rock no lipstick today. When I was done getting dressed, I walked down the hall towards the walk-in closet where Quan would stash all his guns in different shoe boxes and shit. I looked in a few shoe boxes before I finally found one of his pistols that I wanted to use. I grabbed the pistol out of the Nike shoe box and stuffed it in my lime green purse and headed out of the closet.

I grabbed my keys off the nightstand and headed right out of the door over to Yanni's crib.

I pulled up at Yanni's crib ten minutes later. I hopped out and was just about to knock on her door when she pulled me inside. I headed straight towards her kitchen and pulled out a glass and opened her fridge so I could find something to drink. A bitch was thirsty as hell, I was so fucking ready to get the hell on from Taco Bell that I ain't even think to pour me something to drink there. I found a pitcher of lemonade that I assumed Yanni had made and poured me a glass full.

I felt Yanni's presence as she stood at the kitchen doorway. She was waiting for me to explain what we were going to do. After I had swallowed the last bit of lemonade, I put my glass in the sink and followed Yanni back in the living room. I sat down on her couch, and that's when I noticed that she had turned on the TV. Jerry Springer was playing, but the volume was cut down real low.

"I don't know when Jon or Quan is going to get well and

come home," I told Yanni,

"I know it's going to be a long process and I don't have the fucking patience to wait around for them to come home. They almost died both of them, I want to murk everyone of Ken's crew, so he won't have no fucking protection, and I want to save his ass for last. I was going to let Ken walk free until Quan got home but fuck all that shit, as soon as I get that opportunity, I'm going to take that shit." I explained to Yanni.

"We going to handle both Ken and his crew. We ain't letting none of them live. Once they are gone there shouldn't be any more issues. Our niggas can get as much money that they want, and there won't be no more beefing."

"You right Taea, let's do that shit." Yanni agreed.

"But before we put the plan in motion there is one other person that was involved with this shit. I want to personally handle that bitch." I told Yanni.

"Who else was involved? I thought it was just Ken who shot them." Yanni replied.

"Ken was the shooter. Carissa is the bitch that Jon was cheating on me with, she the one who set Jon up to be killed."

"Well damn, in that case, I already know you want to go handle that bitch because I want to handle KeKe ugly ass. She is the one who started all this damn shit by going around lying about Quan. Saying that he hit her ass when I was the one who dragged her ass."

"Right, we can't forget about that stupid bitch. She going to die first, but before I can kill Jon's little side hoe, I gotta know if she pregnant or not."

"It hurts me to my soul to know that some other bitch is carrying Jon's baby. I'm supposed to be the first bitch who has his baby, not no one else."

"Does it matter? She won't be carrying that baby for long." Yanni muttered.

"I just want to know. Jon and I don't have kids, we been trying, but nothing has happened. I just want to put my mind at ease."

"Right, I get what you saying, so what we going to do now?" Yanni asked.

"Bitch, we about to hop in my car and we going to go eat us some good ass food and we going to the Eastside and the Westside tonight. We pulling up on KeKe and Carissa tonight."

"Now that sounds like a plan. Well, let me go freshen up so we can head out. Where we going for dinner?"

"Logan's Roadhouse."

"My favorite," Yanni replied.

After Yanni had headed up the stairs to get dressed, I cut the volume up on Jerry Springer and lit me a cigarette. It was near the ending when Yanni finally came back into the living room yelling that she was ready to head out. I noticed she had one of Quan's pistols in her right hand.

"Is that what you going to use tonight?"

"Damn right. I ain't shot this bitch in a long time."

I couldn't help but laugh.

"You mean Quan stopped taking you outside to let you shoot the cans in the back?"

"Bitch, yessss, the last time he let me shoot this bitch was two months ago. He used to take me once a week on the weekend to shoot, but he started complaining that I ain't need no more lessons."

"He took that gun from your ass for a reason." I joked.

"Bitch, I can shoot good as hell, I want a bitch to try me, I stay ready to bury a bitch."

"And thats why his ass took that gun from your crazy ass." I laughed at her.

Yanni rolled her eyes as she threw the gun into her black bag that matched her black jean shorts.

Yanni had her long weave wrapped into a bun on top of her head and was rocking a grey and gold shirt, with a pair of black and gold shorts. She had on a pair of all black Jordan's on that matched her black Jordan bag that she slid on her back like a tote bag. She was rocking some wine-colored lipstick on her plump lips with no makeup on her face. I already knew when we stepped into Logan's we were going to have all them niggas shook. Bitches were going to be hating that their niggas were staring our asses down, it wasn't shit that we could do about it. We didn't have to clump our face with makeup and shit to get a man's attention we were blessed with natural beauty.

The entire time that we were riding to Logan's Roadhouse we were talking about Carissa and KeKe and what all we were going to do to them.

"I wonder if Carissa going to give you the information you want or if you gonna have to drop kick her ass," Yanni asked me.

"I'm going to have that bitch singing about what happened with her and Jon when I get through with her ass. She was bold enough to try to get Jon to leave me, best believe she been waiting a long time to come face to face with the real bitch who got his heart. I can handle her on my own, but I just want you there to back me up. There is no way, I'm ever going to do no fuck shit without my day one around."

Yanni chuckled.

"You know I got your back. I'm not going to get involved, but I'm anxious to know how all this shit going to play out."

Taea smiled at me evilly.

"You about to experience me on a whole new level, I hope you ready for that shit."

"I stay ready bitch," Yanni said as she pulled up at Logan's Roadhouse.

YANNI

I ate my ass off at Logan's Roadhouse and left with a to-go box.

"Bitch why in the hell are you bringing a damn to go box with your ass. You should be full all that shit you ate," Taea joked.

"Shid, I may get hungry later on tonight."

"When you see me fuck Carissa ass up, you might not want that shit," Taea said.

"Bitch, please, can't shit take my appetite and make me miss out on this good ass steak that I have left over."

Taea rolled her eyes as she hopped into my car. I put my to go box in the backseat and jumped in the front seat.

"Where we off to!" I shouted over Cardi B. blasting from the speakers.

"We headed to the Eastside first so we can take care of KeKe ass first, then we can head on over to the Westside to find Carissa."

It didn't take more than a few minutes to head over to the East Side. I cruised through KeKe's neighborhood, and that's when I spotted her ass. She was walking towards the corner store. She was wearing shorts, a tank top with her hair pulled up in a ponytail. I grabbed my pistol and clenched it in my hand as I slowed down my car.

There that bitch go, it looks like she walking to the store. I'm about to blast that bitch right here.

Damn bitch, you ain't going to follow her ass home? Taea asked.

Hell nall, I ain't got time for that shit, I'mma drop that hoe right here.

As soon as KeKe was about to walk past my car I rolled down my window and shouted out her name.

Bitch, I heard about them lies you fucking spreading, you went and told your fucking brother that Quan beat your ass, why your dumb ass ain't tell the fucking truth.

KeKe walked her ugly ass over to my car popping off at the mouth.

I don't have shit to say to you hoe, my beef is with your lying ass boyfriend. I don't give a fuck about Quan getting shot, he deserved that shiii...

I didn't even let that hoe finish he sentence before I pulled the trigger.

Pow, Pow, Pow, Pow.

I shot that hoe four times at point blank range and ran over her ass twice just so I knew that the bitch was good and dead before I pulled off.

Taea stared over at me and took the pistol from my hand before placing it under her seat.

"Well shit, you weren't playing with that bitch."

"That bitch fucked up when she lied on Quan, and she pissed me off when she walked up to the car talking shit. That bitch is dead dead, I made sure of that shit."

I whipped my car into traffic and sped through the Watson Blvd. traffic until I reached the Westside. We rode around for a little bit before we spotted the projects and rode until we found the apartment number that Jon had given me. I pulled down the road from where her apartment door was at and cut my engine.

Taea immediately reached for her bag and grabbed her gun. I followed the process and did the same thing.

"Are you ready?" Taea asked.

I nodded my head to let her know that I was ready to get this shit over with.

We stepped out the door and jogged slowly towards our destination. As soon as we stepped on her porch, I kicked that bitch door in. There wasn't about to be no knocking.

"What the fuck!" Carissa yelled from the living room couch.

"Get out my fucking house!" Carissa yelled.

"We ain't going nowhere bitch," I told her nastily.

"Just in case you don't know, my name I'm Taea. I'm Jon's bitch. I know about you, and I know about you fucking my nigga," Taea spat at Carissa.

Carissa stood up and crossed her arms.

"I know who the fuck you is bitch, and I want you out my fucking house. Yeah, I used to fuck with him, but I don't no more. He wouldn't leave your stank ass."

Taea didn't even let that bitch say shit else before she smacked her in the face with her pistol.

I posted myself on the wall and stood there just to see how all this shit was going to play out. Taea needed to get a lot of shit off her chest, and I wasn't going to stop her from doing any of it. I had told myself that I wasn't going to get involved unless it was necessary and so far, Taea wasn't in need of my help. But what I couldn't understand was how this hoe was talking this much shit when she had two bitches in her crib with pistols.

After Taea smacked Carissa with her gun, Carissa fell to the floor, and Taea stomped her ass a few more times before snatching her ass up by her long black hair and throwing her back on the half tore up couch that she was sitting on before I kicked her door in.

"I came here for some answers, and I'm not going to leave this bitch until I get them," Taea told Carissa crossly.

"What the fuck you want to know?" Carissa asked with attitude.

"I want to know if you really pregnant by Jon?"

Carissa didn't say shit, she didn't even look at Taea. Taea looked back at me, and I could see the fire in her eyes. Taea was heated and was losing patience with this whole situation, I knew it was only going to be a matter of time before Taea pulled the trigger.

"Bitch I know you heard me talking to you, I know your ass ain't deaf. Is your ass pregnant by my nigga?" Taea asked coldly.

When Taea pointed the gun towards Carissa, I knew shit was about to get real.

"Don't point that shit at me, put your gun away because if you don't, I swear I ain't going to tell you not a damn thing," Carissa replied.

Taea grabbed Carissa by her navy-blue dress and stared her in her eyes.

"Look, bitch, you going to fucking talk because if you don't, you will find yourself with a bullet in the head."

Carissa tried to push Taea off of her, but Taea didn't budge.

I guess Carissa finally began to realize that Taea wasn't to be toyed with because all the attitude changed instantly and I saw nothing but fear in her eyes.

"I'm not pregnant. I just told him that so he would leave you and be with me," Carissa stammered fearfully.

I could tell by how Carissa was looking and speaking that

the hoe was scared shitless. She had every right to be scared if she knew what was going to happen to her.

"But he ain't leave me though, he decided to cut your ass off instead which pissed you off," Taea spat at Carissa.

Taea looked over at me, and I saw nothing but relief in her eyes. I knew that was all Taea had really wanted to know before she blew the bitch brains out. She wanted to know rather the rumor was true, did the nigga she love with all her heart get another bitch pregnant. I didn't know if Taea would have ever gotten over it if Carissa would have told her that she actually was. That was something I knew would tear Taea's heart into tiny pieces. Getting over someone cheating on you was hard but finding out they had gotten the hoe pregnant was something that not just anyone can get over, it took time to process and to figure out what was going to happen next.

"You know I wanted nothing more than to whoop your ass for fucking with my man and getting knocked up by him, but once I found out that your ass was responsible for my nigga being laid up in the hospital, I knew an ass whooping wasn't going to make any of this shit go away. Just because you couldn't have him, you ain't want him to be with anyone else, including the bitch that he belonged to. You one selfish bitch because Jon don't even belong to your trifling ass. That nigga belongs to me, he is my fucking man, I've put three years into what we have, and I'm not about to let you or any other hoe come between what we have!" Taea screamed

Carissa jumped off the couch and pushed Taea hard enough to make Taea fall back for a brief moment. I guess she thought she was going to make a quick exit but Carissa life was about to end, it wasn't no escaping it.

The push was unexpected which knocked Taea's gun out of her hand. Carissa hurried to pick up the gun that had fallen to the floor. She pointed the gun at Taea and was ready to pull the trigger, but I was faster.

Pow.

And that's when Carissa fell to the floor hollering in pain. I had shot that hoe right in her leg just to slow her ass down so Taea could finish what she came here to do. If I wanted to, I could have easily killed her right then, but I decided against it. I knew how much it meant for Taea to make Carissa pay for what she had done.

Taea didn't show Carissa any mercy. She beat the fuck out of her ass. Blood was being smeared everywhere. Tables and chairs were being smashed, and I stood there and watched in awe. I let all that hate and anger that Taea had pent up inside unleash itself. I wasn't about to step in between any of it unless Taea really needed me again. Shooting Carissa was mandatory because I wasn't about to let Carissa take my cousin up out of here.

Furniture was being knocked over, and the living room was being destroyed but not once did Taea stop giving Carissa them hands. Even though Carissa was bigger than Taea that didn't stop Taea from beating the breaks off her ass. When Taea slammed Carissa over the glass coffee table glass shattered everywhere.

Carissa groaned in pain and Taea stared down at her.

"You should have left my fucking nigga alone, and you shouldn't have had Ken coming over here to take him out. Bitch you fucked up when you did that shit."

Carissa was just about to speak, but Taea cut that bitch off when she put two bullets in her head.

"Die, bitch," Taea said coldly.

I walked over to where Taea was standing and kicked Carissa with my feet to make sure she was dead.

"She's dead," I muttered to Taea.

"Good, now let's head home," Taea replied.

Taea and I both ran out of Carissa's apartment and hopped back into my car. I sped back into the main street and swirled in and out and of traffic. Neither one of us spoke, the car was quiet as hell, all was heard was the hum of my engine.

Fifteen minutes later we were pulling up at my crib. I grabbed my food out of the backseat and followed Taea up the stairs towards my house. As soon as we made it inside, Taea headed towards the bathroom.

"I'ma be right back. I need to clean myself up," Taea said.

I nodded my head at her and headed into the kitchen, so I could heat the rest of my food up. Shid, a bitch had worked up an appetite now. After my food had been warmed up, I took a seat in my lazy boy chair and took a bite of my steak while I waited for Taea to reappear. She came out of the bathroom a few moments later with a blank expression on her face.

"Bitch, I know damn well your ass ain't sitting here eating after what we just did."

"What the fuck that got to do with me? Shid, a bitch still got to eat," I told Taea as I continued to chew on my steak.

Taea laughed and flopped down on my couch.

"Do you feel better now that you know Carissa is gone? I asked Taea gently.

"Yes, Carissa is finally out of the picture. I ain't got to worry about that hoe ever again."

"And KeKe thotting ass is gone too, I bet she in hell getting ready to thot down there too," I joked.

Taea and I laughed until tears fell down from our eyes.

"Now the only person we have left is Ken's crew and then Ken himself," Taea added.

"Are we going to let Quan and Jon kill Ken?"

"Hell no, we gonna murk his ass for them. We have no time to waste, Ken's time is up."

"I agree with you," I said to Taea, as I chewed the last bit of my food.

I got up and put my to-go box in the trash and took a seat back in the lazy boy chair.

"I just want to tell you thank you for tonight. You really were looking out for my ass. That little bitch could have really shot me if you hadn't been fast enough to shoot her ass in the leg." Taea said softly.

"You're my day one, you're my family. There was no way I was about to let that bitch shoot you," I told her emotionally.

For the rest of the night, Tae and I both came up with the perfect plan to execute Ken's crew. We were going to knock every last one of them bitches off the map. All we had to do was go to their spot which I was going find out from either Quan or Jon. They knew where Ken hung out at. Wherever Ken was his crew was nearby.

Ken only had five niggas who were in his crew who hadn't folded on him and who did everything he fucking said, so it wasn't going to be too hard to take them out. With Taea with me, it wouldn't take long to blast their asses. Even though the crew wasn't there when Ken tried to kill Quan and Jon the fact that they belonged to his crew automatically made them an enemy. It was a priority that we killed his crew first because if we went for Ken first, we knew it was only going to start a war between Westside and Northside. After we eliminated the niggas who rode with Ken then after Ken was killed there wasn't going to be no more bloodshed.

The plan was going to be simple. Find out the location that they hung out at and light that bitch on fire.

Taea and I weren't going to rest until Ken, and his crew were dead.

QUAN

THE NEXT DAY...

There was no way I was going to continue to lay up in this fucking hospital bed any longer. I wanted to go check on Jon just to see how he was doing. Even though I still had my jaw wired shut I wasn't about to let that shit stop me. I pulled the covers from off my body and groaned in pain. I was hurting, but it wasn't no point in calling for pain meds. I rather suffer in pain then to fuck around and get addicted to the strong medication that the doctors where giving me. So many times, you saw people who had been in accidents being put on high levels of pain medication and becoming addicted.

I didn't want that for myself. Whenever I was released, I wanted to be free to live my life and start back over. I had a business to run and being hooked on pain pills wasn't going to fit into the drug lifestyle that I was living. Yeah, I sold dope and pills, but I didn't use any of that shit that I sold on the streets to the fiends and crack heads. I smoked weed and that was all I was ever going to put in my system. All that other shit was for the birds.

I put both feet on the floor and slowly
and that's when my nurse for that day can

"Where are you trying to go? Mr. Jo
you."

I didn't say nothing to her, I was determined to do it on my
own. I gripped my IV pole tightly and stood on both of my shaky feet. The nurse rushed over to me and tried to talk me into getting back in bed but I shook my head at her and grabbed my clipboard, so I could write out where I was trying to go.

"I need to see my partner Jontavian Monts. He's also in this hospital, let me know where his room at."

The nurse read my clipboard and stared at me as if she was wondering if it was in my best interest to be wondering the hallways.

"You aren't in the condition to leave your room, but I will go check with the main nurse to see where your friend is at," the nurse replied gently.

I watched her as she walked out of my room and headed to the front desk that was located not far from my room.

The nurse today was someone new. I had never seen her before. It seemed that every day I had someone knew who was assigned to me. She was a white woman, with short blond hair. She was tall, slim, and looked to be in her early forties. She seemed to be nice and helpful, so I only prayed she let me have this one request.

She came back a few moments later rolling a wheelchair with a small smile on her face.

"I found out your friend's room number, and I'm going to push you down there. Will you take a seat in the wheel chair for me? I don't want you losing your balance and falling."

I complied and slowly sat down in the wheelchair.

"Now before I take you to his room, I want to check your vitals and make sure everything is good."

I waited patiently as she did her morning tasks.

"Are you in any pain? Do you need any pain medication?"

I grabbed my marker and wrote down on my whiteboard that I was in pain, but I didn't want any more medication.

"Are you sure? I don't want you to be sitting here in pain if you're hurting.

It's bearable. If it gets intense, I will take something. I wrote on my whiteboard.

"Okay, let's go then," she told me.

I grabbed my IV-pole griped it tightly and had my white-board in my right hand, as she maneuvered me through the hospital hallway. Jon's room was located at the end of the ICU hallway. The nurse lightly knocked on Jon's closed door and waited for him to answer.

"Come in," I heard Jon say.

The nurse opened the wood door and wheeled me inside.

"Jontavian you have a visitor to see you."

The nurse pushed me over by his bed and told me that she was going to give me ten minutes to talk with Jon and then she was coming back to pick me up.

I nodded my head to let her know that I understood.

"Quan, you good bruh?" Jon asked me with pain in his eyes.

I scribbled down that I was fine and asked him was he okay.

"I'm trying to fight this pain I'm in. Ken really fucked my ass up, and now your mouth all stitched up, and you can't talk. I'm just so ready to get out this damn hospital so I can put a bullet in his head."

I feel the same way as well, I hate the shit happened the way it did. The shit is fucked up. I scribbled down on my chalk.

"As soon as I get up out this bitch, you and me going to find that nigga and put him six feet deep," Jon grumbled.

I watched as Jon winced in pain.

Try to remain calm, if you keep getting upset you gonna be in here longer then you want to, stress is the last thing that you need to be doing, I scribbled on my whiteboard for him to read.

Jon looked like he was doing okay, but I knew deep down he was hurting and in so much pain.

"Have you spoken to Yanni and Taea, last time I spoke to Taea she was talking about killing Carissa, Ken's crew, KeKe, and Ken?" Jon asked

Yep, Yanni made that shit clear as well. You think they going to do it? I scribbled down.

"If both of them find them, I guarantee you that they going to dead all of them no questions asked," Jon replied truthfully.

I agreed with him on that situation. No matter how much I tried to talk them out of it they weren't going to let the shit go, they weren't going to stop until Ken, and the others wasn't breathing again.

Just mentioning Yanni brought back all the loving memories that she and I shared together. I smiled for the first time that day, and it was all because I was thinking about Yanni. I couldn't wait to see her again, to hold her in my arms and tell her how much I loved her. I know that Jon was feeling the same way. My thoughts were interrupted when Jon began talking about Yanni, Taea, and the Ken situation. I didn't have time to daydream about the past I had to think and worry about the future that Yanni and I were fighting to have with one another.

"I'm not too much worried, but I did tell Gangsta G them to keep an eye out for them. I know how Taea is when she has made up her mind about some shit to get done. It's no persuading her ass otherwise. She made up her mind that she going to eliminate Carissa as well."

I sat there and listened as he explained everything to me. I was far from shocked because I knew that the only way Taea was ever going to be able to move on and be happy was if she eliminated Carissa from Jon's life, it didn't matter if she was pregnant or not, the bitch had to go.

I scribbled down on the whiteboard and told him some real shit.

When we get out of this bitch, I swear the first thing we need to do is marry our girls. They have put up with so much shit, and all I want to do is live the rest of my life a loyal and faithful nigga. I thought I was going to fucking die, but the man above spared my life. I just want to do shit the right way. We were given a second chance at life. I think we need to try to take that shit to when it comes to Yanni and Taea.

"I agree with you. We only have one life to live; it's time we started living it. The only bitch I want is Taea, I ain't never cheating again. I don't even wanna look at another bitch. I just want Taea, and I want to put a baby in her. Taea always wanted kids, and we've tried to no success, but I'm going to give my baby what she wants," Jon said as he stared up at the ceiling.

I nodded my head at him because I agreed.

Jon and I sat and talked for a few more minutes before a soft knock came at the door. I turned around, and there stood Yanni and Taea staring at us both.

"I went by your room, but you weren't there," Yanni told me as she walked over to me.

I could smell her Channel five perfume even before she walked over to me. She planted a kiss on my right side of my face before pulling away from me. Taea was already by Jon's side smiling and kissing on him. I felt nothing but love in the room. After Jon and Taea broke their kiss Jon asked Yanni and Taea was everything okay.

Yanni looked over at Taea.

I knew they had some shit to tell Jon and me, but I had no

clue what it was. I didn't have to wait long to find out because Yanni told everything that Jon and I needed to know.

"We found Carissa and KeKe," Yanni said.

Jon's eyes seemed to widen.

My heart began to beat as I waited for Yanni to tell us more.

"I killed KeKe on her way going to the corner store. I shot her a few times and ran her ass over. I had to make sure that hoe was dead. After we got done with KeKe, we headed to the Westside to where Carissa live. I kicked her door in, and Taea whooped her ass and shot her in the head. Turns out Carissa, was never pregnant; she only lied to keep you," Yanni told Jon.

I looked over at Jon, and for the first time, I saw nothing but relief. It was as if a weight had been lifted off his shoulder.

I sucked in my breath. I already knew without looking at Yanni and Taea that they weren't going to rest until everyone was dead. They were only heating up with Carissa and KeKe, it was really about to get messy soon.

"Taea," Jon said gently.

"It had to be done, the bitch nearly got you killed, there was no way I could let the hoe live after that shit."

"I respect that," Jon replied truthfully.

He reached up to embrace her in a tight hug.

"I love you, I'm so sorry I did this to us," he choked out emotionally.

"I forgive you, Jon, I really do, but don't ever let this shit happen again," Taea told him emotionally.

"I put that shit on my life, it's never going to happen again," Jon replied seriously.

Yanni and I stared as Taea and Jon embraced and made their promises to each other.

I stared up at Yanni, and our eyes spoke volumes. She knew just how sorry I was and just how much I loved her. There were so many bitches that I had fucked, but neither one of them could make my soul move like Yanni. None of them was ever going to have my back like Yanni. I had never in my life been loyal to a bitch, but the love that Yanni and I had required it. My thoughts of love and loyalty quickly were pushed to my back of my brain when I overheard Yanni asking Jon about Ken and his crew.

Jon seemed to be in deep thought as he rubbed his hands over his facial hair. I grabbed my whiteboard and quickly wrote down that I didn't want Yanni or Taea to go searching for Ken. I wanted them to both wait until Jon, and I was released from the hospital. I groaned and lifted the whiteboard in the air to get everyone's attention. Even though I knew Taea and Yanni had taken out Carissa and KeKe and could very well take out Ken and the crew too, something in my heart didn't want them to do that shit by themselves. If something happened to either one of them, shit would never be the same ever again.

Yanni and Taea read my message, but completely ignored everything that I said.

"Quan, I don't care what you say, Taea and I are going to find Ken and put a bullet in his head. You can say whatever you want to say, but that shit isn't going to stop either one of us. I'm your bitch, I'm your day one, I'm loyal to you, and I'm not going to sit here and let this nigga get away with what he did to you or Jon. I want him dead, and I want him dead asap. There is no more waiting. The wait is fucking over, it's time to take action."

During this whole time, Jon didn't speak, he only listened as Yanni broke everything down. When she finished her speech, her and Taea stared at us to wait to see what we were going to say.

"Look, I'm tired of fussing about this shit with ya'll, do what the fuck ya'll want, but I know one thing, neither one of ya'll better not get hurt, ya'll better make it out of there alive because if you don't, we going to be pissed. Ya'll stick together and watch your fucking back," Jon said irritably.

"We know what to do Jon," Yanni and Taea told him defensively.

"Me and Taea needed to know where to find Ken and his crew. I know you ain't never fucked with him on that level, but I know you have to know where to find him and his crew though?"

I cut my eyes at Jon, he nodded his head and gave them the information that they needed.

TAEA

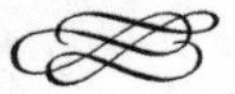

TWO DAYS LATER ...

The bright sun woke me up from a deep sleep. I rolled over to yet again an empty bed. I groaned as I pulled the covers over my head. I wanted Jon back home with me, but he was still recovering from his injuries. I prayed every night and morning for Jon and Quan to be sent home and still, nothing had changed. Neither doctor knew when they were going to release either one.

I pulled the covers off of me and decided that maybe if I talked to Jon's doctor about having an in-home nurse, then maybe just maybe his doctor would let him be released. The fact that Jon's doctor knew that no man stayed with us but me, was probably some of the reason why he wouldn't let him leave either. He knew I had to work and wasn't going to be able to give Jon around the clock care. I may not be able to care for him 24/7, but I was willing to pay someone for it. The thought seemed like a good one, and maybe when I saw Yanni later today, I was going to run that idea through her. I knew she was probably having a hard time without Quan.

I slid out of my California King bed and headed towards the bathroom so I could take care of my hygiene. As I stood in the steaming hot shower, I let the water beat down on my tired body as many thoughts began to run through my brain. I needed to know the perfect way to run up on Ken and his crew in surprise. I needed the right type of guns to get the job down as well. A machine gun seemed like the perfect selection since we were trying to murk more than two people. We were trying to wipe out a damn crew and needed the right amount of ammunition and gun power to get the job done the first time. I ain't want to leave no nigga alive to be able to come back and get revenge. Yanni and I both had to make sure everyone was dead before we left the scene.

I scrubbed my body clean and closed my eyes tightly as I washed the soap suds off my body. Thirty minutes later I was stepping out the shower with a plan. Jon had told us that Ken and the crew always liked to gamble at his crib on Friday nights. Today was Friday and tonight seemed like the perfect time to get the shit over with.

After stepping out of the shower, I hurried to dry myself off. I took care of my oral hygiene and brushed my hair into a low ponytail. I grabbed my phone off my bed and hit Yanni up.

"Yeah," Yanni said sleepily into the phone.

"Bitch get your ass up; I got a plan."

Yanni chuckled.

I could hear her moving like she was getting up.

"Pull up, we got some shit to discuss."

"Let me get clean, and I will be over there," Yanni retorted.

"Cool, see you then," I told her before hanging up my phone.

I threw my phone on the bed and hurried to find me some clothes to put on for that day. I grabbed the first thing that I felt like would match. I wasn't in the mood to dig through all the clothes that I had in my closet to try to find anything else.

I slid on a pair of white Nike shorts, a pair of Nike black socks, with my black Nike's. I grabbed a plain V-neck black shirt from out of my closet and hurried to put it on. I lotioned my legs and put on one coat of pink lipstick on my lips. I stared at myself in the mirror and was satisfied with what I saw. Yeah, I was suffering emotionally with Jon gone, but a girl was still looking sexy as hell, didn't let that shit show on my face at least.

I grabbed my phone off my bed and took a few pictures of myself before I decided it was time to call Taco Bell to let them know that wasn't going to be able to work that day. Normally I took my ass to work every day, but I already knew I had too much shit to do tonight, working was only going to get in the way of all that shit.

Taco Bell phone rung close to five times before someone finally answered.

"Taco Bell, how can I help you?"

Just hearing Mookie's voice in my ear made me roll my eyes.

I hoped this bitch wasn't on this fuck shit today because I didn't mind by getting in my fucking car and coming up there and beating her ass.

"Um this Taea, I just wanted to call to let you know that I'm not going to able to make it tonight. I have a family emergency."

Mookie snorted and seemed to be rustling some paper in the background.

"I'm looking at your attendance and lately you been coming late or not at all. I told you last time that I don't care about your family emergencies, your shift is tonight and it's one of the busiest nights. We need you to be here."

"I'm not able to come if I could come you should know

that I would be there," I told her with a little bit too much attitude.

I just hated that the bitch made it seem that I never hardly came to work. Mookie knew exactly what to do to get under my skin, and she was doing it at that very moment.

"Taea, I'm going to make some shit clear. Either you come to work tonight, or you're fired. Don't come back if you ain't coming tonight."

"You know what Mookie, fuck you and this pissy ass job, I'm done. I won't be coming in," I told her nastily before hanging up on her ass.

I was fuming at first, and I had to try to calm my little ass down. I swear she worked my nerves but never again because she was out of my life. I was in need of a strong ass blunt and was on the verge of digging in Jon's stash when I heard knocking at the door. I already knew without looking outside that it was Yanni. I pulled the door open, and there stood my cousin dressed in red and blue from head to toe. She had on a pair of red shorts, a blue and red top, with a pair of red Air Forces. I stepped aside to let her in and closed the door behind her.

Yanni threw her purse down on my couch and headed straight to the kitchen.

"Bitch, I need a fucking drink, my nerves shot this morning."

"Bitch I need me a blunt. I was just about to roll one, you want to smoke with me?" I asked her.

"Shid, fuck a drink. I'm down to smoke," Yanni replied.

I laughed as I headed to my bedroom and found Jon's stash in our bedroom.

I headed back towards the living room to find Yanni sitting down playing a game on her phone and sipping her a mixed drink.

"Bitch, I'm about to get you high today," I joked.

Yanni looked up and laughed. I separated the weed and rolled us a fat blunt and lit that shit. I took the first puff and passed it to her. Yanni inhaled then exhaled a few seconds later.

I sat back on the couch and tried to relax.

"I got a plan," I told Yanni seriously.

"Don't hold shit back, I want to know every fucking thing."

Yanni squinted her eyes at me through the weed smoke.

"So, you want to do this shit tonight?"

"Hell yeah, Jon said that on Friday's they gamble at Ken's crib. This will be the best time to have everyone in one place."

"Right, I see what you mean. You want to go through blasting?"

"Damn right. We need the machine guns for this hit right here."

"Hell yeah, I'm ready to light some shit up."

I rolled my eyes and inhaled the weed smoke.

"Okay, I'm high as fuck right now, so explain everything to me again," Yanni giggled.

"Omg, your ass only smoked half and you already high, you ain't nothing but a lightweight," I grabbed the blunt from her and began to slowly explain the plan to her again.

"Tonight, around eleven we gonna pull up at Ken's crib and light that bitch up."

"That plan sounds amazing," Yanni slurred.

I shook my head at her before taking the last puff of the blunt and putting it out.

"Enough about tonight, I got some shit to tell you."

"What?" Yanni asked curiously.

"Mookie basically fired my ass not too long ago."

"Hold the fuck up. Fired?" Yanni asked with a shocked expression on her face.

"Yes, Yanni fired. FIRED. I called in to tell her that I had a family emergency and that I couldn't come in later tonight, she started talking shit about me not coming to work as I should and calling out and that if I ain't come then, I was fired."

"That bitch lying, your ass always goes to work. We need to pull up on her ass and show out."

"I know she lying, I wanted to ride up there and beat her ass, but you know what, I'm going to leave that shit alone. I ain't got time for that drama. I can find another job Yanni, but if I go up there and show my ass and beat the shit out of Mookie, I swear I'ma try to kill that hoe."

"I understand what you mean," Yanni told me before standing up and putting her empty glass in the sink.

"Don't worry about any of that shit, you don't need that job anyway. If you want, I can easily get you on working out there with me."

"Um, nall boo, I'm good, I don't do old people."

Yanni chuckled.

"Shid, it ain't that bad though."

"It ain't for me though," I told Yanni honestly.

"Right, I get that. Well, I'm saying if you can't find nothing, we got some positions available. You don't have to do CNA work you can do the cleaning and washing the clothes etc. Money is money boo."

"You right, I'm going to see what I can do first, thanks Yanni."

"You're welcome, you know I got you."

I kicked my shoes off and was just about to get comfortable when my phone began to vibrate in my pocket. I pulled it out and stared at it with a frown on my face when I noticed that it was my mama calling me. I was debating if I should even pick up or not. I finally decided to pick up just to see what she wanted.

Yanni stared over at me and must have noticed the serious expression on my face because she put her phone down and tried to lean over to hear who I was talking to.

"What you want Tanya?"

"I'm just calling to check on you, I ain't heard from you or seen you in over a month."

"Maybe if you laid off the drugs I would come around."

Tanya became quiet.

"I don't know why you hate me so much?"

"Because you were a fucked up ass parent Tanya and you still is fucked up. All you ever cared about was getting high. You never gave a fuck about me or my well-being so if you wondering why I never call or come see you it's because you don't mean shit to me. You dead to me. I'm treating you just how you treated me when I was growing up."

I could hear her crying over the phone which didn't even move me. She had played this role for so long that I didn't even let the tears get to me. Instead, I acted like I didn't even hear it.

"I got to go mama. If you calling for money for you and Lisa to get high with, I don't have any for you."

"Wait don't hang up. I ain't call you for money."

"Then why you called me?" I asked her suspiciously.

The phone got silent.

"Tanya," I called out.

"I'm still here," Tanya replied weakly.

"Stop playing games with me because I will hang up on your ass."

"No games, baby girl. I'm trying to do better with my life. I know I fucked up so much shit and I just want to turn my life around. I don't want to die with you hating me. I just wanted to call to tell you that I'm standing in front of the rehab center in Atlanta. I'm going to be here for a while."

My mouth dropped open. Never had she ever checked herself into a rehab center. Yanni must have noticed that my facial expression had changed because she leaned farther over to where I was at so she could listen. I took the phone from my ear and put it on speaker so Yanni could hear everything that was being said. Tanya went into detail about the rehab center that she was at and I listened not interrupting her.

"I just want to tell you how sorry I am Taea, I hope one day that you can forgive me. I want to get clean, I want a better life, and I want you to be a part of it."

For the first time in years tears fell down my cheeks. Tanya wasn't lying, this bitch was on some real shit, she was really ready to finally change. I had been waiting for this shit to happen for years and finally it was happening. My tongue was tied and I couldn't find the words to speak right then, so Yanni took it upon herself to tell my mother everything that I couldn't tell her.

For six months my mama was going to be in rehab, and she wasn't alone. Yanni's mama Lisa was there with her. She had already checked herself in and Yanni had no clue of it. I could see the hurt in Yanni's eyes when she learned that Lisa didn't reach out to her before she checked herself into the rehab center.

When Tanya told Yanni that Lisa didn't want to tell her until she had completed the program Yanni understood. That was just how Lisa wanted to do things. They both had been on drugs together and they finally were both going to get off of them together and at the end of the day that was all that mattered.

"Ain't God good?" Yanni asked as I hung up the phone with Tanya.

"He too damn good, he finally answered my prayers."

"Hopefully in six months both of our mamas were going

to come back home and be clean and ready to move on with their lives," Yanni said emotionally.

"All we can do is hope and pray that six months from now they come home drug-free without the urge to get high."

Yanni sighed but agreed with me. She grabbed the remote off the coffee table and flipped on the T.V to see if she could find something to watch. After flipping through the channels for a few moments, she finally found LMN. I sat back and cuddled up on my couch as I watched the movie. It wasn't long before I found myself dosing off into a deep sleep.

YANNI

LATER THAT NIGHT....

I was having a nasty dream that I was sucking Quan's dick when Taea shook my ass and told me to get up. I was slick pissed because I was at the point that Quan was about to nut and I ain't get to see the end result. Just imagine not being able to fuck your nigga. I couldn't even remember the last time we had even had sex. So much shit had popped off with me putting him out, and then him being shot, that sex was the last thing on that I thought about, but now my body needed a release. Instead of harping on it, I wiped the drool that had fallen from my mouth.

"Damn bitch, your ass was sleeping hard as hell, sorry to wake you, but it's about that time."

"Ugh," I groaned as I sat up and stretched my limbs.

Taea and I had fallen to sleep watching LMN on the couch, and now my damn back and shoulders were slightly hurting.

"You up here moaning and groaning like an old lady," Taea joked.

"I'm never going to sleep on your couch again. Bitch my

whole body in pain, I feel like them old folks in the nursing home when they be complaining about their arthritis."

Taea laughed.

"How long your ass been up?"

"I been up a good ten minutes? I was getting the guns situated while you slept."

She threw me a black ski mask, and I gently put it over my head. The eyes, nose, and lips were cut out. I applied a little CarMax to my lips as Taea pulled her ski mask over her face. I pulled out my phone and noticed that it was close to eleven pm.

"Let's gone and get this shit over with because a bitch is tired," I mumbled.

Taea nodded her head in understanding.

She handed me one of Jon's machine guns and told me that everything had been loaded. All you gotta do is aim and shoot on sight.

"Do you really think we need machine guns?" I asked quizzically

"Better safe than sorry," Taea replied before grabbing her keys off the table by her front door and walking out of the house. I grabbed the heavy machine gun that she had given me and followed Taea out the door and hopped in her car. I slid the machine gun on the floor next to me while Taea slid hers in the backseat of the car.

Gucci Mane started blasting from the speakers as soon as Taea crunk her car up. She pulled onto the highway cruising slowly towards Westside. She made sure not to draw attention to herself due to the fact we had two guns in the damn car. We ain't want no police pulling us over. We didn't want them type of problems. The type of bitch that Taea and I were, we weren't about to let no police catch up with no weapons. We weren't about to pull over, hell nall if they wanted to pull us over, they were going to have to chase our asses. Rarely did Taea ever drive the damn speed limit but tonight was different.

"Are you okay over there?" Taea asked as she gripped the steering wheel.

"I'm okay, it's just I don't know. I have never done no shit like this before. I ain't never had to take a nigga's life, but killed KeKe without thinking twice."

"I understand what you mean," Taea replied slowly.

"I ain't never killed no one before Carissa, but I knew it was necessary to do because if I didn't shit was really going to get worse. She wasn't going to stop until she had my nigga all to herself or sadly kill him because he ain't want her in that way. Ken has to die. We can't let him live because if he does, shit ain't going to get no better, next time he runs up on Quan and Jon unexpected, they might not come out so lucky. They gonna be dead and once you die, you never coming back. I don't want to lose my man and I am willing to do whatever to protect what's mine, if that means killing someone then I was willing to do just that." Taea said sternly.

I understood what Taea was telling me because I felt the same damn way. It was time for me to get my hands dirty and it was something that I was doing because I loved my nigga just that fucking much, but at the same time, I knew this wasn't who I was. This was a sacrifice that I was making.

Fifteen minutes later we were pulling up at the address that Jon had given us. We parked down the road from his house, and Taea cut the engine. We sat there as if we were trying to figure out what to do next. We both knew what needed to be done, but neither one attempted to step out of the car.

"It shouldn't have come to this, but it did," Taea muttered under her breath.

Let's get this over the with," I told Taea.

We both stepped out the car with our guns right by our

side. Taea grabbed me by the hand and stopped me in my tracks.

"I want to do something different this time."

"What is that?" I asked her quizzically.

"Let us pray, just in case."

"Do you think that shit is even necessary. If you do die, do honestly believe we going to heaven after killing people.

Taea smirked.

"You gotta believe that we are and maybe we will."

I rolled my eyes but said a prayer with her if it made her feel better. After we had finished praying, we jogged toward Ken's front yard that had numerous cars parked in the drive way.

"Looks like everyone is here," I whispered to Taea.

"Everything is going as planned so far," I whispered to Taea.

Taea and I were just about to jog towards his porch so we could shoot Ken's front door off the hinges but got distracted when we heard someone call both our names. I turned around and was stunned to see Gangsta G, Mike Mike, and Richie Boy, running up towards us.

"What in the hell ya'll doing here?" I asked them with a confused expression on my face.

Gangsta G, Mike Mike, and Richie Boy had seemed to appear out of nowhere. They were all dressed in black and had their ski masks covering their face, but left their eyes and mouths exposed. I knew instantly who they were running up on us, without either one of them saying anything to me. Gangsta G muscular ass was the first one who I spotted before any of the others.

"Jon or either Quan must have ordered ya'll to come along? That's the only explanation for why ya'll here, and that can't be the reason because we ain't tell either of them when we were coming."

Gangsta G looked at us and whistled.

"Jon gave us the signal to look out for ya'll so that's what we going to do," Gangsta G told us.

"Look, that's cool. We ain't even mad. Let's split up, someone needs to cover the back and the front while we all go in," Taea told Gangsta G.

"Mike Mike, go to the back and make sure nobody gets pass you, Richie Boy I want you to cover the front of the house," Gangsta G ordered.

The way that Ken's house was set up his yard wasn't very big. That was because he had a basic ass house, nothing fancy, just a place that he sold his dope out of. The house only had a fence tall enough that no one could jump over. I understood the jealousy that Ken must been feeling all these years, but they always said if you couldn't beat them then join them. But Ken had never been interested in that, so with jealousy was coming bloodshed. It was time to take him out of his misery because he never was going to have that number one spot.

"I'm coming in with you to help ya'll out. Be careful and keep your eyes and ears open. When the gunshots started, everyone going to try to flee, don't let any of them get behind you or an opportunity for them to shoot you." Gangsta G warned us.

"What about the neighbors want they hear the gunfire?" I asked Gangsta G curiously.

"Yes, they may hear something, but I doubt it, all the lights are cut out so I assume either they sleep or out. The houses in this neighborhood are spaced out enough to keep sound at a minimal. So, I don't believe nobody going to hear and call the police as fast as you may think," Gangsta G assured me."

"Are ya'll ready?" Gangsta G asked.

Taea and I stared at one another and nodded our heads towards Gangsta G.

"Let's get into position," Gangsta G told the crew.

Richie Boy and Mike Mike jogged towards their positions, and Gangsta G gave us the signal to take a step back while he busted through the front door.

I gripped my gun tightly with my sweaty hands. The hate I had in my heart was strong for Ken, but I wasn't a killer by nature. It was necessary to pull this trigger since this was the man who was responsible for my pain and nearly killing Quan. This was the only thing that was going to get me through this shit. As we neared the porch of Ken's house, loud music seemed to be blasting from the inside, which let us knew that either they were alone or they were having some type of party. Well if they were having a damn party, the party was about to be crashed.

As I was getting my mind right, Gangsta G kicked Ken's door in with his boot. I aimed my gun and came face to face with Ken's crew, they were snorting and smoking. They were caught off guard which was good for us. They didn't even have time to grab their guns before we let the bullets start flying.

Rat It Tat, Rat It Tat, Rat It Tat.

Tat It Tat, Tat It Tat, Tat It Tat.

Taea went on one side, and I went on the other. Little did either of us know that Ken's crew wasn't there alone. There were others that were in the house, and they were indeed having some sort of party, but us seeing that didn't deter us of our plan. Ken was considered to be our enemy and whoever was there in his damn house had to be close to him so in that case, they were going to catch these bullets as well.

As the bullets began flying people started running and screaming, some shots were fired back at us, but Taea and I took cover as well as Gangsta G. Taea didn't show anyone any mercy, this bitch was aiming at everyone which meant she was thinking like me. Ken was our enemy and whoever was in his house was considered our enemy as well. When the gunfire finally seized there were nearly fifteen people that we had killed.

Gangsta G went through every room of the house in search of Ken because he wasn't one of the fifteen that was now dead. Gangsta G told us that he had to make sure that Ken wasn't nowhere hiding out, but after waiting over five minutes for Gangsta G to search the house, he came back to the living room empty handed. I stepped over a body and started helping Taea count Ken's crew that had been shot. We all breathed a sigh of relief when all five of Ken's crew was identified by Gangsta G.

Even though Taea and I had seen all five of Ken's crew on a few occasions. They were always with Ken and following him around like he was their master. So even though we knew them by face, we still wanted to make sure that we popped every last one of them niggas. We didn't want any fuck ups that would lead back to us. The smell of drugs and blood filled the air was beginning to cause a foul odor, which was making my head spin. I didn't dare sit on the blood-stained couch. Instead I stepped over the blood that was on the floor and followed Gangsta G and Taea out of the house.

"Do anyone have any idea where Ken could be at?" I asked no one in particular.

"Well, we all know he ain't escape so apparently he ain't here or had just left before we pulled up," Taea muttered under her breath.

Richie Boy and Mike Mike jogged over to where we were posted up at on the porch.

"I know he's going to come back, he got to, he left all them people in his house," Gangsta G said as he pulled on his goatee.

Everyone agreed.

"I'm not going back in that house, I swear I feel as if I want to throw up," I complained.

Gangsta G chuckled.

"Amateur," he joked.

I rolled my eyes.

"I got a weak stomach," I defended myself.

"This ain't a bitch's job anyway, so seeing ya'll both out here, lets me know just how much ya'll committed to ya'll niggas. Right or Wrong ya'll both putting ya'll lives at risk, that's real love right there."

He looked down at me and Taea's heavy machine guns and grabbed it from us.

"I don't want ya'll to hurt ya'll selves. I know you know how to work it and all but you got my ass feeling some type of way with ya'll carrying this shit. I got two more pistols I keep in my car, let me go get them for you," he told Taea and me.

Taea and I stood there as Gangsta jogged to his car that was parked a few houses down from Ken's house. I watched as he popped the trunk of his car. He threw the two machine guns in the trunk and grabbed two pistols and jogged back towards us and handed them to us.

"Okay, I know how much ya'll want to murk Ken, so Mike Mike, Richie Boy, and I are only going to stand by just for protection we ain't going to fuck with him, we going to let ya'll handle that shit. If something goes wrong, we got ya'll back."

Taea and I both nodded our heads to let him know that we understood.

Since you ain't going back in the house, keep a lookout and let me know when you see some headlights coming," Gangsta G instructed me.

"I will make sure to yell out to let you know when I see headlights," I told Gangsta G.

Mike Mike, Gangsta G, and Richie Boy headed back inside and closed the half-busted door shut behind them. I stood out there on the porch in silence with Taea standing next to me.

The silence was finally broken when Taea began to talk.

"We did good back there, it's good that Gangsta G and the crew came. Neither one of us was expecting them to have that many folks in the house."

I nodded my head but didn't speak.

"Are you okay? Are you still shook about what just happened?" Taea asked.

"No, I'm not shook, I just thought that I couldn't do it, but I did, and I don't feel bad about any of it. I'm just waiting for Ken to reappear. I can taste the revenge on my tongue. My heart will rejoice when he dies."

"Mine will too, but looks like the moment is finally about to come here come some headlights, Taea informed me.

I grabbed her by the arm, and we ran inside the house to get into position.

"I see headlights," I told everyone as I gently closed the door up behind me.

Taea and I positioned ourselves as well as Richie Boy, Mike Mike, and Gangsta G. The headlights of Ken's car lit up the living room as Taea, and I hid behind his long living room curtains which were right next to the front door that Ken was soon about to push open. We had the perfect hiding spot because he never was going to see either one of us coming.

When the car door slammed shut, my heart began to beat erratically. I had been waiting on this shit for so long, and finally, it was about to happen. A few moments later, the door opened, and I was the first bitch who jumped out gun drawn. Ken didn't stand a fucking chance with me. He didn't even have time to pull his pistol out from his hip.

"If you move one fucking inch, I swear I will load your body with these fucking bullets."

"What the fuck happened?" Ken asked in an enraged voice when he noticed his crew and everyone in his house was dead.

"None of this shit would have ever happened if you wouldn't have tried to kill Jon or Quan," Taea replied nastily as she stepped from out her hiding place.

If Ken even thought for one moment that he could beat Taea and me because we were some bitches all them thoughts was shot dead because that's when Gangsta G, Mike Mike, and Richie Boy made themselves visible.

"Come sit your stupid ass down," Gangsta G demanded him.

"I'm not sitting no fucking where; you didn't even have to kill my fucking crew they ain't have shit to do with it," Ken spat angrily.

I laughed evilly.

"We ain't just kill your crew, we killed your lying ass sister first, then we killed that little hoe, Carissa. The crew had everything to do with it, anyone who dealt with you had everything to do with it. I'm a street bitch nigga but work a nine to five job. I know how this shit works, if we would have come for you, and not offed them first they were going to come for all of us, and it was going to be a bloody war in Warner Robins, we don't want none of them problems, nigga. Your crew had to go, and anyone in this trashy ass house had to go right along with them." Taea spat

Ken was about to speak, but Taea interrupted him.

"Look, nigga, I got shit I got to do, I need to hurry home and get some sleep so I can go visit my nigga in the fucking hospital in the damn morning. Your stupid ass wanted to off Quan and Jon so bad, but you were sloppy with the shit, both lived and was able to come tell us what exactly happened. I know you ain't believe that hoe ass thotting sister of yours when she told you Quan hit her ass. Quan ain't touch that hoe, it was me, I beat that hoe ass because she was in my house and was talking hella shit about she had fucked my damn man. You knew that hoe was lying, but you wanted to use that for a motive. Then you get Carissa involved, you thought ya'll was so fucking smart, but ya'll was far from it. I wouldn't even call your ass a street nigga. It don't matter how much you wanted to replace Quan and Jon in these streets, even if you would have offed them both, your product is trash, and you don't know they fucking connect to get the information to their plug, so what was killing them was going to do, but cause you even more problems. Now do what the fuck Gangsta G said, take a seat on that blood-soaked couch so we can have a fucking chat." Taea said crossly.

Ken moved slowly towards the couch and took a seat.

Taea and I stared at each other, and I nodded my head that she could take over from there.

Gangsta G now had his gun pointed to the pack of his head while Mike Mike and Richie Boy had their gun pointed at the side of his head. Ken knew his time was up, he knew he was going to die, he was outnumbered and there was no way that he could get to his gun in time to blast anyone without being killed instantly.

"You killed Carissa and KeKe?" Ken asked emotionally.

"Nigga you think this a game? I told your ass KeKe and Carissa are dead. Matter fact Yanni shot your sister and ran her ass over. That bitch is dead dead. I killed your little Mexican bitch Carissa, the bitch had to go, she fucked with the wrong nigga and had the nerve to lie about being pregnant with my nigga's baby. The fact that she set Jon up, really sealed the deal with her life," Taea spat at him.

Ken didn't speak, but I saw the horror in his face and the sadness in his eyes.

I chuckled.

"I can't believe that Quan and Jon sent their bitches to do their dirty work," Ken stated in confusion.

"Let's clear some shit up first, Jon and Quan didn't send us, we sent ourselves, our niggas can't off you themselves, so we gonna do it for them. That's true love right there and loyalty right there," I told him seriously.

"I'm going down without a fight, Ken replied before grabbing his gun from his hip. He was about to pull the trigger before I shot him in his stomach."

I walked over to him and watched him as he started to bleed out on the blood-soaked couch.

"You shot my nigga in his fucking face and stomach, he didn't die, but you are about to."

"Any last words?" Taea asked him as she walked over beside me with her pistol aimed at his head.

"Fuck all ya'll," Ken said as blood spluttered from his mouth.

Taea and I didn't flinch once, as we blew his brains out, splattering it on Gangsta G.

"Shit, your ass can actually shoot, I should have known Quan and Jon had taught ya'll. He's definitely dead," Gangsta G said as he walked over to Ken and looked down at him.

"Damn, well everyone is dead in this bitch, so I'm about to dip," Richie Boy told us.

"Yep, it's time to dip, we don't want to stay too long," Mike Mike replied.

Everyone began to file out of the house except for Taea and me. She gripped my hand as we stared at Ken's dead body. Blood continued to spill out from his head wound, and the smell of death began to fill my nose.

"We finally did it, he's dead," Taea said softly.

I wasn't trusting myself to speak, so I remained silent.

"Come on, let's get out of here like Gangsta G said," Taea said softly.

Taea pulled me by my arm, and I followed her out the house. I broke out in a cold sweat as I stepped on the porch. It was only then that my brain began to process what had just happened. Gangsta G and the others were standing on the porch waiting on us to leave out the house. Me and Taea handed over the pistols he gave us, and we all headed back to our cars. As soon as Gangsta G made it to his car, he popped his trunk to give Taea and me back our two machine guns. I took both guns and told Taea to pop her trunk so I could lay them in there.

"Be safe," Gangsta G told Taea and me as I slammed the trunk down.

"Thanks for tonight," I told Gangsta G and the others.

Gansta G saluted me and hopped in the car and pulled off.

I slid into the passenger seat next to Taea just as she started her car.

"Let's head home and try to get some sleep, we got to go see Jon and Quan in the morning."

As Taea cruised through the neighborhood to get back to the main highway, I stared out the window, it was quiet, and everyone's lights were off, there was no movement at all. We had gotten in, did what was needed to be done, and had gotten out unnoticed. Whenever Ken was found, I already knew the police wasn't going to investigate it. They had no point in investigating, it as one last dope boy they had to catch and try to lock up. It was going to be an open and shut case, they probably were going to think that it was a drug deal that had gone bad or that Ken had crossed the plug which why he ended up dead.

It brought relief to me knowing that Carissa, Ken, KeKe, and his crew was now dead and there was no one left who would come for either of us, not even the law was going to be looking for our asses.

I closed my eyes just to rest them, but I knew there wasn't going to be any sleeping for me tonight.

QUAN

I had just finished eating breakfast and decided today I wanted to get out of the bed and actually get a little walking done. My wound was healing and knowing that information had me hyped to get my ass up and actually get a little exercise. I was finally getting to the point that I was able to go to the bathroom on my own without a nurse helping me out of bed. I slid out of the hospital bed and slowly walked to the bathroom where I took a leak and took care of my hygiene. I needed to shave badly, but I didn't have a way of getting to my shavers to trim myself up. Whenever Yanni came back through, I was going to make sure that she brought them from the house. I had never been the type to like a lot of hair on my face anyway, I kept my shit trimmed as well as my locks twisted. I rubbed my hands through my long locks, and I knew within a week I was going to have to get them retwisted.

After leaving the bathroom, a knock came at the door and then the sound of someone walking in. A few seconds later I spotted Gangsta G, and he was by himself. I gripped my IV cord tightly as he walked over to where I stood and dapped me up.

Gangsta G was dressed today in just a plain white t-shirt, with a pair of black shorts, and some white Air Forces. He wasn't rocking a hat, but he was rocking his silver jewelry with his silver grill that was made of silver diamonds.

I could tell just by looking at him that he was tired, but I was grateful that he was here because I was dying to know if Yanni and Taea were both okay. I ain't heard from either one of them since they last time seeing them in Jon's room when they were trying to find out where Ken lived.

"What up Bruh? How you feeling? I see you up and moving around, so I see you probably feeling somewhat better."

I still had my mouth bandaged so I still couldn't speak without it sounding muffled.

I wasn't in the mood to grab the whiteboard that was lying a few feet from my bed. I guess Gangsta G knew that too because he told me that I ain't have to say anything, he just came to let me know how everything had gone down with the Ken situation.

"Well Bruh, you can now be at peace, Ken and the crew is dead. We all made sure of that shit. Me and the crew pulled up just when Taea and Yanni were about to break their door in. We gave them a hand, but shid Taea and Yanni aren't to be fucked with. Yeah, they some bitches but shid, they as hard as a nigga. They didn't play no games with nobody in that house. I'm glad that me and the rest of the crew pulled up when we did because Ken had a little party going on. He didn't just have his crew there he had some more folks, but Taea and Yanni killed every single last one of them. We didn't want to leave nobody alive to be able to tell shit, even though I ain't know any of them personally, they just were at the wrong place at the wrong damn time. Everyone that fucked around with Ken was at that party, and they all had to go bruh."

My heart was beating rather fast, but I knew it all came from thinking about Yanni, and wondering was she okay emotionally. Never had she ever killed anyone before, I knew how it could affect anybody when you had to pull the trigger to end someone's life. The first nigga that I killed, I was only seventeen years old, I was deep in the streets slanging dope on the corner when I ended up being robbed by some nigga for my dope. Flashbacks of that nights still haunted me to this day because up until then, I was the type of nigga who didn't get myself caught up in no bullshit, all I wanted to do was sell my dope and get my money, but here I was getting robbed by a nigga I ain't even fucking know. Back then I always made it my business to carry a pistol on me where no one was able to see it. Nigga thought that I wasn't carrying when actuality I was.

The nigga robbed me at gun point in fear of him shooting my ass without being able to pull my pistol on him first, I relented and handed over my product, but the nigga fucked up when he turned his back and ran back to his beat-up old Box Chevy. I pulled my pistol out with quickness and shot him right in the back of his head, killing him instantly. I grabbed my drugs that had fell to the ground when he had fell, and I took off running.

Killing was necessary in the game sometimes and the fact that Yanni wasn't in the game and wasn't a dope girl, really made me worry about her. If it affected me back then when I was only seventeen, I knew she as probably going through somethings. I wanted to see her to talk to her, just to make sure she was okay. I hated that she had to do any of that shit. She wasn't ever supposed to get her hands dirty, and she had. I only hoped that she didn't hold any resentment towards me for any of this shit. If she and Taea had just waited, she wouldn't even have had to go near Ken or the crew, but Yanni was one stubborn ass bitch and had made up her mind that she was going to seek revenge herself. I loved her ass more than I ever had and I was going to do everything in my power to prove it to her.

Another knock came at the door, and then it slowly pushed open. It was Doctor Harvard. He came into the room smiling and shit.

"I have good news," Dr. Harvard told me.

I took a seat at the edge of my bed and waited for him to say what he had to say.

"It looks like you are healing up rather fast and you no longer have to be stuck in this hospital. I believe if we discharge you that you can manage on your own as long as you have someone close by."

"Yes, he has a live-in girlfriend. She will be there with him," Gangsta G told Doctor Harvard.

"Well, in that case, I believe I can get them discharge papers to you by tomorrow. We have so many patients coming in that really need attention and the hospital has a policy to release any patients who have recovered or can do recovery at home."

I could only nod my head, but my heart felt as if it was about to burst. This was like a dream come true, I was finally going to be able to go back home for the rest of my recovery and get a chance to start things over with Yanni. She deserved so much more then I had given her in the past. When the doctor walked out of my room Gangsta G dapped me up and told me that he was going to let me rest and to call him if I needed anything else.

Gangsta G was just about to walk out of the door when he turned around and looked at me.

"I'm glad you finally coming home, I'm going to head over

to Jon's room to see if his doctor going to let him go home as well."

Gangsta G closed the door behind himself and left me with my thoughts.

* * *

I MUST HAVE FALLEN asleep because when I woke up, I spotted Yanni sitting next to me. I groaned, and that's when she stopped looking at her phone and gave me her full attention.

"Hey boo, how you feeling?" she asked me as she placed a kiss on my forehead

"Your doctor told me about the good news. You finally coming home tomorrow, you just don't know how long I been waiting to hear that."

I tried to smile but failed.

"Don't worry baby, I will make sure to take good care of you."

A few moments later the door opened, and Doctor Harvard stepped inside with his nurse. He had a pair of scissors in his hands while the nurse held a clipboard.

"I think it's time we can remove your bandage," Doctor Harvard said.

I sat there making sure not to move as he removed the gauze that was in my mouth as well as the bandage.

"It's not bleeding, so that's a good sign," he told me as he pulled my bandages off my wound and threw them in the trash that was located near his foot.

He ran his hand over where he had to stitch my jaw and told me that my wound was healing just fine.

"Can you say anything, with it hurting?" Doctor Harvard asked.

My mouth felt like cotton, and it was dryer than the desert.

I tried to form a word but found it hard at first, it had been a while since I had last been able to speak.

"Take your time, Doctor Harvard told me."

I looked over at Yanni as she stared back at me. She had so much hope in her eyes.

"Will you marry me?"

I watched as Yanni expression changed from being hopeful to something that I couldn't explain.

Tears ran down her face and I knew I had touched her. I had said some shit to her that she never thought that she was going to ever hear from me. Shid to be honest, I never thought I would be saying these words at all.

The doctor moved away from my bed to give us space and pretend to busy himself but I knew him and the nurse didn't want to leave right off because they wanted to know what Yanni's answer was going to be, shid, I was still trying to figure out what she was going to say.

I wiped the tears from her cheeks, and that's when she grabbed me by my hand.

"Yes, I will marry you," she replied emotionally.

"As soon as I get my ass out of here, I want to make things official," I assured her.

"You just don't know how happy I am, you just don't know how long I've waited to hear these words."

"I'm sorry to interrupt, but I just want to say congrats to you both. Quantavious is lucky to have someone who he knows will be there for him. I wish you both the best of luck. He will be released tomorrow by twelve so make sure to be here around that time to pick him up," Dr. Harvard told Yanni.

"I will make sure to be here," Yanni replied as she stared down at me.

She didn't seem to take her eyes off of me until she heard

Dr. Harvard closing, the door behind himself when he left out of the room.

Yanni bit down on her lip as she took a seat in a chair that was next to my bed.

"I have so much to tell you, I don't know if Gangsta G them told you yet, but Ken is dead," she whispered.

"He just left baby and he told me everything, but I rather hear your side of the story, are you okay?"

"I never thought I could kill someone, but I shocked myself. At first, it bothered me, but now I'm getting through it, I love you so much, if I would have lost you, I swear I would have never gotten over it. Killing him now puts my mind at peace knowing that he can never hurt you again."

"I understand baby, I just want to make sure emotionally you can live with this."

"I'm no killer Quan, but I'm willing to do anything to protect what's mine," Yanni muttered.

I already knew what she was telling me, so I decided to drop the conversation.

"I appreciate everything that you and Taea have done, and I promised myself that when I was able to get out of here, I was going to make you my wife, my one and only. No more hoes and no more fuck ups. You deserve nothing but my loyalty."

I grabbed Yanni's hand and placed a kiss on each of her knuckles.

Yanni smiled down at me before pulling her hand away from mine.

"I guess I need to tell Taea that I'm going to be getting married before her."

I chuckled lightly.

"I wouldn't be so sure. Jon made it clear last time that we talked that he was going to put a ring on Taea's finger as well."

Yanni eyes sparkled.

"You mean that we can have a double wedding."

"Whatever you want baby, I will make that shit happen."

"Getting married to you and having Taea next to me is a dream come true. She has always had my back and has never folded. Just because she's family don't mean nothing. Family can be shady and on some fuck shit, but Taea has always been there."

"I know she has."

Yanni stood up and placed a kiss on my cheek before grabbing her Gucci bag that I had gotten her last Christmas.

"I will be here tomorrow to pick you up and bring you home, I got to head home to get some cleaning done. I've been so depressed and lazy that I haven't even cleaned up since you been gone."

"I don't believe you," I joked.

"You don't want to be living in our house right now if I brought you home with me, you will be in disbelief."

"Go home and clean up then baby, but don't overwork yourself."

"I'm going to head down the hall to visit Jon right quick and then I'm going to take my ass to the house."

"Okay then baby, hopefully, Jon and I both will be getting out of here."

I watched as Yanni made her way to the door.

She turned around a few moments later and blew me a kiss before walking out of my room.

JON

I was sitting up eating a little lunch when I spotted Yanni at the door.

"You came alone?" I asked her as she headed inside.

"I left Taea. She was taking too long to get dressed," I said with a smile on my face.

Jon laughed.

"You look tired."

"Taea ain't about to leave the house looking crazy, but yeah, I am, I'm very drained but learning that Quan will be released tomorrow has given me life. Doctor Harvard feels he has healed enough to head home, but someone is going to have to be there for him."

"I'm glad for him, I ain't heard shit from my doctor. I don't know when they going to release me," Jon said in frustration.

"I know you ready to get out of this bitch, but you know how these doctors are, they ain't going to release you until they think you well enough."

"I ain't got time to be sitting in this damn hospital any longer, I got shit that I want to do when I get out."

Yanni raised an eyebrow at me.

I chuckled softly.

"Almost dying changed me, it let me know that Taea and I are not going to live forever. I did some stupid shit and almost lost her, but I promise I'm never going to fuck up what Tae and I share ever again. She has proved her loyalty to me, and now I must prove my love for her. I want to marry her as soon as I get out of this hell hole."

Yanni smirked.

"Well, Quan was telling me the truth."

"What you talking about?" I asked Yanni.

"Quan just asked me to marry him."

"Congrats to you Yanni, you deserve it and so much more."

"Thank you, but he also told me that you were going to ask Taea to marry you as well."

"That's the plan if I can ever get out of here."

"Whatever you do, don't tell Taea my plans, I want it to be a surprise."

"I'm not going to tell her shit; I'm not even going to tell her that Quan already proposed. I'm going to wait on all that."

"Thanks for that."

"You're welcome."

A knock at the door brought the conversation to an end.

When Taea walked inside the room, my heart began to beat erratically.

"I'm going to give ya'll some time to yourselves," Yanni said before walking out.

Taea didn't speak until she heard the hospital door close.

She was rocking a smile on her face, but I couldn't help but notice the bags under her eyes.

She walked over to me, bent down, placed a kiss on my lips, and whispered into my ear.

I wrapped my arms around her, I didn't want to let her go, I wanted to be tied to her for forever.

"Ken is dead."

"I figured that much when you walked in here smiling and shit. Plus, Yanni would have told me if the mission had failed."

"Yeah, I guess you right," Taea replied as she moved away from me.

"But I'm here because I'm eager to know when you will be coming home."

"Baby, to be honest, I have no idea. I ain't heard shit."

Taea sighed, and I could see the frustration written out on her face.

"How are you feeling? Do you want me to bring you anything?"

"I feel like shit because I'm not with you. I'm just ready to head home so we can start a family."

"I will love that," Taea replied emotionally.

Taea bit down on her bottom lip and began to caress my leg under the covers. My dick grew instantly hard as soon as I felt her hand brush up against it. It seemed as if it had been forever since my dick had gotten any action.

"Baby what about???..."

Taea hushed me as she pulled my rock-hard manhood out of my boxers that I was wearing under my hospital gown.

"I know you need a release because I damn sure do. Sit back and relax."

I didn't respond. Instead I did exactly what I was told.

As soon as her mouth closed down on my manhood, I felt as if I was in heaven. It had been forever since I had this feeling of pleasure and I wanted to make the shit last, but as she sucked and slurped on my dick, I began finding it hard not to bust. I gripped her by her head and guided her up and down on my wood until I heard her gag.

"Shit," I groaned.

I closed my eyes tightly as and moaned out her name as she began to stroke my dick with her hand before spitting on it and placing it back in her mouth. As she sucked, she even started moaning which let me knew that she was enjoying this shit just as much as I was.

She pulled my dick out of her mouth a few moments later and stroked it with her hand as she sucked on each of my balls.

"Fuck, I'm about to cum," I choked out.

It didn't take long before I filled her mouth with my milk. She sucked the soul right from out of me and swallowed every last drop.

She wiped her mouth with her hand and placed my now semi-hard dick back in my boxers, just before she leaned down towards my ear.

"When you get home everything you thought you knew about our sex life is going to be different," Taea replied as she grabbed her purse from the chair that was next to my bed.

"Shit, you mean you going to be taking my soul like that?"

"Hell yeah, so rest up boo, you going to need it," Taea said as she headed out of my room.

* * *

HEARING about Quan getting out tomorrow and me not hearing shit from the doctor on my recovery was beginning to make my ass worry. The tube that had been in my chest for the first few days had been removed but still no word about when I was going to be released. I was beginning to get irritable because I wanted answers. Instead of sitting there and being angry I decided to buzz a nurse, just so they could find my doctor and see what he was going to do about my release date.

I buzzed the front office close to four times before someone finally came to check on me.

"Damn, if I was in this bitch having a heart attack, I would be long dead by now," I grumbled with attitude.

"I'm sorry, we just have been very busy, and we are short staffed. What can I do for you?" The nurse asked me.

"I just want to speak to my doctor; I want to know when I can be released."

The nurse checked my paperwork before staring back at me.

"Give me twenty minutes, and I will have the doctor to come in and talk with you about it."

"I mean you can't tell me about it, you are the nurse."

"I'm sorry when it comes to things like this it's for the doctor to do."

I grunted.

I sat there fuming as the white girl with the long dark hair left out of my room.

Twenty minutes later just as she had promised, she brought Doctor Coleman into my room.

"How you doing today Jontavian?"

I wasn't in the mood to chit chat, I wanted to know when I was going to get up out of this bitch, so instead of making small talk, I quickly got to the point of why I wanted to talk to him.

"I just want to know when I'm going to be released. I'm not wearing the tube anymore, so I assume my lung is healing just fine."

Doctor Coleman confirmed just what I was thinking by nodding his head.

"Yes, your lung is healing just fine and so are your chest wounds. You were supposed to have been released two days ago, but the staff has gotten behind on some paperwork, I got to shuffle through the paperwork later this evening to find your release papers so I can sign them for you. So tomorrow around noon you should be able to go home. Who do you want me to call to notify to pick you up tomorrow?"

The whole time this nigga talking to me, I'm talking hella shit in my head about his ass. This nigga was actually telling me that I could have been home two days ago and the only reason why I wasn't was because he ain't signed my release papers. I was pissed as hell but told myself to calm down. The fact that I was well enough to go home was a blessing, but the fact that I could have been home and laid up with Taea was what really had me heated.

Taea had just come to my room and had given me some A1 head, and this nigga was telling me that I couldn't be released until tomorrow at noon. I calmed myself down and told myself that tonight was going to be the last time I was going to sleep in a bed alone. Tomorrow night I was going to be with Taea and trying to make a baby.

YANNI

THE NEXT DAY...

I had tossed and turned almost all night; I woke up the next morning anxious to get dressed so I could pick up Quan. I rolled out of bed and hurried to the bathroom so I could take care of my hygiene. After showering, and taking care of my oral hygiene and pulling my hair into a ponytail, I headed towards my closet and found me something to wear for that day. It was way too hot for jeans, so I decided to wear a pair of white shorts with a red shirt with the phrase ***"Don't Fuck With Me"*** written on there with white letters. I still had a few hours before I could actually bring Quan home so instead of sitting there pacing the floor, I decided to call Taea just to see if she was already up.

"Hey bih, you up?" I asked into the phone.

"Yeah, I'm glad you called, I'm close to your house, I was going to come pick your ass up so we can get some breakfast."

"I can't eat right now, I'm so ecstatic about Quan coming home."

"You might as well eat, you going to need all your energy when he comes on," Taea told me as she joked into the phone

"What in the hell are you talking about?" I asked her as if I didn't know what Taea was trying to say.

"I swear when Jon gets home, I'm going to ride his dick into the sunset, it has been a while, I'm in need."

"Bye bitch," I laughed into the phone.

A few moments later I heard Taea car horn blowing to let me know that she was outside.

I grabbed my purse and headed out the door, making sure to lock the door behind me. I was just about to slide into the passenger seat when I noticed a small dent in the passenger door. I couldn't even hold my laughter in when I slid into the car next to Taea.

"Bitch, you got a dent in your fucking car," I laughed.

"I don't even want to hear the shit, I accidentally sideswiped something on the way home yesterday."

"Right," I told her as I shook my head.

"Your ass still can't drive right," I joked.

Taea rolled her eyes.

"Your ass can get out and walk if you want to," Taea joked.

"I ain't about to walk no fucking where," I laughed.

"Then hush all that shit up. I'm hungry as fuck, what you want to eat?"

"I'm not too hungry, so we can go where ever you want to go."

"Shid, I'm thinking about being petty and heading on over to Taco Bell to get us some breakfast."

"Your petty ass," I mumbled under my breath.

It didn't take no more than ten minutes for us to pull up at Taco Bell. Taea cut her engine and stepped out the car with me following behind her.

"Yep, that bitch car is here," Taea hissed

I rolled my eyes.

"Please don't go in there and show your ass."

Taea just stared at me with an innocent expression on her face, but I knew the bitch to well that she had a reason why she was coming to Taco Bell for breakfast. She could go anywhere to get breakfast, but Taco Bell is what she chose to go.

After stepping inside Taco Bell, I followed her to the front so we could order something to eat. Mookie, the bitch who had fired Taea was standing up front taking orders when we walked up. Mookie tooted her nose up at Taea and asked her what she was doing there.

"Last time I checked I could come here if I wanted to. You fired me bitch, but I'm not banned from coming here to get something to eat."

"You could have easily gone to the other Taco Bell on Watson," Mookie added.

"I don't like how they cook. I'd rather come here."

I could tell that Mookie wanted us both gone, but she kept her mouth closed and took our order. After taking our order, Mookie handed us two large cups, and we headed over to pour us some coffee, a few seconds later I heard a loud splash. I looked down and noticed that Taea had spilled her coffee and looking at her face I knew that she had done that shit on purpose.

I held back my laughter as Mookie began shouting about Taea spilling the coffee and making a big mess.

"Well, bitch it looks like you need to get your fat ass out here and mop it up. Don't fucking talk to me disrespectfully. It was an accident bitch," Taea said rudely to Mookie.

Mookie stepped from behind the counter, I saw the anger on her face, and I was waiting for the bitch to get stupid and swing on Taea because I wasn't about to allow that shit to go down that way.

"I will make a complaint to the GM to let them know that

you were rude as hell to me, didn't they tell you that the customer is always right."

"Fuck this damn job, bitch you picked the wrong bitch today!" Mookie shouted as she ran up on Taea with her hands balled up.

Just when she was about to make that first swing, I pushed Taea aside and threw my hot coffee on Mookie, which brought her to her knees.

Taea took that opportunity to drag that bitch up and down Taco Bell. There were only a few customers who were inside Taco Bell who witnessed what was going on. They were older people who looked to be in their sixties and seventies. They all stared at the commotion that was going on with interest. I bet this was the most commotion that they were ever going to see for a while. A few of the team members ran out of the kitchen and was recording the entire fight that was going down at that very moment between their shift leader and Taea.

I watched as Taea beat the brakes off of Mookie when Taea was done, she left that hoe on the floor groaning in pain and bleeding.

"Someone needs to call the police," an old white woman said in a squeaky voice.

"Ma'am no one will be calling the police, she deserved that ass whooping one of the Taco Bell team members told the old white woman who looked to be in her seventies."

The older white lady looked over at Taea and shook her head. I could tell that she disapproved, but the woman kept her mouth shut.

"Come on George lets go, the old lady said as she grabbed her husband hand and headed out the door towards their car."

The other older people didn't leave; instead they sat there with their mouths wide open.

I grabbed Taea and told her it was best that we got the fuck out of there before the police really did show up.

"I don't trust that old bitch that just walked out of here, I'm sure she may call the police as soon as she gets her old ass in that fucking car."

Taea agreed.

We hopped in Taea's car and sped off.

"Shit, I'm hungry as hell," Taea muttered under her breath.

I laughed.

"I thought we were going to Taco Bell for breakfast but shid, we did everything but eat."

Taea smirked as she pulled up at Krystal's which was right down the road.

Taea ordered us both something to eat before pulling into a parking lot and eating breakfast. I picked at my sunriser while Taea devoured hers.

We talked and joked around as Taea basically stuffed her face.

"I can't believe we took our asses to Taco Bell for you to whoop her ass," I laughed.

"I had to do it, she had all that mouth over the phone when she fired me. I wasn't about to let that bitch get away with that shit."

"Are you satisfied?"

"Very. I feel better now." Taea admitted

"Good," I laughed.

"Are you ready to head over to the hospital, it's still early but shid, I'm ready to go see Quan."

"I'm done eating so let's gone and head over there," Taea replied.

Taea hurried and crunk up her car before easing it into traffic.

Ten minutes later we were pulling up at the hospital. We

headed inside and split up when we got on the floor to where Jon and Quan were both at.

"When you ready to go, just let me know," I told Taea as I headed towards Quan's room.

Quan was already dressed and had his bag packed when I stepped inside.

"Damn, you ready ain't you?"

Quan gave me a half smile before nodding his head.

I walked over to him and placed a kiss on his lips and took a seat right beside him on the bed.

"You look like you barely got any sleep," Quan said softly.

"I didn't. All I could think about was you," I told him as I took a seat beside him and laid a head on his shoulder.

"I didn't sleep much either, I can't believe it, but Jon and I are finally about to get up out this bitch. I'm so ready to get my ass home so I can dig deep into your pussy," Quan added.

I pulled away from him and laughed.

"Why you staring at me like you in shocked, shidddd, you know what time it is."

"But aren't you still in pain?" I asked him gently.

"Fuck all that, my dick still works, and I want it inside you as soon as we get home."

Just hearing him saying some shit like that had my pussy leaking with anticipation. I wanted the dick, but at the same time, I didn't want to cause any strand on his body or hurt him in any way. We didn't have to wait too long for the doctor to barge in with a thick booklet of release papers that he wanted Quan to sign. I sat there and watched as Quan went through each piece of a paper as Doctor Harvard instructed him to put his signature.

When Quan was done, Doctor Harvard gave him a small packet of information about his injuries and assured me that as long as Quan did as the paperwork instructed him, then he was going to be okay. The doctor shook both of our hands and told us that we could leave whenever we were ready.

"Thanks so much for all you have done," I told Dr. Harvard just before he walked out of the room.

I stared down at Quan and grabbed the light tote bag that he had filled with his personal items.

"Are you ready?"

"Hell yeah," he told me as he followed me out what use to be his room

We walked halfway down the hall and came to Jon's room which we found Jon and Taea embraced in an intense kiss. They both pulled away from one another when they spotted us standing at the door.

"Has Jon been released yet?"

Taea didn't even take her eyes off Jon as she nodded her head yes.

"Well let's get up out this bitch," I told them.

Taea finally tore her lustful gaze away from Jon and moved away from the chair that Jon was sitting in.

Jon and Quan dapped each other up, and we all headed out of the hospital at the same damn time.

"I find it so ironic that both of ya'll come in at the same time and leaving out at the same time," I said to everyone as we all headed to Taea's car.

"It's a fucking blessing that they both are alive, and well, I thank the man above every day. It could have been so much worse," Taea said aloud.

Instead of sitting in the front with Taea, I decided to sit back in the back with Quan. After Quan and I had gotten into the car that's when Jon must have noticed the dent in Taea's passenger door.

"Damn bae, what you do to the car, what you hit?"

"Nigga, get your weak ass into the car, don't start asking all these questions, you ain't even been out of the hospital ten minutes good and you already trying to joke my ass," Taea said in a joking manner.

"Baby, I just wondered what happened to the fucking door, shid, I know it wasn't like that when I brought it," Jon replied.

We all laughed inside the car.

Taea rolled her eyes and crunk her car up.

"If you want to know what happened then I guess I better tell ya'll since ya'll are going to keep asking."

"Damn right, we going to keep asking, my nosy ass want to know," Jon joked.

Taea sighed before finally mumbling that she had swiped something that caused her to dent her car door.

"What did you swipe?" Jon asked curiously.

I remembered Taea telling me she had swiped something with her car, but I never asked her ass what she had hit.

Taea groaned before mumbling that she had swiped her car when she was leaving the gas pump.

The entire car interrupted in laughter.

Even Quan was chuckling right beside me, with his mouth still healing he could only open it so wide.

"Well I see some things are never going to change," Jon joked.

"What the fuck that supposed to mean?" Taea asked.

Jon didn't bother by responding; he only smiled at Taea.

Taea rolled her eyes and pulled into traffic as we headed in the direction of me and Quan's crib.

Ten minutes later Taea pulled up at the crib and Quan, and I got out.

"We heading back to our house and maybe we can get together and hang out later on!" Taea yelled out just before I closed the door behind myself.

Quan headed into the house with little to no help. The

first thing he did when we got inside was pull me into a tight embrace.

"Baby, don't hurt yourself."

"I'm not bothered by any of that shit."

"Do you need a pain pill or something?" I asked with concern.

"I don't need shit but you," he whispered into my ear before caressing me sexually.

I followed him to our bedroom and watched him as he eased himself down on the bed.

"Are you going to join me?"

I didn't think twice about sliding in the bed next to him. He held me close as he caressed my body with his hand.

"You just don't know how much I've missed you," he whispered into my ear.

"Prove it to me," I told him boldly.

"I plan on showing you for the rest of my life," he said just before he pulled down the shorts that I was wearing.

My pussy instantly began to drip with just the thought of him finally being able to touch me again.

"I wanted to dick you down when I first got home, but I rather wait until our wedding night. What I want you to do is ride my face like you would this dick."

I wasted no time by sliding on top of his face and riding it. This nigga tongue game was so strong that it never took me long to reach my peak. I closed my eyes and squeezed them shut as he licked and sucked on my clit.

"Shit baby," I cried out as he made love to my pussy with his tongue.

I felt myself going weak, so I knew it was only going to be a matter of time before he made me cum. When he began to apply pressure to my clit, I cried out his name as my body began to shake.

Quan made sure to lick and suck every drop of cum from my body before he gently moved me off of his face.

I laid there beside him not able to move after what he had just done.

"Shit, I can't even move," I mumbled to Quan.

"Where are you trying to go? You right where you need to me, you here with me."

TAEA

Finally, I had my man back home with me where he belonged, and I was never going to let him go. As soon as we stepped into the crib, I grabbed his bag and headed towards our bedroom so I could put his stuff up. I had just finished putting the last of his personal items in the bathroom when he walked into the bathroom and embraced me in a hug.

"You just don't know how good it feels to be back."

I looked up at him and kissed him gently on his lips.

"Let me run you a bath baby so you can relax."

"Baby, you ain't got to do all of that shit we can save that shit for later."

I eyed him up but folded when he stared me deep into my eyes.

"What you had in mind to do on your first day home?" I asked him curiously as I headed out of the bathroom.

"All I want to do is lay under you for the rest of the day.

"We can do that baby, I'm all yours. I no longer work at Taco Bell, it's a long story that I will save for another day," I told him as I walked over to where he was standing.

I caressed his face with my hand as he placed his hands around my waist. He slowly began to rock with me from side to side.

"I want to spend the rest of my life with you baby, I want to have a family with you. I never knew what love truly meant until I met you, I never knew how it felt to be heart-broken until you left me, and I never want to be without you ever again. Will you marry me, baby? Will you be the mother to all my kids?"

I pulled away from him briefly just to make sure that I had heard him correctly.

I stared at him, and I saw nothing but love in his eyes.

"I can't believe this is happening, I never thought that this would happen," I whispered to him.

"It's about that time don't you think? I know I've fucked up and you may not trust me no more, but marry me anyway because I want to prove to you that I'm a changed man. I promise that I will never hurt you ever again. All I want to do is love you until the day I die."

I stood there not able to speak for the longest time. Tears fell down my face because I was finally getting everything that I ever wanted.

"Yes, I will marry you," I cried to him.

He grabbed me and pushed his tongue into my mouth as I wrapped my arms around his body.

The kiss deepened, and the passion of having my man here with me had my body in overdrive. I pulled away from him only briefly just so I could catch my breath.

"When are we going to get married?" I asked Jon breathlessly.

"Tomorrow."

"We can get married that fast? I asked him. Isn't there paperwork to be filled out and procedures to go by?"

"Yes, there is, but I ain't about to let that shit stop us from marrying tomorrow."

I raised my eyebrow up at him.

"Your nigga got money, them hoes gonna take that money and process that paperwork the same day, I put money on that shit. These females always looking for a quick way to make some fast cash, so don't worry about anything, let me take care of everything."

My eyes lit up; I knew then without a doubt that what Jon was telling me was the truth. He really wanted to get married and start a family with me, and the best part of it was he wasn't holding off on the wedding, that really put my mind at ease. Even though I knew he loved me and wanted to be with me, I didn't know if he was ready to marry me until that very moment. I was thinking this nigga was going to wait some months down the line for us actually get married and make the shit official.

I guess he knew that I was having a back and forth battle within myself because he quickly put my mind at rest.

"I know you may be shocked that I want to marry so soon, but baby, life isn't guaranteed. I take my love for you seriously; you are the only woman I want to spend the rest of my life with. I know you may want a big fancy wedding, and you can have that later on if you want that, but I want us to start our lives together as soon as possible."

"I don't need no fancy wedding, all I need is you," I admitted to Jon.

Jon smiled down at me, before pulling out his phone and punching in a number.

"She said she will marry me bruh, we gonna get married tomorrow."

I stood there already knowing who was on the phone.

When the phone call ended, Jon gently pushed me down on the bed.

"I just got off the phone with Quan. He and Yanni are going to get married with us tomorrow at the courthouse."

Yanni and I had been through so much with our men, and now we both were going to be marrying the men we couldn't live without.

Thoughts of Yanni was pushed to the back of my mind when Jon began to undress. I watched him as he pulled off his red shirt, his white shorts, and even his boxers. His naked body stared back at me, and I instantly got wet. I gently caressed each of the bullet hole wounds that he had on his chest just before he slowly began to undress me.

As he sucked on my neck and caressed my naked body, I knew at that very moment that life just couldn't get any better than this.

* * *

I WOKE up the next morning to an empty bed. I called out for Jon but got no answer. I rolled over to my side of the bed and grabbed my phone, so I could call him to see where he was at. He picked up on the first ring, Yo Gotti blasted in my ear before I heard my man's voice.

"I woke up, and you were gone. Where you at?"

"I'm okay, I left to take care of some business before the wedding, and I got us some breakfast."

"Baby, you need to be home in the bed, you shouldn't be out."

Jon chuckled.

"I'm okay baby, don't stress over me boo, I have come a long way, I can handle myself."

"Umhm," I said into the phone.

"Give me five more minutes, and I will be pulling up."

After ending the call, I hopped out of bed and headed straight to the bathroom so I could take care of my morning breath. I didn't want to kill him with my bad breath.

I had just finished taking care of my oral hygiene when I heard him walking towards our bathroom.

"You look so fucking fine," he said to me as he stared at me.

I shook my head.

"I look horrible this morning," I complained.

"Baby, you're beautiful. After today I'm going to be waking up to you every single day."

I couldn't help but smile at his comment.

"Now, follow me so you can eat some breakfast. We have a big day today."

I left the bathroom and followed him towards our kitchen. The smell of grits and sausage filled my nose. My stomach immediately began to grumble when I spotted the Huddle House carry out box. I wasted no time by sitting my ass down and digging into my food.

"Damn baby, slow that shit down," Jon joked.

I slowed down on my chewing and swallowed.

"My bad, you just don't know, this is my first real meal in a long time, the entire time that you were gone, I couldn't eat like this, I was so stressed, and I missed you so much."

"I know you missed me, baby, you weren't the only one suffering so was I."

As we ate, we talked about our future and even talked about the kids that we were going to one day have.

"The wedding will be at noon; everything has already been arranged."

I couldn't help but smile as he stood up and threw our empty food containers in the trash. I stared over at the clock and noticed it was already ten a.m.

"Only you can pull off getting married on such short notice."

"What can I say, I got that pull like that."

"Oh, I'm not complaining," I replied happily.

"I'm going to go and let your ass get dressed and get yourself beautified. I'm about to roll this blunt and think about our future together."

I couldn't help but laugh as I watched him walk out the back door.

After leaving the kitchen, I walked towards my bedroom and went straight towards my closet so I could find something to wear for that day. After searching for over twenty minutes, I decided to wear a pair of all black shorts, with a red top that had Love written in white letters. I grabbed my red and white Jordan's and put them beside my bed and placed my clothes on top of the bed. I grabbed my red thong out of the drawer along with a matching bra.

I headed towards the tub and ran me a hot bath. After the tub was filled up to the max, only then did I step inside. I slowly eased down in the hot water and soaked my body for a few moments just before I actually started to bathe myself. After taking my bath, I stepped out of the tub and dried my body off.

I rubbed my hands through my shoulder-length hair just before I grabbed me a comb and began to comb out my hair. For an entire hour, I stood inside of the bathroom and did my hair and took care of my other personal hygiene before the wedding.

I stepped inside my bedroom and had just finished putting on my clothes before Jon walked into the bedroom. I licked my lips as I watched him. He was wearing a pair of khaki pants, a red polo shirt with a pair of red Nikes.

"Damn, look at us, we both rocking red."

"Great minds think alike," he told me just before kissing me on my lips.

His cologne tickled my nose, and I wanted nothing more

than to push him down on the bed and throw the pussy on him at that very moment.

"Damn you look so fucking good," I told him as I pushed up on him.

"Thanks, baby, your looking super sexy boo. Can't wait until we get back home," he whispered into my ear before flicking his tongue over my earlobe.

I swear that shit set my soul on fire. I was tempted to give him some ass before the wedding, my coochie was screaming for a release.

"I'm about to head out to the courthouse, will you be good by yourself?"

"Yes, I will be good," I told him sweetly.

He placed a gentle kiss on my forehead before leaving me with my thoughts. Thirty minutes later, I finally grabbed my keys and my cell phone and headed out the door.

I was just about to hop in my car when my phone began to ring.

I picked up when I noticed it was, Yanni, calling me.

"Bitch this is the best day of my life!" Yanni yelled into the phone.

I smiled because I felt the same way.

"Are you on your way to the courthouse yet?" Yanni asked me.

"Yes, I just hopped in the car, Jon already left."

"Yeah, Gangsta G and Jon rode by and picked Quan up."

Yanni and I talked and joked on the phone until we pulled up at the Houston County courthouse. I stepped out my car and headed straight towards her car and knocked on her window. She stepped out her car and threw her arms around me in a tight hug.

I pulled away from her and complimented her on what she was wearing. She was dressed in a pair of white shorts, with a lime green top with a pair of white and lime green Air

Forces. Her long weave was pulled back and was in a tight bun on top of her head.

"Here we are, we are finally about to get married," Yanni said excitedly.

"I'm still speechless and can't believe the shit either," I admitted to her.

"I'm going to always remember this fucking day."

"So am I, I just wish our mothers could be here," Yanni replied sadly.

"I know, but once they get out from rehab, we can always have a bigger wedding that they can attend."

"I think that will be a good idea." Yanni agreed.

"We will make sure to make a phone call to let them know. Plus, we need to check up on them anyway."

"I wonder if they still there? Yanni asked.

Shid, even if they ain't they always going to be our mothers and we always going to love them, I know they ain't perfect, but I'm better now, and I want to have a better relationship with Tanya, no matter what."

"I feel the same way about Lisa, but something in my heart tells me that they still there and they really trying this time to get clean," Yanni said seriously.

"All we can do is hope for the best," I told Yanni.

After stepping into the courthouse, we spotted Quan and Jon both waiting on us. Jon was dressed just like Yanni each of us color coordinated with our mate. Jon was rocking a pair of lime green cargos with a white and lime green shirt, with a pair of white Air Forces.

We took a seat next to each other as we waited for the judge to call us into the back so we could be married. We waited nearly twenty minutes before I started having a panic attack.

"How we going to get married, we ain't got no rings," I said as I groaned in disbelief.

"Baby, will you please calm down, we got the rings, Quan and I both got the rings this morning."

"Shid, you up here stressing about a fucking ring, I didn't even think about it," Yanni replied.

"What the hell was you going to wear on your fucking finger bitch?" I asked her in disbelief.

She laughed.

"A rubber band hoe."

Everyone laughed even the security guard that was near us joined in.

"Bitch, I can't with you," I told Yanni.

It was so fucking funny because I knew Yanni wasn't lying.

Ten minutes later after my breakdown, the double doors towards the back opened, and a bailiff told us to follow him. As we followed the bailiff, I tightened my hand around Jon and walked alongside him. As soon as we had made our way into the back of the courthouse, I let out a deep breath when we were met with the man who was going to be in charge of marrying us.

He introduced himself as Pastor Henry. He was tall and slim, dark in complexion, with a low haircut that was faded on the side and in the back. When he smiled, I noticed he had a gold tooth in the front of his mouth. He looked no more than fifty and was dressed in a grey suit and tie.

"Will this be all who attending this ceremony?" the pastor asked gently.

"Yes," Jon replied.

"Very well, let's get started," the preacher said happily.

"Before I start the ceremony, I just want to tell each one of you that I wish you nothing but the best and I hope you have a wonderful long-lasting marriage."

We all told the pastor thank you, and he even offered us his card with his information if we ever needed counseling or guidance. After everything had been discussed only then did the ceremony began.

I stared into my man's eyes as I said my vows, I knew without a doubt that I was making the right decision.

Yanni and I had suffered so much heartache and tears throughout this relationship, but finally, we were going to get everything we ever wanted.

When Jon placed his lips on mine, I knew without a doubt that he was going to be mine forever.

THE END

CONNECT WITH ME ON SOCIAL MEDIA

Subscribe to my mailing list by visiting my website: https://www.shaniceb.com/

• Like my Facebook author page: https://www.facebook.com/ShaniceBTheAuthor/?ref=aymt_homepage_panel

• Join my reader's group on Facebook. I post short stories and sneak peeks of my upcoming novels that I'm working on https://www.facebook.com/groups/1551748061561216/

• Send me a friend request on Facebook: https://www.facebook.com/profile.php?Id=100011411930304&__nodl

• Follow me on Instagram: https://www.instagram.com/shaniceb24/?hl=en

BOOKS BY SHANICE B.

- Feenin' For That Dope Dick
- No One Has To Know: A Secret Worth Keeping
- Meet Me In My Bedroom: A Collection Of Erotic Love Stories (Volume 1 & 2)
- All I Need Is You: A Christmas Love Story
- I Wish You Were My Boo: A Tragic Love Story
- Your Love Got Me Shook: A Novella
- Married To The Dekalb County Bully
- Love, I Thought You Had My Back: An Urban Romance
- All I Ever Wanted Was You: A Twisted Love Story (Part 1 &2)
- He Loves The Savage In Me: A Twisted Love Affair (Part 1 & 2)
- Kiss Me Where It Hurts (Part 1-3)

ABOUT THE AUTHOR

Shanice B was born and raised in Georgia. At the age of nine years old, she discovered her love for reading and writing. At the age of ten, she wrote her first short story and read it in front of her classmates, who fell in love with her wild imagination. After graduating from high school, Shanice decided to pursue her career in Early Childhood Education. After giving birth to her son, Shanice decided it was time to pick up her pen and get back to what she loved the most.

She is the author of over twenty books and is widely known for her bestselling four-part series titled Who's Between the Sheets: Married to A Cheater. Shanice is also the author of the three-part series, Love Me If You Can, and three standalone novels titled Stacking It Deep: Married to My Paper, A Love So Deep: Nobody Else Above you, and Love, I Thought You Had My Back. In November of 2016, Shanice decided to try her hand at writing a two-part street lit series titled Loving My Mr. Wrong: A Street Love Affair. Shanice resides in Georgia with her family and her six-year-old son.

CPSIA information can be obtained
at www.ICGtesting.com
Printed in the USA
LVHW010719270521
688662LV00001B/87

9 781690 987413